The Loophole

The Loophole

NAZ KUTUB

BLOOMSBURY
NEW YORK LONDON OXFORD NEW DELHI SYDNEY

BLOOMSBURY YA
Bloomsbury Publishing Inc., part of Bloomsbury Publishing Plc
1385 Broadway, New York, NY 10018

BLOOMSBURY and the Diana logo are trademarks of Bloomsbury Publishing Plc

First published in the United States of America in June 2022 by Bloomsbury YA

Text copyright © 2022 by Naz Kutub

Bloomsbury books may be purchased for business or promotional use. For information on bulk
purchases please contact Macmillan Corporate and Premium Sales Department at
specialmarkets@macmillan.com

Library of Congress Cataloging-in-Publication Data
Names: Kutub, Naz, author.
Title: The loophole / by Naz Kutub.
Description: New York : Bloomsbury Children's Books, 2022
Summary: Sy, a seventeen-year-old gay Muslim boy, travels the world for a second chance
at love after a possibly magical heiress grants him three wishes.
Identifiers: LCCN 2021056228 (print) | LCCN 2021056229 (e-book)
ISBN 978-1-5476-0917-8 (hardcover) • ISBN 978-1-5476-0935-2 (e-book)
Subjects: CYAC: Gays—Fiction. | Friendship—Fiction. | Love—Fiction. | Muslims—
United States—Fiction. | East Indian Americans—Fiction.
Classification: LCC PZ7.1.K898 Lo 2022 (print) | LCC PZ7.1.K898 (e-book) | DDC [E]—dc23
LC record available at https://lccn.loc.gov/2021056228
LC e-book record available at https://lccn.loc.gov/2021056229

Book design by John Candell
Typeset by Westchester Publishing Services
Printed and bound in the U.S.A.
2 4 6 8 10 9 7 5 3 1

To find out more about our authors and books visit www.bloomsbury.com
and sign up for our newsletters.

To my mom;
thank you for letting me go.

AUTHOR'S NOTE

I don't know where you are in the world as you're reading this, but if coming out poses a potential danger, then please make the safest decision, and come back to this book when you're living under safer circumstances. I promise you it'll still be here.

And when you do come out, just know I will be here. Waiting.

We all will be.

To welcome you to your new family.

CONTENT WARNING

Please skip the following chapters if they may open up wounds.

Chapter 13 contains a scene where the seventeen-year-old protagonist experiences physical abuse from his dad.

Chapter 14 sees him kicked out of the family home.

Chapter One

If I could make a wish, it would be for less blah in my life. Seriously, it's been a bit much.

My boyfriend broke up with me three months ago.

My dad's a tyrant I can't wait to escape from.

And I've just burned this hipster's croissant. For the second time today.

"I'm so sorry, sir," I say to the bearded-to-the-neckline LumberChad, while half a dozen other patrons look on with disinterest. "I'll heat up another for you."

But he gives me the dirtiest look, his beard quivering with every word he spits out. "Are you serious? Do you really think I can wait five more minutes for you to burn it *again*?"

Ugh. "I promise you, this time it'll be perfect. You see, I'm by myself right now—"

"I don't care. You just burned it twice!"

Ugh, ugh, ugh. Where the heck is Dzakir when I need him? "Let me throw two croissants into the oven, just in case?"

The McJoe throws his hands in the air. "So you're going to burn a total of four now? What's going to happen if—"

"Sir, I need you to back off," comes the voice of my savior.

And there he stands by the glass door entrance: Dzakir, D, my BFF—"Best Fighter Friend." Two hundred pounds of brown muscle, sass, and lip gloss, coming to my defense. And a fist firmly planted on one hip. All of it squeezed into a My Little Pony T-shirt.

The beardy hipster takes a moment to assess the situation, but before he can say another word, I pop yet another croissant into the oven and busy myself with milk for the cappuccinos, lattes, and ice-blendeds for the others huddled around the blue velvet couch of the Grounded café (where the brews are semi-modest but the prices aren't).

Dzakir makes his way in and around the corner, ties on his apron, all the while never taking his eyes off my antagonizer.

When the oven dings, I hand a warm, golden-crusted, buttery croissant to the man, who leaves with one last angry look and his overbrushed beard in tow.

"Thanks for saving me, D. Again," I say, scanning the remaining crowd.

Dzakir whispers, "You need to get a grip and forget *you know who* already. So you can actually focus. And quit looking like you've got a cactus up your butt."

I swallow a grunt while emptying a bag of Oaxacan beans into the grinder. "I'm trying, D. Like, really, *really* trying."

"It's called breaking up. He did that when he left you a quarter of a century ago—"

"It was three months."

"Like, full-on severance. But you can't stop staring at his skinny face on that broken-ass phone of yours. I mean, sleepless nights are way cliché."

I twist my thumb ring, the one my ex gave to me. My cheeks feel hot even in the full blast of the AC. "I know. Can you please just stop?"

"*Can you please just stop? Really? That's the best you've got?*"

"You're the drag-queen wannabe with the glib tongue. I'm just the emaciated sidekick with the flaccid comebacks."

"Us brown boys need to stick together, Sy," Dzakir says, and then his eyes soften. "I don't want to see this aura of hurt on you anymore."

"I know, D, I—"

BANG!

The jolt from outside seems to rattle the whole café, shoving the caffeine-starved zombies awake and nearly stopping my heart.

Every head in here, mine included, swivels in the microsecond after that bang. The source is a ponytailed girl, right about my age, now sliding down our front door, smudging the glass I'd Windexed an hour ago with a vertical streak of makeup.

There's another split microsecond where everyone's just staring at the curvy, beautiful mess as she sits back in (what looks like) a bra and miniskirt, obviously dazed, clearly figuring out what her next move should be. But she gives up and slams her upper body on hard pavement, gaze fixed on the blue sky, while just three feet away on the street behind her, cars fly past.

And what do these people do? They snicker, crane their phones upright, and, with a few taps on their screens, immortalize the poor girl's tragic accident.

Worry stabs my chest. I want to scream at them, but nope, can't do that. I need this job bad. So I huff a tiny "Eff this shit" under my breath and scrabble behind the counter past Dzakir, littering a dozen *excuse-me*s on the Unhelpful Ursulas as I scramble out the door.

"Hey, how're you feeling?" I ask, lowering myself to my knees next to her right arm.

The girl's deep, dark eyes are a perfect complement to her only-believes-in-SPF-4 kind of tan, which pairs with a ruby-red lip color that now scars up her right cheek. Her black ponytail has fanned out on the floor, forming a crown. And both her hands float like wild tentacles, trying to grab on to something. "What. Where. Who. Huh?" are the only words she can muster as she appears to swim up to an imaginary surface for air.

Poor thing must've fractured her skull—although, from my vantage, the door glass doesn't look like it's suffered the tiniest crack. But that lipstick-colored smudge will require a few hundred calories to rub out. "Can I help you up?" I ask.

Her right hand grasps my shoulder with definite triumph, latching on. "Do forgive me, young lad," she says, "but I must've suffered an obtuse concussion. Or is it an acute obtrusion? Now, where is my purse?"

She kinda looks like if Rebel Wilson and Mindy Kaling had a biological teen together, although she sounds like that old dame from . . . that PBS show? *Downton Abbey*? What's her name . . . Maggie Smith! Which is kinda odd, because she doesn't look much older than I do.

I prop her upright the best I can and scan the ground all around. The gawking crowd on the other side of the glass retreats behind their cell phones the moment they catch my questioning glare.

There it is, next to the ficus plant by the door: an angry yellow rectangular thing with . . . foam spikes? "Is this it?"

She balances herself to a seated position, legs flat out on the sidewalk. When her eyes narrow in on it, she brightens up, her ponytail dancing a merry jig. "That's it, love. That's the one."

And then the sour smell slams into me. "Is that tequila?" I ask. *Damn*. That explains the accident, although how rough must her morning have been for her to indulge this early? "Are you hurt? Is there anything I can get you?"

She stuffs the angry purse under a bare armpit. "Oh, no need for that. My head's sturdier than Hugh Jackman's arse." She smiles as if contemplating the image, and suddenly the smile becomes a devilish grin.

"Um, I really have to get back to work."

The girl shakes her head, her ponytail swinging wildly. "Oh, right. Where were we? Ah, Grounded." She cranes her neck, stares at the signage, puckers her lips. "I have to say, that's not a clever name, is it? Anyway." She holds out her left hand as if waiting for it to be kissed. "Well, help me up, then, my dear."

I help her scramble to her feet, and once up, she dusts herself so hard, I fear she may accidentally peel off her tight black skirt, even though it looks painted on.

She checks her reflection in the window, licks her front teeth, then pats away the bright spat of lipstick on her right cheek, ignoring curious eyes staring at her beyond the glass. "I've lost my need for coffee, thanks to my make-out session with the door." She holds out her hand. "Thank you, Sayyed."

"No worries. Wait, what? How do you . . . ?" I glance at my name tag, which has always read "Sy." No one but my family calls me by my actual name.

She grabs my hand, and as her thumb brushes my ring, her dark-brown irises get even darker. "Who's Farouk?"

What the . . . ? How does she know my ex's name or that he has anything to do with the ring? A ring I shouldn't even be wearing, since he gave it to me as a symbol of undying and eternal and never-ending love.

But before I can get even one question out, she departs with a strange wave and a hop, skip, and more skips down Santa Monica Boulevard.

I could run after her. I want to, just to ask my questions. But I'll be in trouble with Dzakir if I don't get back to pumping out lattes.

Suddenly, I wonder if I was the one who bonked my head on the glass door, because now it's pounding real bad.

I stumble back inside, my whole world a little askew, while the customers glare at me for making them wait two and a half minutes longer than they're used to. All I can do is slink behind the counter, back to work.

Dzakir raises his hands to the high heavens and mumbles, "Thank you, God, for bringing my sister back from his hiatus so he can help me help all these other sufferers."

"Okay, Ariana. Mellow your drama."

"Watch it, you. I can claw you to death with these manicured hooves," he says, motioning at me with a hiss.

"So shall we?" I rub my temples before getting back to the crowd, satisfying their desires for this strangely legal drug.

Meanwhile, the mystery of the ponytailed girl widens. Who is she, and how did she know about Farouk?

Chapter Two

The scent of lentils and sounds of a Bollywood movie soundtrack stew in the air as I step in the front door. "Umi?"

There's a clang in the kitchen. "Sayyed?" the voice calls out.

More bangs this time—maybe the wooden stirrer against the pot—and then she appears in the doorway to the kitchen. "Let me see your face."

Welcome to the ritual. The obligatory greet-your-son-from-his-extended-presence-away-from-the-safety-of-home dance.

Umi stands before me, face lined with wrinkles from a son who tries her patience simply by existing. "I'm fine. Nothing happened," I say.

"It's my job to worry."

"You say that every day."

"That's what mothers do." She wipes sweat off her brow.

"And sons just want our freedom."

Umi does so much: in the kitchen, in the laundry room, in the living room. She won't let me raise a hand to help. She's "given" me the freedom to do well in school and to concentrate on doing well in life. But every time I try to wash a plate, she grabs it and tosses it in the sink and tells me to sit on the couch and just relax and watch TV.

I wish I could do more.

She balks, ties her hair up in a bun. "You're free when you find a wife. That's the rule."

My eyes roll themselves, I swear. "Where's Sofia?"

Umi finally ambles away, back to the kitchen. "In her bedroom. Doing homework, what else? Even though it's summer and she's on vacation."

I head to my room first to set my backpack down and decompress for a minute. It's small, with the twin bed, and the desk, and the tiniest of bookcases, but it's mine. Although the door's not allowed to be locked, which makes for some awkward attempts at privacy. Getting walked in on while staring at another boy's face is . . . kinda cringe-making.

Eventually, I make my way to my sister's room and creep up behind her. "You suck so hard at trig," I say.

Without even turning around, Sofia lashes out a fist behind her, striking me square in the stomach.

"Ouch!"

"That's what you get for insulting me," she says while delivering a face of utter satisfaction. "And don't try to get violent with me. Remember who's better at pinning the other down in a wrestling match?"

"Boys aren't supposed to wrestle girls anymore in this house."

"That's so sexist, brother. What next? I can't be an astronaut?"

"Not when your math sucks that bad."

I leap back before she has the chance to launch both fists at me, which leads to her growling and whipping her braid at me instead.

"Calm down, sister. Maybe I'm just faster than you."

Sofia is a tinier version of me. Her nose is slightly stumpier, and my eyebrows are a lot bushier, but we both have the trademarked Nizam family straight white teeth.

She turns back to her homework. "Oh god. What are you here for anyway? Trying to bait me into talking about Farouk again? Either stay and help me with my problems or get lost, brother."

"Have I been talking too much about him? Damn."

"Don't say damn."

"Fine. Why're you studying so hard?"

"Gotta get a head start before the new school year. Surprised you haven't done a thing, since you start college in what . . . a month?"

I sit on her bed, trying to avoid the idea of life in college without Farouk, while almost drowning in a hundred Hello Kitty pillows, until Umi calls out that dinner is ready.

We both rise like two obedient little children to head to the table.

The front door swings open just as we take our seats.

Suddenly, it feels like winter in our tiny house in sunny Los Angeles.

Baba.

This mustached man with dark eyes is my father. And this is his domain. Everything goes according to his rule of law.

Sofia and I watch as he swings the door shut and drops his keys in the ceramic bowl on the stand next to the door. He marches around like a general, full of purpose: to the living room to turn on the TV, setting it to the same sports channel for the latest in soccer news, then to the bathroom for a quick washup, then to join us at the head of the table, waiting for his food to be served. My umi has timed its presentation perfectly for his arrival.

And then, right on schedule, come the barking words that fall out from that waggling mustache: "Sayyed. You need to start coming home early."

I can't help but quake in my shorts. "Yes, Baba. But sometimes I have to work late."

"I go to Mumbai in two weeks, and you cannot leave your mother and sister by themselves."

Two plates of rice materialize in front of Sofia and me.

"Okay, Baba. I'll tell my boss at work."

Sofia leans into me and starts meowing.

I plant a heel on her toes.

She almost yelps but coughs instead.

Umi brings out the lentils and turmeric fried chicken. She knows these are my favorites. We dig in, silent except for the sound of my father's grumbles at failed goal kicks and strange soccer terminologies I'll never understand—I mean, what the heck is an offside, and why would anyone want to be on it? Anyway, I'm way too distracted by the juicy thighs on the screen to care about a score. *I shall settle on these skinny chicken thighs instead.*

And the thought is automatically followed by a pang as Farouk creeps back into my mind, and my thumb ring grows heavy.

As I slowly consume my meal, I drift away to the other side of the world.

Wondering where he is right this minute.

Wondering how he's doing with all the freedom he's swimming in.

Chapter Three

Relax, Sy. They're going to love me," Farouk said, his shoulder rubbing against mine as we walked up to my front door.

How was he taking it all so easily?

I couldn't help but stare at this tall boy next to me. Seriously, he towered a whole human head above me. The curly hair that swept across his forehead and those big brown eyes that refused to look away from me every time our eyes met.

"You're telling me to relax? I'm bringing you home for the first time ever. I just know something bad's going to happen. I can feel it. I can smell it. It's oozing out of the ground like a pile of dead skunks swept in by the sewer tide and—"

Farouk poked my rib. "Where the heck does your imagination come from?"

"You can thank my mother. 'Overactive' is the best way to describe hers."

"Ah. So should I turn back?"

"If you do, I'll make sure you die from a lack of kisses."

"Like I said, relax. You're going to give yourself a hemor-rhoid. They're not pretty, you know."

"Ew. Where'd you get *your* sense of humor?"

"Not from my parents, that's for sure."

It took us, like, three hours to walk up the steps to finally get to the front door. Maybe it was three minutes. My finger hovered over the doorbell. *Please please please, God, just don't let them hate him. Not my Roukie.*

Light touch on the doorbell. The ding. The shuffle of har-ried feet. And finally, the door slid open the tiniest of cracks.

"Sayyed. It's you," Umi said as she pulled the door clear open, unlocked the gate, appraised my sacrificial lamb and me. "So this is your friend Farouk? Look at you. So tall. Come in, come in." She withdrew, letting my "friend" and me through.

As far as she knew, he was my "best friend" after a month of knowing each other. "Auntie, your house is so cute," Farouk said.

Umi blushed, covering her mouth with a hand. "Cute? Really? Sayyed, did you hear him? He likes my knickknacks that you hate so much."

Farouk swung his backpack around, unzipped it, and pulled out a paper bag. "I hear this is your favorite chai."

Umi's face got even redder. "Oh, Farouk, you shouldn't have. But thank you. Sayyed, entertain your friend while I turn the kettle on."

She took off for the kitchen.

I was just about to lay a hand on Farouk's face but stopped short at the sharp intake of breath behind me.

"Sofia." I turned to catch her peeking at me from the hallway, before stepping out into the open. "Come meet Farouk."

She pasted on a sickly grin, and suddenly I knew she knew.

My dirty, not-so-little secret. *Ugh. I should just dig a grave and bury myself right this minute.*

But she was her oh-so-sweet self. "Nice to meet you, Farouk. Sayyed has spoken very highly of you. Brother, can I get your help with something for a quick second? I'm stuck on this one calculus problem. Promise it'll be, like, two minutes tops."

I wanted to throttle her neck, then feed her to the sewer skunks, but I needed to address this. "Sure. Have a seat, Farouk. Anywhere you like."

Farouk shrugged and planted himself on the couch. Taking it all in, really absorbing our humblest of abodes.

"What, Sofia?"

She shut the door behind me. "He's your boyfriend."

I. Hate. Her. So. Much. "You're talking out of your skinny behind, like you always do."

"I've got eyes and ears, brother. Two of each. I can see the way you look at him, hear the way you talk about him."

"He's a super-nice guy and just a friend."

"It's a sin to be gay."

"You have no idea what you're talking about. And stop butting your nose into my dealings."

I finally stormed out of her room, stopping to calm myself before I faced Farouk again.

"What's wrong?" he asked.

I sat next to him, steam leaking out of my pores. "My sister knows." I looked around, then lowered my voice. "About us."

"And?"

"I'm afraid her big mouth might tattle unexpectedly."

"Are you sure? She seemed kind of nice."

"A baby viper is never nice."

I wanted to hold his hand so badly, run my fingers through his curly hair, stare into those deep, dark, beautiful eyes. Forget everything. Everyone. But I couldn't. Not until we were out of the house.

Dinner came and went. Sofia said nothing, though she eyed Farouk all night. Baba said even less, his mustache bristling every now and then, other than a few aggressive nods at the soccer match on TV and the stranger in his house. Umi was cordial, as always.

So it all went fine.

I summoned the courage to walk Farouk to the bus station, where we stole a kiss before he got on his ride. Glad we survived the evening.

And I ran home right after.

Oh, the thrill of danger.

Back home, Sofia came into my room and sat next to me as I tried reading Homer's *Odyssey*. It was completely yawn-worthy, but Farouk had given it to me. "What is it now?" I asked.

"Brother, it pains me to say this—to actually tell you that I care for you—but I don't want to see you get hurt."

"How would I get hurt?"

She grabbed her braid. "If Baba finds out, he'll disown you. We have no relatives here, so you'll be on the streets."

I slammed the book shut. Took in a deep breath. "I know."

With that, she gave me a curt smile and let herself out.

It was probably the nicest moment I'd ever had with my sister.

But I thought she didn't know what she was talking about. There was no way my dad would ever find out.

No way at all.

Chapter Four

The next morning, I'm zoned out to the monotonous hum of foams and grinds when there's a sudden moment of quiet.

"Finally," D says, staring out the front door, as he wipes down the counter.

Ah. Sweet respite that we're in desperate need of and that we hardly get, and who knows how long it'll last. "Do you think people will ever rid themselves of this addiction?"

D tosses the towel over his shoulder. "Coffee's a great drug. You know what else is?"

I turn my back to him, while still dealing out a side-eye. "I smell something lecture-y seeping out of your skin."

There's a blur of white and a stinging swat at my back that makes me go "yeowch" as I spin on my heels.

"That's what you get for giving me an ounce of sass," D says, wagging the towel in my face. "You know what I'm going to say."

I've known him so long—since junior high, when I caught him staring at Michael Owens, the ultra-hunky school bully who played basketball, and realized how our thought bubbles mirrored each other's.

Thus, the accidental and mutual outing of Sy Nizam and Dzakir Abdullah made us compatriot mo's for life. We weren't exactly outcasts, but Michael Owens did make anyone smaller (me) or larger (Dzakir) than him targets of shoves and name calls. Dzakir and I weathered it all—him with his acid, brusque persona that could wipe a smirk off any blossoming mean girl and me, who coasted along, meek and subservient.

All to say, he can read me and vice versa.

But back to our discussion, and it isn't the time to roll my eyes. "Love. Love is a drug."

"Precisely, my fair gaydy. And it's something you need to wean yourself off of."

"What're you talking about?" My shrug is miles high. "I've only looked at his pic twice this morning."

"That's twice more than necessary. You need to be like me."

"An angry bulldog?" I leap to the side before the towel can schwack me again.

But he retires his weapon this time, throwing it into the sink. "I mean, think about it. We've seen all the movies and read the books. No one ever makes it with their blippity high school sweetheart."

Two things I'll never understand: D never, ever using a curse word (something I don't appreciate) and D always trying to perk up his extra-downer of a friend (something I totally appreciate). He's been there since the very beginning, and there's no doubt he'll be there till the end. "So you're saying . . ."

"I'm saying Farouk's just one frog. There'll be plenty more."

"Oh my god. Did you really just call him an amphibian?"

The evil in D's smile glimmers like the North Star. "Life's one big fairy tale, Sy. You've got to kiss a lot of them to find your true love. Trust me."

"Ew. That explains your cold sore."

"What? No. What?" D's quick to swipe a finger on either side of his mouth. "There's nothing there."

I raise my hands in surrender before he can jump me. "I'm kidding. I'm so kidding."

But he's already grinding his teeth.

That's when my phone vibrates in my pocket. "Time-out. It's that time, D."

His eyes take in the clock on the register as the steam hissing out of his ears dissipates. "Fine. Go take your lunch and talk to Mama."

Phone in hand. Slide to answer. "Umi? One sec." I cradle it between my cheek and upraised shoulder, stuff an egg salad sandwich into a paper bag, and grab a bottled water. Oh, and the trash from the bin.

"Sayyed, did you hear what happened?" Umi says, her voice slick with panic.

Uh-oh. "No, Umi." I haul the trash and my lunch through the back door of the café and into the bright sunlight. "I've been too busy with work to even check the news." Which is a lie, since occasionally—or maybe somewhat frequently—I grab my sad phone with its spiderwebbed screen to do quick searches of one Farouk Hameed. "Yes, busy, busy, busy," I say, flinging the bag of trash into the dumpster.

"Are you okay? I'm just so worried about the protests!"

"Why wouldn't I be okay, Umi?" I heave the trash into the dumpster, and I'm already sweating in the August heat. "Wait, what protests? Where did this happen?"

"London."

Oh, Umi. "Los Angeles is not really next door to London, you know."

"I know that, but you didn't call, so I got worried."

"Sorry. I'm just going for lunch now."

A contented sigh. "Sayyed, come home early, okay? I think it's just strange out there, especially for people like us, you know, and I get all these thoughts in my head and—"

"I know, Umi. I will try to leave early. I promise."

"Okay, good. Also, get some turmeric and chili powder at Raju's on your way home. I need to make my special curry powder to give to your baba for his trip. I want to make his other wife jealous of how good it tastes compared to hers."

Ugh. It's always about his other wife and family in Mumbai. *Sayyed, come home early and take care of your umi and Sofia, so I can take care of your stepmother and two half siblings.* I'd like to think if you can't really afford to have one family, why be so horny as to have another? "You should just let Baba go and not come back."

Another sigh, a tired one. "Sayyed, you have to respect your baba. Don't talk about him like that. You wouldn't be on this earth without him."

"Yes, yes. I know." I grab the water out of my back pocket and take a few good gulps.

"Okay, Sayyed. Be good, and don't forget: come home early, okay? Bye."

"Yes, Umi. Bye."

"Okay, bye."

"Bye, Umi."

"Okay, bye, Sayyed."

I have to hang up, because Umi will never do it first.

A photo of Farouk and me wallpapers my lock screen. His arm is wrapped around me, his six-foot-three frame clearly and absolutely dwarfing my tiny five-foot-eight(ish) body. Hasn't helped that I've shed ten pounds in the last three months, having subsisted only on the tiniest café sandwiches, a light dinner at home, and a regular flush of Diet Coke.

I'd love to show Farouk the black hole he left behind. The one I can't fill with any amount of wishing and hoping and praying and starving.

I'm sure he's having a basket load of fun. But he hasn't Instagrammed in more than a month, the bastard. Maybe it's time I peel him off from my lock screen.

"He's a handsome one, that Farouk."

What the . . . ? A head hangs out from behind the dumpster, ponytail swaying, saying those words.

It's the same girl from yesterday, blinking at me. *But how did she—?* "Oh. It's you. Again."

She steps her entire body out and . . . she does look slightly refreshed, not tipsy at all, and kinda cute in a body-hugging green onesie. "Aww, love. At least show *some* excitement at my reappearance," she says, strutting over and swinging the end of her ponytail in my face.

I push down on the nerves clawing their way out of my stomach. "What are you doing here? How do you know about Farouk?"

"Farouk? Farouk who?" She scratches her head like an old-timey cartoon character.

"You've mentioned my ex, Farouk, twice now, but . . . we don't even know each other. So how—?"

"Hush," she says, finger on her lips. "Do you hear that?"

"Hear what?"

She shakes her head. "I thought I heard someone whistling at my curve-tastic bodyliciousness." She traces a finger slowly from the base of her shiny black ponytail, down the side of her ample bosom, all the way to her hip. "Or it might've been a plane, actually. Say, darling, what've you got in your hand there?"

I side-eye my paper bag. "Lunch."

"What's in it?" she says with a squint.

"Uh. Egg salad sandwich."

If I've never seen a murderous grin before, I'm surely seeing one now.

"Would you offer it to me?" she asks. "I haven't eaten in ages. I mean it. Literally ages. And my tummy's a-rumbling and a-tumbling."

"Uh . . ." What would I eat, then?

"What if I offer you something in return?" She hoists her purse from her left armpit—the angry yellow thing looks slightly soggier than it did yesterday—unzips it, and peers in. "Well, that's not going to work. Oh, wait." She pulls out a card and hands it to me.

There's a phone number on top and the words:

> Regina, but preferably Reggie.
> *(Because that's the name I usually answer to. Preferably.)*
> Here to make your wishes come true.

Oh god. "I'm sorry, but—"

"Did you not read the 'wishes' thing?" she asks with a flit of her lashes. "You could wish for me to be your best friend."

A billboard with neon lights should flash BAD IDEA over her head. "Thanks, but I have enough of those." I actually only have Dzakir, but I take a step back, trying to find the door handle behind me with my hand, to slip back into safety. Because my lunch break is about to turn into a slasher flick.

"Okay, how about this? In exchange for that thing you did for me yesterday—you know, that scraping-me-up-off-the-floor thing—*and* for the sandwich, I'll offer you three wishes."

"What? Are you serious?" Where is that dang door handle? It used to be somewhere right about butt-level . . .

"Oh, get on with it." Before I can stop her, she grabs the paper bag, tears open the sandwich wrapper, and takes a large bite. "Make your first wish."

It's exactly this kind of thing that Umi says is the reason I should stay in my bedroom and never leave. "Please don't make me call the police."

Her eyes go dark, with a sparkle of menace. "I said, *make your first wish.* Do it."

"What? What would I wish for?"

"Dammit. Just wish."

So, in the sorriest effort at an escape, I utter the first thing that comes to mind. "I wish for a million dollars." This is the moment the scene turns, and tonight they'll find me knifed to death for complying with a stranger's wish-granting.

She pulls a phone out from her other armpit and, with eyes fixed on me, her fingers dance a hypnotic salsa on the screen. "Done."

"Done what?"

"I really do like that thumb ring, by the way. I'm off to get myself one now. Ta, darling."

The ring Farouk gave me. The one he made me promise to never, ever take off. The one I can't seem to stop twirling around my meatless thumb.

But she takes off, although not before crashing into the dumpster next to us, recovering, then hop-skipping her merry way out of the alley and almost getting run over by a honking convertible.

Um . . . what?

I sink against the wall for support. Flabberblah . . . that's what I am . . . with a bunch of " . . ." filling my brain as I drag my sorry, hungry, confused ass out of the alley.

A million dollars. Okay. What a joke. Now I need to figure out how much I have left in my account so I can get something else for lunch, since the café gives an allowance of one measly food item per shift.

I log on to my bank app under the glare of the intense sun— *please please please it's almost payday*—braving a squinty eye, hoping for more than fifteen bucks, enough for a new sandwich, plus the spices Umi wanted me to get. But that's funny.

The cracked screen must've finally given up on me, because for some strange and unknowable reason, my account balance is a little more than I expected:

One million dollars more.

Chapter Five

HAMZA AND THE DJINN

The city of Salamat sat in a lush oasis clustered with palm trees in the middle of an otherwise barren desert. It was ruled by the well-established Mansour family, who owned Salamat's wells. Because water was the spring of all life, they harvested gold, rubies, and diamonds from merchants all across the land.

Hamza Mansour was the sole scion of all this wealth and one half of our tale. A victim of privilege, he was afforded interests in the arts and settled on being a flautist. Hamza gave little concern to earning a living and spent years honing his craft, fingertips brushing and rat-a-tat-ing on his silver flute, showcasing unmatched talent to peers of his rank and to the adoring public.

Delima, the other half of our tragedy, was a plucky orphan with cunning and wit to match Hamza's talents. She was born of the alleys, a wily street urchinette with a face gummed by dirt but with a lithe body carved by hunger. She haunted the winding streets of Salamat and had learned to pick pockets and fruit stands at a very young age.

But their fates were twined in a moment of pure kismet.

One evening, Delima stood outside the arena where Hamza played and basked in the melody as it floated into her ears and echoed within her soul. So what if she couldn't pay with silver and gold for a seat inside? Delima had learned her own ways to indulge in the otherworldliness of the rich. Like how she'd watch sunsets and munch on stale bread while savoring the delightful smells as she leaned against the outside walls of fine restaurants.

Because there was no way their two worlds should ever collide.

If she hadn't been daydreaming and humming to herself, eyes closed in the shadows, and if Hamza hadn't stepped out at intermission, they might have never met. When he slipped outside for a breath of smoke-free air, Hamza saw the curves of Delima's body slinking away from the colonnade. He tried to stop her, but it was too late.

She was gone.

The next night, he snuck away again at intermission and once again saw her silhouette. With a tinge of curiosity, he begged her not to leave, to stay and keep him company.

But Delima knew no good would come of it. And once again, she sprinted away, but promised herself she would be more careful and would not make the same mistake again.

Hamza wanted to try for the final time. So the next night, when he saw her faint shadow at the farthest colonnade, he raised his flute to his lips and played. His fingers flew with a sureness as he took step after step, afraid of making the smallest mistake on the journey.

He was but a step away, his breath so soft as he played, as he watched the lines on her face, eyes closed but filled with contentedness.

That was when he knew he had to know her.

He stopped playing, and her eyes flew open, filled with sudden alarm.

But he raised his hand and begged for her to stay.

As torn as she was, Delima saw something in him that instilled calm in her. So she planted her bare feet into the sand and stood her ground.

They hovered in the shadows, eyes locked in the moonlight, and he asked permission to rub the dirt from her cheeks. They spoke about circumstances—what lives they had lived that had brought them there, to that very instant of happenstance. And when his name was called by the conductor, he asked to see her again the following night.

And the following night and the following night.

Their love bloomed and blossomed over weeks. But the rule of the land forbade rich and poor to stand side by side, as Delima had known from the very beginning. She wasn't at all surprised when Hamza's parents objected to her presence, since it stained him of poverty.

There were threats of rejection, ejection, and disownment. Yet Hamza and Delima's story wasn't of their enduring love or of their eventual departure from each other's arms but of the dire results of a moment of indecision.

It was thanks to a tear-soaked moment in the garden surrounding one of his family's wells on the outskirts of Salamat.

With faces buried in the other's shoulder, drenching shirt and blouse with salty streams, they argued about their future. She couldn't have him live by her side, begging for scraps, and he couldn't imagine a life without her.

Through a heated exchange of words, they'd forgotten to heed their surroundings. And it was then that one of nature's most potent predators made its approach: the dreaded sand viper slithered toward them, singling out the scent of human sweat. Before either of our lovers could hear the grass shake beneath them, the viper struck, lashing at Delima's heel, injecting a stream of venom.

Our young hero watched the life of the woman who held his heart wither in front of him. And when the light left her eyes, it left his too.

It was a tragedy of his own making but one he promised to spend his whole life undoing.

After her burial, he searched for ways to ease his pain, and when none came, he bundled gold coins into his pockets—gold could pay for anything; perhaps it could find someone to bring his dead Delima back. So he stepped onto the sands of the desert, embarking on a journey with unknown destination.

It was luck that, a mere day after leaving lush green grass, his slippered foot dislodged a crystal-blue bottle from under a mound of sand. His eyes blurry from dehydration and all curiosity piqued, he crashed to his knees, picked up the bottle, and peered into its murky depths. With one twist, he unsealed the stopper, and whoosh . . .

An olive-skinned beauty appeared, her eyes as bright as the moon, hair in a tight ponytail, and body wrapped in a shimmering silver robe that jingled. She blinked curiously at Hamza. A beam of a smile lit up her face as she bowed, revealing that he was, from that moment on, her master, and she—a djinn—was in deep gratitude for the release from her prison.

His act of kindness would be rewarded with three wishes.

A mystified Hamza rubbed his weary eyes, dug at invisible sand pouring from his ears, and mumbled incoherent words through cracked lips, wondering if he needed water to ease this hallucination.

The djinn helped him rise and guided him toward a bubbling spring just around a dune.

When he asked if he'd used up a wish for that offer of water, she laughed and admitted that she was tasked with keeping him alive until all his wishes were granted.

A strange phenomenon she would call a "loophole."

Hamza did not have the energy to decipher her words but simply asked if he could wish his fiancée back from the dead.

The djinn took on a dark visage and shook her head. Resurrection was forbidden within all laws of the universe.

Hamza hung his head over the puddle, his tears tainting its pure water. But the djinn, being of a kind soul, offered advice for our weary hero. There was a way for him to bring his precious Delima back, but the journey would be arduous.

If that was the only chance he had to bring her back, then so be it.

And there he made his first wish: Hamza wished to go to the Underworld.

Chapter Six

I feel a waterfall of bile coming up.

I've just sprinted five blocks, braving early-afternoon traffic, to the ATM. An ATM that verified I have a whole million dollars parked in my account, earning me real-time interest—which is totally beside the point.

The point is, I have a million dollars. And I have no idea how. Did I accidentally hack someone else's bank account?

Or was that Reggie girl really telling me the truth, even though I was totally kidding and obviously she was, too, right? Except she wasn't, because I have a million freaking dollars in my account.

Breathe. Don't spew.

I need to slap my cheeks, smack them with a dab of reality. I mean, that's money I can use to move out, gain independence, escape from my father—

And maybe figure out how to get Farouk back?

But I can't; there's no way. I wasn't ready to leave with him. That didn't mean he had to disappear.

Roukie. I miss you. What do I do?

Calm down.

If that ponytailed girl got me involved in some shit nugget of an FBI sting, God help me, I'll . . . I'll . . .

I don't know what I'll do.

My hands shake as I dial her number. "Hey, it's Sy. How did this . . . how did you . . . please tell me I'm not . . . going to jail?" I huff from my tired lungs.

"Jail? June-gloom gray wouldn't be a good color on you, dearie. That shade is only compatible with one queen, and that is the late Queen Victoria's pale complexion, not your beautiful brown skin. No, no, darling."

So far, this call is failing miserably at allaying my fears.

I stop walking just a block away from the West Hollywood Mall. "Please be serious. This is my life you're toying with. I've got a long one—hopefully—ahead of me, and I'll probably need all the years I have left to take care of my mother."

"What is this talk? Of course you will live a long life. Hold on."

"Hold on? For what?"

The pause is five seconds long, but it sounds like she's chugging something. "Your wish was granted. Don't you remember? You wished it. You. Wished. It. Do I have to repeat myself, hammering you with exclamation points instead of simple full stops, or 'periods' as you might call them in this strange land where—"

"What if the secret service comes after me? Or the FBI? What if I go into the bank and the manager wants to have a *chat* with me about my new account balance? No one has a *chat*; that's what they want you to think when what they really want to do is cuff you to the chair and pull your tongue out and jam toothpicks under your nails."

"Torture? You think they might resort to torture? Which bank is that again?"

"You're not taking me seriously."

"And you keep ignoring what I'm saying."

"I'm not ignoring you." Cars whiz by like Santa Monica Boulevard's a racetrack.

"So listen, then, instead of pretending like none of this makes any sense. It was your wish, so go to Best Buy and get yourself a new phone and throw that cracked piece of garbage away."

Best Buy's right there. Literally across the street. "How do you . . . ?"

"The mysteries of the universe are not yours to comprehend but only for the most studious of minds to—"

And the line goes dead. Did she just hang up on me?

I fidget-dance on the sidewalk. What if I do go to jail? But, like . . . what's wrong with getting a new phone until that happens?

Farouk would do it. He'd want me to just enjoy, to live life in the moment. He always said the saddest book he'd ever read was my unstamped passport. He'd want me to *do* something.

I feel an internal shrug and a meh coming out . . .

Okay. Best Buy.

Here we go.

✦ ✦ ✦ ✦ ✦

Half an hour later, and what do I have in my hands? A top-of-the-line iPhone, a top-of-the-line Nutri Ninja for Umi, and a top-of-the-line e-reader for Sofia. Because this shit is real.

The only wish I ever had that came true was for a wonderful boyfriend who loved me as much as I loved him. Too bad I couldn't wish for him to stay forever.

But this. This total stranger decided a measly helping hand, along with a paper-bag sandwich, were worth a million dollars.

How did this even happen?

Chapter Seven

I think karma is a pretty shitty thing actually," Farouk said. He munched on fried dough, his mom's easiest go-to snack for her son, as we browsed through the YA fantasy aisle at the bookstore.

My lips went from "o" to "O"—like, absolute shock. "How can you . . . ? Karma's going to spank you so hard."

Farouk subscribed to his own nebulous philosophy. At that moment, he was digging into my belief that you had to do good to be repaid with good.

He shook his head. "Sy, it's probably the most selfish thing. I mean, think about it. Karma dictates for the regular person to do good so that they will have good done unto them. And you only have bad things happen to you if you do bad things. Can't you hear how wrong that sounds?"

"As opposed to what?" I asked.

"As opposed to doing good just because you want to, because

you should. Meaning, without expecting anything good or bad in return. Doesn't that sound more sensible?"

I kind of wanted to fold my arms across my chest, but that'd look super defensive. "Ugh. Hate it when you're right."

Farouk blinked at me twice with those huge brown eyes, grinned his cheeky grin, then swooped in to kiss me deep, his aquiline (took me forever to find the perfect adjective) nose brushing against my stubby one, in front of everyone at the bookstore.

Fire burned my cheeks as I dragged his tall ass behind an art book display that didn't do a thing to hide his towering height. "I know you're totally cool with that, but you know if my dad catches me, he'll skin me alive, right after boiling me in hot tar."

Farouk laughed it off. "You need to lighten up. If that ever happens, you'll come and live with me. My mom will want you to."

"Your mom hates me. She knows I'm Indian."

"That's some archaic thinking. My parents are third-generation Pakistani. Super-progressive Muslims. They don't think like that."

"Maybe it's because I'm making you sin by forcing you to commit all those unmentionables and unspeakables whenever I stay over?"

He spun me around to face him and draped his gorilla arms over my shoulders. I could feel them hang behind me, fingertips caressing my upper back. "Silly Sy. That's the good kind of sin. A sin I'll have your damn karma pay me back for many times. Besides, you really shouldn't worry. Mom loves you. She's just adamant about me becoming a surgeon like her."

"So she thinks I'm beneath you. I knew it. I don't even know what I want to do for the rest of my life. Our marriage won't last long."

"Who said we were getting married?" he asked, as stern as he could, but cracking before he could let me even land a punch on his broad swimmer's chest. "We've got to live together and sin together first."

"Live together? Like, how?"

"I was thinking . . . it makes the most sense to live near campus. So I'll get an apartment—my parents will want me to anyway—and you'll obviously . . ." He winks, expecting . . . something?

"And I'll . . . really? We'll actually live together?"

"Yeah. If you want to? I'll find something close to a train station so it'll be easier for you to get to SMC."

Wow. Was it really happening? "You're not just asking because . . . of all my problems with my dad. Are you?"

He leaned in close. "Of course not. I'm asking because I want you with me. All the time."

Speechless. Tongue-tied. Absolutely shushed-out. All the words to describe me.

He went on. "Anyway, what should I get you for our third month–iversary? Thought I forgot, huh? How about your favorite? A book?"

I couldn't stop the grin from touching my eyes. Farouk

knew my obsession, even though I couldn't really afford to buy new books.

"By the way . . . ," he continued. "You, mister, are not beneath anyone. You're more noble than anyone I know, and that's why I love you. And if anyone ever tries to say anything bad about you, do anything wrong to you, I'll make sure these Thanksgiving turkeys of mine"—his seriously apelike hands—"will do what the universe wants them to do. So, going back to what we were talking about. Don't expect anyone to hand you a million dollars just because you helped some old lady cross the street. Or gave food to the needy."

"Did you just say you love me?"

He smirked. "Did you just ignore everything I said? And no, I didn't say that. I said I love you."

"You love me."

"No. I love you."

"Fine. 'I love you.'" *Ah! Did I really just say that?* Heat spread across my cheeks, even as I silly-grinned. He had tricked me into saying the words, but they were true, and there was no turning back. I was his. Forever. And ever. And ever. And ever.

He was the boy who made the world a little less scary for me, and in return, I gave him all the love I had to give.

Chapter Eight

O r, at least I tried to give him all the love I had.

Because then he turned eighteen and decided to leave the country, crushing my heart and our dream of sharing a new life together, even if we could only go to different institutions.

Now, my only connection to him is through Instagram stalking. His last few posts were in London a month ago. Of him waltzing around the town, hanging out with new friends. One at a fish-and-chips shop with some older Middle Eastern guy. Guessing he's the owner. Selfies in front of the London Eye and some street shops. And then a final post. A photo of him in front of a bookstore with a caption saying "signing off for a while." And that was it.

I can't even ask him if I should keep the million dollars. To see what he'd think about the karmic retribution I might inherit by keeping what might not be rightfully mine.

Meh. And ugh.

But maybe I can use that money to convince him to come home so we can have a life together—can I do that? We could start an animal sanctuary, or a scholarship fund, or . . . ?

Gosh. Those seem a little too far off in the future for me to even consider.

And what good will any of it do, since I'll just be using it as bait? Karmically, that's pretty sleazy.

Maybe I should just blow it all on a lifetime of cocaine and alcohol. I hear that's what celebrities do.

Did all of this seriously start with an egg salad sandwich and a helping hand? Why would someone give me all those dollars for food and a bit of assistance?

I'm still on the Boulevard, hauling gifts, wondering if this might be a good time to text Farouk, to ask him all these questions, instead of letting them muck around in my head, when my new phone buzzes.

Reggie: YOU'RE NOT GOING TO BELIEVE WHAT I JUST SAW. SERIOUSLY. HOLD ON TO YOUR VICTORIA'S SECRET PANTIES. YOU'RE GOING TO DIE! CLICK ON THE LINK I'M SENDING NEXT!

I'm not usually one to fall for clickbait, but I have been waiting two minutes for a follow-up. When none arrives, I can only vent my frustration:

Me: Well?

Nothing. Then finally:

Reggie: I told you to hold on to your panties. But clearly you're of the "in a bunch" kind. Anyway. Here you go.
Grinning face

It's the same photo of Farouk in London. In front of the street shops—an ALDI and some others. Ugh.

Me: This is an old photo. What about it?
Reggie: You're such a twonglehead. Do you know where that is? *Scratchy head face*
Me: London
Reggie: Yes . . . and? *Shrug face*
Me: And what? Also, haven't you heard of emojis? Instead of typing all your reactions out in between asterisks?
Reggie: Emojis? Sounds made up. Anyways, you have a million dollars now. What's stopping you from visiting Londontown to win your ex back? *Questioning face with a hand scratching chin*

Uh . . . my umi for one. That and the fact that I've never traveled beyond a ten-mile radius without my parents. I've never even been on a plane.

But maybe she's right. Is all this money worth it if I don't have the boy I'd love to spend it with?

Reggie: Anyways, don't forget. Two more wishes. I'm off now to

I wait two more minutes until I realize that's all I'm going to get. I'm so close to ripping out my eyeballs and stuffing them in my ears. It's only our third conversation, and I get the sense that Reggie will always be the giver of more questions than answers.

I pace the sidewalk, my eyes and fingers glued to my phone with its perfectly zoomed-in, pixelated rendition of my Farouk. Is he still somewhere in London? Still within my universe?

I have to do it. Maybe I don't have to *go* to London. But she's right. I have to tell him.

So I message him. On Instagram (meh). Then Twitter (meh). Then Snapchat (meh). Then Facebook (ew!). Then Twitch, and Discord, and every single possible thing I've found him on. Even something called Myspace—not even sure what that is.

I'm still walking the streets, googling his damn name and coming across a hundred thousand quintillion Farouk Hameeds—because, London—doing what private investigators probably do best, and there's no way I'm going to find anything more about him than what I've already gathered.

Super. Annoyingly. Blegh.

Maybe I can use some of the money to hire an actual private investigator? Will that help?

This money has me thinking about possibilities and what

ifs on overdrive. Can't help it. Going to call him. A quick hit of the speed dial (yes, he's still programmed in my phone).

But my heart drops.

Those harsh beeps. It just goes dead.

Why is his line doing that?

A thread of panic weaves into me. Is his phone disconnected? Or has he blocked me? Or did he sell off his phone in a final attempt at truly signing off, like his last post said?

No choice but to go for the nuclear option. I look through my contacts and dial the only person who might know:

"Assalamualaikum."

"Wa'alaikumsalam, Auntie. It's Sy . . . Sayyed."

Breathy silence. "Why are you calling?"

So awkward. "Auntie, I'm sorry for not calling in a few months, but I wanted to know if Farouk is . . . ?" *Home? Alive? Hating me?* "Okay?"

"You still dare call this house?"

The words crystallize my spine. What is she talking about? "I didn't do anything to Farouk, Auntie. I—"

"You didn't try hard enough and because of that, he gave up everything and ran off halfway to the other side of the world. And now . . . he's . . ." There's sniffling. "Never call here again!" The line cuts off.

What the . . . ?

What was she about to say? Did something happen to Farouk while he was in London?

Questions burn holes in my brain. How the hell am I going to—?

Dzakir: WHERE THE HECK ARE YOU? DO YOU KNOW
WHAT TIME IT IS?

Uh-oh. I'm a half hour late. Which means Dzakir's been
waiting all this while for me to be back so he can take his lunch.

I start to run but can manage only a hobbling sprint with
my new packages flying around. What the heck am I going to
do to make up for this? Dzakir spits fiery insults when he hasn't
been fed. Plus, he's had to work by himself this whole time,
which will make him exponentially hungrier and angrier.

Just. Freaking. Great.

Chapter Nine

The café's familiar glass door looms—totally smudge- and streak-free once again—but something burns in the air. Not coffee beans but maybe the glower homed in on me. It's bad. Oh, it's that bad. "I'm sorry, D"—my voice comes out as a squeak—"but you've got to let me explain."

There's just one customer in the café. A petite woman with pigtails and overalls, staring at us with sudden interest.

There's no doubt D's got all the drama covered—he doesn't need a larger audience. "What in the freaking blippity bleep's godforsaken name is wrong with you, sister? Do you know how long I've been waiting for you to come back?"

"I know; I'm sorry. Just let me—"

"Three hours. I've been waiting for *three dangity hours*. I almost ate that bowl of sugar packets."

Uh-oh. I fear he's on the verge of actually cursing. "I was

gone less than an hour. I mean, it was just over an hour, which I don't think is all that bad, and—"

Heat is fuming forth from Mount Dzakirious.

And my insides are all knotted up. "I know, I know, please—"

"Stop saying 'I know' because you obviously don't. What kind of inconsiderate person would do this to his best friend?"

I unlock my new phone and quickly switch to my bank account, so my balance is on full display. All those zeros getting me into so much trouble. "Look, this was what happened just after I stepped out for lunch and . . . okay . . . I . . . guess . . . we're . . . not . . . listening."

Dzakir stares at the phone with slits for eyes, taking in every square pixel, and for a quick moment, he looks away, then back at me, before setting his hands, thumbs forward, on his hips. "I. Am. So. Sick. Of. You. And Farouk and all the stupid crap that you get yourself into because of one freaktastically useless bumbum who freaking left you and forgot about you and went and did his own thing without worrying that you're still here not realizing how foolish you are being. So. So. *So* foolish"—he breathes—"and I can't believe I have to listen to you make up bull like this some more for god knows how long because you managed to figure out how to hack an ATM and I thought you were broke"—another breath—"so where the heck did you get the money to buy a new phone, you whore?"

I have no idea what the string of words means, but I've retreated to the door by the time he's done, and the tiny pigtaily thing has also disappeared from sight and site, coffee be damned.

"D, that ponytailed girl from yesterday, the one who banged into the door? Ugh, I don't even know how to explain even though I'm trying to, so please let me just gather some of my thoughts and I can maybe lay it all out for you to see, including how I got this new phone during my lunch break, and I promise you, I didn't have to whore out my undernourished body on the Boulevard to get it."

Dzakir's body quivers with fury, like a freshly plucked guitar string. "Go on. Explain. All of it. I'm listening, because clearly I have nothing to do but keep listening to you until the moment you decide you're not more important than everyone else. Go on. Go. I said G-O. Go."

"I . . . you see . . . the girl who banged herself . . . front door . . . lying on the floor . . . wishes and egg salad sandwich . . ."

The words become mush in my mouth.

"Precisely," Dzakir concludes before I can try again. "You were just being your selfish self again. It's always 'Farouk this' and 'my needs that' and 'I'll be alone until the end of time' and 'you'll never understand how it feels' and 'boo me.'" He drags in a breath. "No, Sy, my life is not perfect and I have my own problems too, but you'll never understand. So I think you should go home."

I'm speechless. Defeated. Giving up. "Are you being serious right now?"

He just stares at me.

I slink behind the counter and stuff Umi's and Sofia's presents into my backpack.

And make my way out, wondering how long this one storm will last.

✦ ✦ ✦ ✦ ✦

Never in the history of my years with Dzakir have I seen him that mad.

Dzakir eats his feelings, but he also works out all of it at the gym, which has caused a cycle of eat, hunger, eat, hunger, and given him a strangely beefy, muscular physique.

In our history, his hunger has caused many an outburst, usually directed at others, but I've never seen him as mad as he was just a few minutes ago. I can only guess something terrible must be going on at home with his dad.

Something we little gay boys share.

See, he and his dad moved from Singapore all the way to Los Angeles after Dzakir's mother died, but the man was no longer the same person he used to be, and often takes his anger out on my poor friend. Who's learned to deal with it.

The thought makes my stomach drop. I wish Dzakir would talk to me instead of bursting like that. I don't really have a choice right now but to wait it out, hoping he'll forgive me, because it was my damn fault.

No. It was that girl's fault. Reggie. Here I am, waiting at the bus stop, so so so mad that I can feel the fury radiating, seeping out of my core like some evil bonfire. But hang on a quick minute.

Here's a tiny twist.

What am I doing waiting for the bus when I can take a taxi home? It's only four, and Umi did ask me to be home early.

I go to the ATM to withdraw cash for all her spices and treat myself to a sad, lonely, but very swift ride home.

All the way thinking of how I have become the loneliest person in the world so very quickly.

Chapter Ten

After a quick stop at Raju's, I burst through the front door, safe again from the evils of Outside. The neighborhood I live in isn't too bad, but shit still happens. Umi keeps reminding me about the college kid who got shot a few months ago—although that was two miles away, so technically nowhere near in this big, sprawling city.

Stuff like that can send Umi into the tizziest of tizzies, and here she is, latched on to me with what I thought would be a hug, but no, it's practically a body lock. This close, that familiar mothery smell of spices and rices and care and concern wafts into my nostrils. "Umi . . . let me at least . . . put down my backpack."

We're not supposed to be typically affectionate—because, Asians—but Umi will show her embarrassing love whenever she damn well feels like it. Not her exact wording, but that's the easiest way to describe the ferocity of her love.

"Sayyed, I'm so glad you're home. I've been worrying non-stop. I heard someone threw a bottle at a Muslim and now the poor man's in a coma, because it hit him right in the head. And this was outside a mosque."

"Umi, where did this happen?"

"Berlin."

My mother also wins the gold at hurdling to conclusions. "That's a million miles away, Umi. We're safe here in LA." I kinda want to believe that, but . . . eh?

She tsks me, her eyes widening, while she ties her graying hair up into a bun. "We're safe nowhere. Do not take anything for granted, Sayyed. This world is not always good."

I can't help it; a lot of Umi's fears have rubbed off on me, although I'm less irrational about it. "Umi, I know there are murderers and racists out there, but I always look over my shoulder, and I know that if a car pulls up right next to me as I'm walking, I should—"

"Take off at a sprint and don't stop running until your lungs give out, preferably to somewhere safe, hopefully with a security guard."

That's our mantra for walking home alone, especially at night. "Yes, Umi. Anyway, what did you cook?" Asking about food always distracts her quick. "Anything ready yet?"

"Want me to heat up yesterday's fried chicken and rice for you?"

I can never say no to that. "Sure. I'll go shower."

I spend ten minutes seated on the toilet, lamenting my BFF's overreaction while searching for we-know-who on

my phone, then spend only the last two minutes actually show-
ering. The bathroom is one of the few places I can have privacy
in the house. I'm not good at a lot of things, but anyone can
quiz me on a speedy self-cleaning.

God, I can't wait to move out. Whenever that day may
come.

Sofia finds me as I exit the bathroom. Her left eyebrow
quirks up in accusation. "You're home early, brother."

Uh. "Thank you for checking in on me, dear sister. They
didn't need me this afternoon. The big boss came in and helped
out."

Soooo mannnyyy liessssss.

She squints at me, tugs at her braid. "You did something
bad, didn't you? Spill it." Sofia isn't too great with math and the
sciences, but she makes up for it with Sherlockian powers of
deduction. This teeny spitfire can smell an untruth, or a con,
or one of those creepy older men hiding around a corner. She's
smarter than me on so many things.

"I did nothing wrong. D got mad at me over something
blegh. Anyway, Umi wanted me home early."

"You were late coming back from lunch and he got mad
because you let him get hungry, didn't you? Why didn't you tell
him to just down a dozen sugar packets on the spot or when he
started to feel the stomach acid attack his empty brain?"

What? How? Did she bug my phone? "Go to your room."

"Nicely played, brother. You really are the wimpiest person
I know."

"I'm not wimpy. I'm merely a pacifist."

"In all the history of mankind, pacifist equals wimpy nice guys who never win. Umi says food is ready. Go eat."

She's right. The earthy burst of turmeric and cardamom and chili powder spikes the air. I dash to my room with a towel still clutched around my waist and exchange that for a raggedy Captain America T-shirt and basketball shorts that have never seen a court in their lives.

Deep in my dear umi's kitchen, which has always looked frozen in time with the same rice cooker, same fridge, same stove, and same dining set among other relics from when I was born, she sets out a steamy plate of last night's rice with lentils and fried chicken. I wash my right hand real quick and, as Umi watches—her most favorite thing to do, since she gets so much joy out of watching her children savor the years of honed crafts-manship—I say a quick "bismillah" before digging in, scooping up a mound of food into my mouth.

"Still good?" Umi asks.

"You know your cooking's amazing. Even the next day." Another clump of lentil'd rice hovers an inch from my mouth. "And you don't always have to stand there and make sure I eat every grain of rice every time, you know."

"Stop complaining, Sayyed. Or I'll get your father's second wife to send over some of *her* cooking."

"Speaking of unnecessary family members, why don't you just get a— Ouch! Why'd you hit my arm?"

"I'll give you a tight slap next time you start to say anything like that again."

"But he—"

"No more talk. Eat. Or I'll twist your ear so hard, it'll get as large as an elephant's."

We've had this argument too many times, although I secretly clap my hands in glee every time Baba leaves, because it always feels like the monster has finally left the village and its people. Anyway, Umi's bark is much harsher than anything she's ever done to us (although her pinches might come close). She's the kind of mother who'd dole out punishment and then cry afterward. Because her heart is mushier than a ripe mango.

I so wish I could protect it. "By the way," I say, pointing to my backpack. "Got you a present. And the spices you wanted as well."

She grabs my bulbous bundle, unzips it, pulls out one of the boxes inside. "What's this? Oh, Sayyed, I don't need a new one."

"Of course you do. Everything you put in the old blender now tastes like ground chili and onions. I tried to make apple juice the other day and it tasted so ew. This model's pretty cool, I think. It doesn't absorb strong flavors, since the container's made of this super-durable, curry-resistant glass."

"You're such a good son." She sticks her head into the hallway and shouts out, "Sofia, come look what your brother got for me."

The TV in the living room is set to CNN, which has been broadcasting the current protests in London. Umi tsks at the screen. "I thought they were peaceful there?"

My sister drags herself out of her room and appears at the kitchen's threshold. "What is it? I've got so much math to do, my eyes are starting to spin. Wait, is that a new blender? Where did he get the money?"

In an effort to shut her up—I swear she needs a lip zipper—I rush over to my backpack and pull out her gift and hand it to her with my clean left hand. "This is for you."

She narrow-eyes the box before grabbing it as if it's booby-trapped. "An e-reader? Is it the one with enough space for ten thousand books? Where'd you get the money for all these gifts, brother? No, don't tell me. Is that why you got sent home early today? Did you steal money? Did you get fired for stealing money?"

My eyes must be so big, because they feel like they're about to pop out and bounce against the walls. "What are you talking about, you ridiculous girl? I did not do such a thing."

Umi coaxes the blender next to my plate. "Sayyed, she's right. How did you get all these things? They're not cheap."

It is at this very moment that the front door swings open. All eyes turn to Baba.

Oh no.

He scans the three of us for telltale signs of treachery, collusion, and deceit. "What's going on here?"

Chapter Eleven

Nothing, Baba," I say. "Got a bonus at work. For being such a hard worker that my boss decided to reward my hard work. With a bonus. For all the hard work." I'm trying so hard not to gulp, because that's the ultimate giveaway for nervousness.

He eyes Sofia's e-reader and Umi's blender, scratching at the left side of his mustache. "Where's mine?"

Uh-oh. It'll come to me. Please let it come to me. "It's on special order. Out of stock or something. It's this new, uh . . . mustache trimmer that has a laser that can guide your trimming or something like that. Something-something laser beard mustache something-something trimmer."

He narrows the distance with just a step, and it suddenly feels like he's an inch away. This is the man who's more intimate with the backhand than a hug.

I can only cower, trying hard to not run off and escape.

"I do need a new one," he says. And then he's off to the

living room, remote in hand, planting himself into the worn pleather couch until he's ready for dinner.

"Like I said, Sayyed, you're the best son any mother could ever want," Umi says to ease the tension.

I summon a smile, even though it feels like the slimiest ever. I hate lying to her, but right now, I kind of have to with what I hope is the most bleached white lie ever.

Seriously. *Alllll the lieeesssss.*

"Brother, thank you for my wonderful gift," Sofia says with a meekness that's so transparent. "Can you help me with my math homework now? Please? I'll be waiting because it's due tomorrow. Thank you." And she's gone.

My appetite's gone out the window. I wash my hands and try to help Umi clean up, but she shoos me out. Sofia wants something. Either that or she's about to interrogate the hell out of me. Because she's got no homework at all. Since there's no school.

I tiptoe into her room. "You don't want my help. Spill it."

She's in her desk chair with her back to me, and she swivels it around slowly like the evilest villain. "No, you spill it. I want to know where you got all the money. Or I tell Baba. Stealing is a sin, brother."

"Ugh. You're such a righteous and nosy bee." I brave a glance in the living room. Baba's tuned in to his soccer match. Good. He'll be glued to his seat for the remainder of the game. I shuffle to Sofia's side. "You can't tell anyone. Promise?"

"I cannot promise. If you're involved in something criminal

that might lead to our family's downfall and send any one of us to jail, then—"

"Okay, fine. I'm not going to tell you anything."

"BAB—"

I slap my palm on her wide-open mouth. "Incorrigible. Do you know that word? I'll spell it for you."

"I know the meaning. Now tell me everything."

Sofia's the best at blackmail.

I sit on the edge of her bed, grabbing one of her plush Hello Kitty pillows to hug—a shield against a worthy opponent. "I helped someone, and she gave me some money."

"How much?"

"Doesn't matter. Just think of it as a reward. Maybe even enough to . . ."

She eyes me. "Let me guess. Farouk? What, enough for you to chase after him?"

"All he did was love me, and I betrayed him when I wouldn't leave with him."

She spares me for a second. "Enjoy this one time where I try to be nice. You know there's no way you would ever do a thing like that—leave home at seventeen to travel the world or whatever. I don't even know why you got that passport. And it was a blessing he left you. As much as you annoy me, you're still my brother. Your love for him was leading you astray from the true path of Islam."

"He never led me astray." I let the words sink in. "And . . . Iloveyoutoo."

"So how much money did you get?"

Just to shut her up, I pull out my phone and show her my account balance. She wide-eyes it, then goes all squinty—it's her favorite facial expression—and instantly folds her arms across her chest. "I knew it. You hacked into your boss's bank account, didn't you?"

"No! I told you, I helped some girl, and then all hell kinda, sorta broke loose."

I spend fifteen whole minutes explaining every single ridiculous thing that happened while her face holds a stony stare. I can't even tell how she's taking it. The story ends with Dzakir's outburst, which really was my fault because I could've gotten him a sandwich or something on the way back as a peace offering.

She looks like she's about to empty her dinner onto my face. Finally, she says, "You are truly the most frustrating brother to have in the world. Someone gives you a million dollars and you don't report her to the police? That is obviously drug money. Next, one of her henchmen's going to pick you up and stuff you with condoms packed with cocaine, all the way into your intestines, and you'll have to fly all the way to, who knows, maybe Lithuania and deliver it to someone there, where they account for every single gram of the drug that they put inside you. Unless one of those baggies ruptures before you get there, because then you're really in a ton of trouble as your body starts to die from the inside. Oh, brother, when your brain stops working, it really stops working."

Uh. I'm not the only one Umi's rubbing off on. "Nothing

like that's going to happen. Reggie doesn't seem like the kind of person to . . ."

Except . . . Reggie can barely hold on to a sentence to save her life and can barely walk a straight line to pass a DUI. What the hell did I just get myself into?

Sofia rambles on. "So she's going to grant you two more wishes? It's the twenty-first century, brother; nothing like that will ever happen. You seriously think she's trying to help you find your male lover, the guy you were fooling around with and sinning against our religion and God for, even though it's clear, so clear that he's done with—"

She stops short, and before I know it, I feel it too. The air in the room has changed. There's electricity buzzing, crackling, and I can't help but shudder.

Both our heads swing toward the door at the same time, and my heart sinks right down to my bare soles.

Because standing at the threshold to her room is the one man I fear most.

Baba.

And by the way that mustache bristles, it looks like he's heard everything.

Chapter Twelve

Hamza stood in front of a rusty gate, where a garden of wilted blooms lurked beyond. Darkness sucked every ray of light that entered.

The djinn pointed out the gate to the Underworld and swung it open.

Hamza took a step forward but was immediately shoved back by an invisible hand. He tried again, and again, and again, his strength waning with each attempt, until he asked the djinn how he could step through.

Simple, *she told him. She had taken him to the gates of the Underworld, but he couldn't pass through because he was still human. All he would need to step inside was to die.*

Hamza, distraught, lamented his futile first wish and how he was ill-equipped for the Underworld to claim his soul. Setting aside his confusion, he demanded to know why he must open the gates at all, if he couldn't enter.

The djinn explained to his mortal mind that the gates were designed to deter accidental entry against those enslaved by curiosity, for they housed creatures that humans wouldn't survive against, especially alone. Hamza wanted to know what awaited him once he stepped through, but the djinn would tell him no more, for she wasn't born of that world either, and her knowledge of that realm, though deeper than humans', was still shallower than others of her make and kind.

As Hamza contemplated his next decision, knowing he might not last long in there, a hushed but sustained whisper crept out of the gates, slithering its way down the tunnels of his ears. There were no discernible words in the airy voices but sensations instead. He could feel them within and without. His body began to sweat and squirm as if encased in ecstasy and horror all at once. He glanced beyond the gates and at figures shuffling around, darker than the shadows, again sucking in all the dying light from where he stood outside the gates, all of them anxious. Waiting. But for what?

The djinn snapped her fingers and cleared her throat. She said that it was a mere example of what he could face once he stepped through, but if he were ready, he should decide to make his second wish right there and then.

Delima's face crept into his mind, and all doubt evaporated into the ether. He knew his entire happiness hinged on bringing her back to life, back into his arms. He told the djinn that he was ready.

She shook her head and raised a finger and, with a curious smile, told him that she might be able to sentence him to a gentler punishment, all the while retaining his humanity, if he were to simply wish to be half dead instead.

He didn't think it sounded bad, until her warning that it was a feat no one had attempted before and the results could be disastrous.

Hamza wept a tear, for reasons he couldn't understand, and it felt like a farewell to everything he knew behind him. Salamat, his parents, his friends. And so, with flute by his side, he took a breath and said the words.

The djinn nodded and blessed him with the granting of his second wish.

Hamza felt no different, but he took his first steps toward the gates. After a few breaths to galvanize his confidence, he chanced a finger past the threshold and, when he felt no resistance, slid the entire arm through. He gave the djinn the most wan of smiles, then transported his entire body past the magical barrier, taking a minute to drink in all the darkness the Underworld had to offer.

They relied on the djinn's shimmering silver robe to light the way. But the whispers grew with excitement, and the same sensations crept across and into his body, but before they could take root, Hamza glued his flute to his lips and his fingers took off.

The trills echoed around them, and the dark creatures—all with seemingly humanlike silhouettes—took off, as if pained. Hamza watched their retreat with a glee so triumphant, regaling at the ease of it all. He turned around to take a step outside to explain what he'd just done but found his exit barred. Again by an invisible barrier.

The djinn, alarmed, rushed to his side, stepping through the threshold with ease, explaining that the constitution of her spirit allowed her to weave through the barrier, a feat few other creatures could accomplish.

But she had only sad news for him: upon further inspection of the barrier, she could only conclude that its path was one-directional, and his current physical state was blocking the way out.

Hamza allayed the panic latching on to his throat from inside, as the reality of his situation sank in.

The djinn reassured him that he would simply need to wish for his and Delima's transformations to full human form for the gate to allow them reverse passage, back to the world they'd always known.

Hamza held on to his faith, a rope he hoped would lead him out of the darkness. He placed a good measure of that faith in the djinn, and on he went, through what looked like a garden of wilted black roses.

He had taken fewer than fifty steps in when he heard laughter that chilled his blood. His eyes darted across the dark landscape. A rank odor of rotted meat wafted through and made Hamza's stomach roil. He was fortunate he had not eaten in days, and all that came up was a sour burn. It stung his mouth as it exited, a pool that was immediately absorbed by the soft black soil under his slippered feet.

Hamza played his flute again, and the laughter died, but not before he felt a sharp whack on his back, as if struck by a sharp pebble. He screamed more out of pain than fear, but the djinn laughed and pointed to a slight creature, no bigger than a child, hiding behind a glittering bush.

But the dark being flashed its fangs, and Hamza's heart lurched into his throat.

The creature leaped at him, kicked him on the chest, and sent him crashing to the ground. It perched atop his chest as he landed, and it stayed there, surveying Hamza's face, weighing its options with those very sharp teeth.

Chapter Thirteen

Once, when Sofia was a toddler, she walked up quietly to Baba, who was busy spanking me for one thing or another. Then, when she got close enough, she yelped and threw her empty milk bottle at him, hitting him squarely in the nose. She tumbled to the floor, letting out the most ear-piercing cry. Baba had to let go of my arm so he could cradle her in his, giving me a chance to escape to my room, where I scrambled under the bed. Umi was busy cooking dhal, with Rishi Kapoor belting out some tune on her phone—from the movie *Bobby*, I think—so she had no idea what had happened just yards away.

I've always faced the brunt of his anger. She's always had a hand in stopping it.

"Sofia, leave." The words spit out of Baba's mouth now, his mustache trembling.

"No, Baba. I don't want to," she says.

"Sofia, I've never laid a hand on you in your life, but if you don't leave this room, that will change. Five."

The countdown. Oh no. Sofia's gaze flicks back and forth.

"Four."

She hangs her head.

"Three."

With one last look at me that spells resignation and an unspoken apology, Sofia pushes herself from the swivel chair and walks out.

Because this time, she can't save me.

Baba watches her leave. In this house, everyone does everything he says.

Now that it's just the two of us, me suddenly cowering on Sofia's bed, a few inches too big in every way to stuff my body under the wooden frame for protection, I can only wait. A hundred mouthless Hello Kittys stare anxiously, waiting for what will happen next.

Baba swings the door shut. There's no escape.

He unbuckles his belt. Slides it out with a rustling of the loops.

Our dance is about to begin. The one I hate most in my unfortunate life.

My hands shuffle me back to the headboard, the sturdy wood propping me up, whispering, *It's finally time to fight back. You are younger, stronger, braver.*

"Tell me, Sayyed. Everything your sister said, was it true?" Baba asks.

I blink so fast and so hard, I start to see constellations. It's a trick question, and I have no idea if there's a right answer. "Baba, please."

"Is that a no? Then why did she say all those things? About your friend Farouk? Are you a homo?"

"I don't know what she's talking about."

He spares just one second before he leaps across the room.

My tiny hands can't shield my entire body from the lashes that swing in every direction, at my arms, my legs, my torso. I squirm on Sofia's thin mattress with every hit, a little earthworm dying out in the afternoon sun, struggling against the hot rays striping its body.

Thwack. Thwack.

The screams tear themselves out of my throat—*Baba, no!* Is it possible to scream so loud that you burst your own eardrums? All I can smell is my familiar uselessness, which is a hint of salty sweat and snot running down my nose and into my throat.

He times every stroke with words that leach my sanity.

"Don't lie to me, you filthy boy." *Baba, don't.*

"I can't even imagine what you do with him." *Baba, stop. I didn't do anything.*

"You make me sick." *No, Baba, that hurts.*

I don't even know how the words leak out of my mouth. The words that spell my doom. "We never had sex!"

And there it is. In his eyes. No way to describe that look. "Get up," he whispers.

There's a point, in crying, where you're just racked with sobs, when breathing becomes a ragged chore, chopping up all your words into worthless syllables. "I'm . . . sorry . . . sor . . . ry . . . I pro . . . mise . . . Please . . . no more."

"I said *get up*." Baba grabs me by the arm, lifts me off the bed. "Pack your things and get out of my house."

What? But I'm not ready. My departure's supposed to be on my own terms. Not like this . . . as desperate as my need has always been.

There is a wounded yelp behind him.

Umi rushes forward, planting herself squarely in the aim of fire, between her husband and me. "No, Baba, don't. Sayyed has nowhere to go. Our closest family is in Mumbai."

"He should have thought of that before he decided to become *this*. I don't have a homo for a son." His words, all of them, spit disgust and contempt.

Umi falls to the ground, wraps herself around his legs. "No, he's not. Sayyed?" She plants a questioning look at me.

"Umi . . ." But I can't look her in the eyes. "I . . . I . . ."

Umi's face sinks with defeat. "Baba, he's our only son. If it's true, I'm sure he can change. He'll go back on the righteous path. Allah has the power to change hearts. Don't hurt him anymore."

"Get off me." Baba spreads his legs out so Umi loses her grip, then steps aside. "If you want to go with him, then go. Otherwise, stay out of this. I don't want a son who behaves the way he does." He then shoves Umi out the door.

It's time for the worst decision ever in the history of me. If I stay, Umi and Sofia may be in terrible danger; Baba might take his lashings out on them. Plus, there's no way in this damn universe he'll let me stay anyway. But if I go, I'll be faced with who knows what out there. A whole world of unexpected surprises I have no idea how to navigate, because I've been so damn sheltered my whole life.

Guess there's only one thing I can do.

I keep my distance from Baba as I stumble out of Sofia's room and into mine. My entire childhood has been plastered by welts, usually hidden under T-shirts and jeans, and today my body bears the same scars as way back when. All bandaged over calloused old ones. The one thing I can never understand, ever, is why Baba would take out his anger on me. I know I can sometimes do inconsiderate things and make mistakes, but do I deserve to have the shit slapped out of me? Do I deserve to be called demeaning names? Do I deserve to be kicked out simply because . . . I'm gay?

T-shirts, shorts, jeans, underwear—they fly from the dresser into my backpack. My room is pretty bare—I've never had a knack for decorating, so it's just the used books Farouk had gifted me in the bookcase. Unfortunately, those have to stay.

They are a luxury that won't help me on the streets.

Wait a sec. Almost forgot my passport. The one thing Farouk made me get just before things went to shit. He said not having a passport is like being chained to the ground.

Haven't I been a good son? Taken care of my umi? I never really talked back. I adore my little sister, because I know she loves me to the ends of the world.

I can't help but twist the thumb ring furiously. It has always been my wish to get the hell out of here ASAP. And I'm about to have my wish granted.

Except Fate can be the cruelest joker ever.

So can I really do this?

Chapter Fourteen

Carrying my entire life on my back (and limping a little from the déjà vu pain of new bruises), I drift into the living room where, standing solemnly, like pallbearers, are the remaining loves of my life. Baba glowers by the door, waiting, his eyes pinned to the street outside. Guess he doesn't like the look of his homo son.

I want to scream. We shouldn't have to live with this. I suspect neither Umi nor Sofia even bears an ounce of love for Baba, because he's never given a reason for us to.

I also want to tell Umi: *Please come with me. Maybe we can figure out a way for my million dollars to pave a path for us to live successful lives. Maybe I can learn to stop being afraid so that I can become a confident man and learn to take care of us. I don't know if I can do it, but if you give me a chance, I'll give it my best.*

But I know she won't. She's bound by silence, her eyes fixed on mine, begging me to promise to change my errant behavior so I can stay.

Meeting Farouk did not help things one bit. In fact, it's only made everything worse.

I have one card left to play. Her love for me is stronger than anything else I've ever known, and I hope it'll sway her in my direction somehow, even though I know she bears zero power in our stinking family dynamics. "Umi, I can't lose you. Please?" I whisper, tears raging down my face again. I don't know how many more I have left.

She throws herself onto me. "I promised myself I would take care of you and Sofia as much as I could . . . Sayyed, I love you more than the world, but I have to do what your baba says. It is my duty."

I guess that a son's love just isn't enough.

Can't argue with any of it. Can't argue with what she believes in, for the belief is part of who she is. Asking her to abandon that would be like ripping the wings off a butterfly.

Umi kisses me on the forehead, a gesture I return in kind.

Sofia still has a hand on Umi's shoulder, so I grab it and kiss it lightly. "Sister, take care of Umi, since I won't be around any longer. You must figure out how to be good in math so you can graduate and make her proud."

Sofia can only dig her face into Umi's back while her body shakes with tremors that don't seem to end.

"I love you both," I say, knowing how much I'll miss them.

And just like that, I've lost it all. I truly have.

✦ ✦ ✦ ✦ ✦

I'm out the door in a sprint, tasting freedom at last, but it's a bitter freedom, and I suddenly don't know if I want it anymore.

The door slams behind me. Outside, it is still bright, but the sun will set soon.

I huddle into the collar of my T-shirt. Why does it feel like the winds of winter have swooped in when it's still August?

Guess it's all about the little steps. One step away, and then another, and on the third, a thump reverberates from the house. Sounds like Baba's starting the tantrum throwing, something he's pretty good at when he's been ticked off good. I have a feeling he'll be miffed for a long time to come. How will he explain the shameful son his virile, macho, manly sperm produced? No doubt he'll keep it secret from cousins and aunts back in India. Maybe my half brother can save him from embarrassment.

My flesh pulses a dull ache, my skin stinging with rising welts, but at least I won't be the subject of any more beltings. I guess that's a positive, even though it's a pretty raw silver lining.

Where do I go? I've never had to take care of myself, and the sudden infusion of a million dollars doesn't guarantee I won't mess things up.

Time to face the horrors of the real world.

Chapter Fifteen

Farouk and I had just left some late movie. It was a few minutes after midnight, and we were walking to the bus stop. Even though his family did well as surgeons, their nice, big house was still on the same route but north of the freeway. And he could've driven, but he'd always choose to keep me company on the bus as much as he could.

He was so down-to-earth, he was at ground level with the rest of us. Including me.

I was bumping shoulders with him, since I still wasn't feeling the whole hand-holding thing. "Don't they all start to get the same, superhero movies? The heroes gain these amazing powers; go through some door of no return; fight the villains, who exploit their weakness; then they go through their dark night of the soul and finally regain a revamped superpower to defeat the Boss. Isn't that how it always plays out?"

Farouk snickered, swung his arm over my shoulders. "It's

not about superpowers. It's about character. Constitution. How you brave the same world knowing you're a changed person. And also love."

"Never seemed like that to me."

"It's pretty obvious. Take Superman. He's strong in every way, but what's his greatest weakness?"

"Uh . . . Kryptonite."

"Nope. It's Lois Lane. Or simply . . . love. He can always overcome Kryptonite, but he can never bear the thought of Lois getting hurt. And he's also at his strongest when he's with her."

"Okay. How about Batman? He's got no superpower."

"Even though he's human, love is his greatest strength. He fights the bad guys to protect the city he loves so much."

I tried hard not to roll my eyes. Figured I'd throw him a stunner. "Fine. Venom?"

Farouk gave me the meanest but playfulest side-eye. "That one's unfair. He's not really a superhero, more of an antihero. But in any case, Venom's so much in love with his host, Eddie Brock, that he'll do anything to protect the guy. So there you go."

I guessed it was true with most superheroes—as powerful as they were, they would almost always give it all up to protect that one thing they loved. Like Farouk would protect me.

But his body stiffened beside me, his hand gripping firm onto my shoulder.

As a trio of rowdy guys approached. "Um, Roukie?"

Few cars passed us by on 3rd Street, and we were still, like, a hundred yards from the bus stop. We kept walking anyway. "Don't look at them, Sy. Keep your eyes on me."

I wanted to take off, retreat back to the movie theater, because it was either that or just die of nerve-racking heart palpitations on the spot, but I kept my breathing normal and eyes glued on him and pretended I was laughing at one of his groanworthy jokes about why I was afraid of every damn thing. I babbled something like, "Oh my god, you are hilarious with those witty puns and seriously, no one would ever truly understand why you part your curly hair that way, and you really need to cut down on the cologne sprays; maybe just one is enough for—"

"You can slow your anxiety roll now. They're gone."

It must have been the sigh heard around the world, what erupted from my lungs. Farouk's arm across my shoulders felt like an invisible cape that could've protected me from bullets.

"Thanks, Superman. What would I do without you?" I said. And for the first time, I flung . . . no, catapulted . . . all caution to the midnight wind of ye public arena, and I nuzzled his neck.

Farouk let out a throaty laugh that vibrated through me. "Anything for my Lois Lane."

Chapter Sixteen

But this time I am truly alone, trotting through the darkening streets of South LA to the bus stop three blocks away. I text, call, FaceTime, everything, to get in touch with Dzakir, but nope. Even when I try to explain my situation, leaving him what feels like hour-long voice mails, nothing. My BFF has zeroed his way out of my life.

I text a few of my other friends from school, no one I'm particularly close with and of course, they're all so busy right now with the last summer before college, I don't even bother telling them my situation. Just a quick *what's up?* only to get these replies:

Hanging with the fam
Gaming
Napping

No one's bothered to ask me how I'm doing. Sure, I'm about to get shot, bro, so thanks for checking in. I'm not going to ask them for help, with whatever little pride I have left.

So I call Farouk's mom again. "Hello, Auntie? It's Sayyed. I know you don't want to talk to me, but please, if there's anything you can tell me about Farouk—"

"Sayyed." Her voice is labored and then angry. Very, very angry. "My beautiful boy. He hasn't spoken to his mother in a month. Do you know what that means? We've called the embassy, and they said he left the UK a few weeks ago. And he hasn't . . . Farouk hasn't replied to anything since then. Not a phone call, not a text. And his phone is disconnected. We've gone through his bank accounts, and he's not withdrawn a single cent. Do you understand now? You had the chance to convince him to stay and become a surgeon and you didn't. And now he's *missing*. If you call again, I will call the police."

And the line goes silent.

What? Missing?

I don't know if it's because of the call, but my skin's really starting to burn, and it's pretty uncomfortable to even walk. I kind of want to just dip myself in an ice bath, or maybe drown in it.

But where the hell could my Superman have gone?

By some heavenly guidance, a green-and-white taxi races up the street from nowhere. I flutter a hand, and it screeches to a stop.

My first instinct wants me to be taken to the nearest any-thing with a security guard, so I ask for the nearest somewhat-reputable hotel so I can also stay there, because right now, I can't think about my future and what might've happened to Farouk. Because if I do, I'll end up doing the unthinkables.

The Eastern European driver tries to strike up the smallest of talks, but my mind's spiraling. And I'm too busy texting.

Me: Hey Roukie, r u ok?

Me: Pls just talk to me

Me: I just need to know ur ok

Ten minutes later, with a trail of unanswered texts behind me, we pull up to the brightest of lights, and it takes me three seconds to realize where I am. The JW Marriott. *What the fly-ing fish sticks?* Super fancy. Oh well.

I have no cash on me, so I pay the driver with a swipe of my debit card and surprise, it goes through. Nothing else to do but pretend I may actually belong here, in my faded Captain America T-shirt, basketball shorts, and backpack. I walk in through the sliding doors, marveling at the miracle of air-conditioning on this muggy August evening, the scent of vanilla warming my nostrils. Mood lighting showcases boldly colored couches and wingback chairs. Escalators escalate up to the glitzy world of corporate conferences. Tons of people mill about, drinking, eating, laughing, clinking glasses—just doing regular rich-people things. They have it so good. Unlike the woe that is me.

There's a front desk, a concierge, and a guest services. Don't they all do the same thing? Guess we'll start with the front desk.

I creep on up, stand in an empty line. A pearly toothed lady at the counter with a short bob beckons me over. "Are you checking in, sir?"

"Uh, yes. How much is a night?"

She scans me, says, "Our rack rate is four hundred and forty-nine dollars."

My eyes want to punch out of their sockets. That's a week's pay. Before taxes. A small part of me wants to try and find something cheaper, but the idea of the ice bath is really appealing right now, and I don't know how much more I can push myself today. "Okay. One night, please."

"Sure. May I see your ID along with a credit card?"

I slide over my passport and debit card, amazed at how easy this is.

But she does a very visible double-take as she scrutinizes the tiny blue book up close, like within an inch from her nose. She then lays both items on the counter and, with a curt smile, says, "Regrettably, sir, you're too young to stay here. Do you have a parent or guardian who can check in for you?"

"No. My dad just kicked me out."

A shadow passes over her face, and her eyes lose the tiniest bit of luster. "I'm sorry to hear that, but unfortunately, we cannot accommodate minors without adult supervision. I hope you understand."

I don't. I really don't. Because I'm homeless. Why can't she understand that this is my only option, that I have nowhere else to go? I don't have any words for her as I collect my sad passport and my sadder debit card.

Until I realize that just because I've lost my family, it doesn't mean I've lost everything.

I've still got an important tool left that no one can take away: my words.

And I'm going to use them to start rebuilding the "House of Sayyed."

Chapter Seventeen

What're you doing here?" Dzakir asks, peeking out his window, his eyes squinted so they're invisible under his brows. "My dad will kill you if he sees you. We've already had a huge fight because I had to work late, which ruined his evening out."

I raise my hands in full supplication. "Please, D. I know I've been an inconsiderate prick to you. But you're my best friend. My dad kicked me out. I have nowhere to go. I tried going to a hotel, but they won't let a seventeen-year-old stay without an adult present. Please please please please please?"

He scratches his head, then crosses his arms, really wrestling with this. A pause as he sucks in a huge breath. "Fine. I'll think of something. Maybe we can stay at the café."

My shoulders sag a little. They'd been so tense this whole time. "Your heart's bigger than your hair, you know."

He sneers at me, but I leap back. "Stay there and keep quiet," he says, canines still bared.

I watch as he climbs out the window, panting and not-cursing. "Don't look at me while I huff and puff. Haven't done cardio in a month."

We're finally face-to-face again, and I can't help but give him the tightest hug ever. "I'm so sorry, D. I know I haven't been a true friend, but I promise I'll try harder."

Dzakir hugs me back, then pushes me away. "You'll never change. So maybe we just need to communicate better."

"Ew. You sound like you're thirty."

"I know, right? I am so cringe right now," Dzakir says. "You know that money's going to get you in trouble, right? I think you should return it. You don't even know who that girl is."

"If I do get in trouble, I'll give it back."

"You're a stubborn little turd, aren't you? Just stuck in your ways."

I hold back a snort. "I'm not stubborn. I'm just . . . not used to my life being different."

"Like today instead of yesterday."

"Right. I'm fucked, aren't I?"

"Listen, kid—"

"We're the same age. How dare—"

"Right now, I'm being your drag mom for two seconds and giving advice, so do you want to listen or not?"

My lips are zipped. And locked tight.

"Your dad is a special kind of buttnugget."

"I still don't get why you don't curse. Can you just say 'asshole'?"

"Stop interrupting me. He doesn't deserve your love.

There's a saying that many in our community have adopted as gospel. 'Friends are the family you get to choose.' And you, Sy, are my family. My mister-sister. I will get mad at you, but I'll never get mad enough to break up with you."

Friends are the family you get to choose. "I like the sound of that." I'm quiet, thinking. About family. About what I want to choose. That's when the pang hits me. The deep, dark black hole inside telling me that, even with Dzakir by my side, my heart will never be filled. "You're right, D. I think it's time for me to build the family I choose."

"Yes! Exactly—"

"With Farouk."

"Not quite what I was going for." Dzakir sighs. "You're going to try and get him back, aren't you?"

I can't believe I'm doing it, but it actually feels like I'm nodding. "He's my family too. And . . . please just listen . . . I made the mistake of letting him go. Because I was too afraid. But now, I really have nothing to lose and everything—him—to gain. I just need your support."

Dzakir huffs and glowers. "Have you ever thought that he might not want you back?"

Uh. That never occurred to me. "I guess we'll just cross that bridge when we get there."

"The bridge you burned?"

"I'm rebuilding it. With the million dollars."

"You should really reconsider this, Sy. You don't know where he is. He can be anywhere out there." He says this while staring up at the empty night sky.

"I love him. I just don't know what else to do anymore. I can't rent an apartment. Can't find new friends. A month till I'm a college freshman. But if I can get him back, maybe we can start a life together somehow? He did promise we'll find an apartment and I'll come live with him."

"It all sounds a little too perfect for me."

"I know. Like I said . . . maybe it's time. For me to grow up."

He scratches his head roughly. "And . . . how exactly are you going to do this?"

I can't help the hesitation on my end. "Well. That Reggie girl . . . said I have two wishes left. As demented as she sounds, I honestly don't think she's a bad person. A little odd, maybe? But she's not going to hurt me."

Dzakir is quiet. "You're braver than I am."

"Brave? You're saying I'm brave to want Farouk back because I'm afraid to be alone? Because I have no home here, and he was the only one who promised he'd take care of me and give me shelter but instead chose to leave me and everyone behind just so he could teach English in a foreign country? I also can't even believe I'm freaking homeless right now. Like, did it actually happen? It did, didn't it? My entire life is right here, on my back, and the only person who supports me is in front of me. And I wish I could stay and just be with you, so we can figure everything out together, but you've got your own problems with your dad, and I don't have the knowledge to help you out. So no, I don't know what I am. Foolish? Ridiculously naive? Weirdly hopeful? All of those, but definitely not brave."

Then Dzakir gives me a quirk of his eyebrow, his dark pools

of eyes seemingly drinking in my whole soul. He even takes a step back and looks at me up and down. "And there he is."

Yet those four words accuse me of being the biggest liar to myself.

"I know you have to go. Just . . . remember to take care of you." He reaches out and hugs me tight. A long minute later, he releases me. And huffs and puffs his way back into the window. "Sy, this may sound a little dark, but you better not die on me. Because if you do, then I'm going to unbury you out of your grave so I can kill you again."

A surprising smile carves its way onto my lips. "There's no way I'm getting hurt. I have a feeling she knows what she's doing."

Evennnn morrrre liessss.

But whatever. Time to go make my second wish.

Chapter Eighteen

Reggie? It's Sy."

What sounds like a football stadium's worth of noise floods out of my phone. "Who? Di? Princess Diana? Are you back from the dead? Tell me you're joking."

"No. Sy. Sayyed. You gave me your card . . . and three wishes and then a million dollars. We spoke earlier, and you told me to go to Best Buy to treat myself?"

There's also loud bass pumping through. "Sayyed? Does not ring a bell, darling. But tell you what, if you have my number, it must mean you have my card, which also means you're invited. I'll text you the address."

She's my absolute last resort at the end of my apocalyptic world. She didn't answer my texts, so I finally gathered the courage to call her. A tiny surge of hope burst in my chest when she answered.

Well, maybe not courage but desperation, which fuels me

into doing really sucky things, like call someone I've only just met who coincidentally gifted me with the most money I've ever seen in my life.

So . . . I am going to be kind to myself.

Here comes the text with no fanfare whatsoever and a whole lot of words in between asterisks. Really need to teach her how to use emojis. I map the address and . . . where exactly is that? Lots of windy roads and some greenery. Looks pretty near, so I flag down a cab and show the driver the location. She looks at it, at me, gives a tiny nod, and again, off we go.

God only knows what this will bring.

What did Farouk get himself into? And is the blame on me? I guess the indecision I'm so famous for probably did us in. Ugh. He better not be involved in anything bad.

The driver drops me off on Sunset Plaza Drive, after complaining that the road up is too dark and narrow for her failing eyesight and I'll only have to walk three minutes to get to the address. I swipe my card while muttering to myself how even *she* is abandoning me now.

I shoulder my backpack and trudge past house after house—twisting my thumb ring while jumping at every single potentially creepy noise—the numbers increasing slowly until I get to what sounds like an elephant horde stamping around within the grounds. Bass pounding. Treble screaming something of a Mediterranean flavor. The road is lined with Lamborghinis, Ferraris, Maseratis, and a flock of other luxury cars.

The house is ridiculous. Three floors, tough concrete walls, windows from floor to ceiling. Does this Reggie girl really live here? Yes, yes she does, because . . . I mean, she did grant me all that money, and seemingly just for fun. Or to toy around with me.

Screw it.

I stumble over stray pebbles up to the heavy gate while four supermodels in stilettos and body-hugging outfits glide past and hop into a waiting limo. A straggler donates a casual glance my way, because I'm obviously a nobody, before getting into the vehicle and taking off.

I make it through the reverberating front door. To say the place is a zoo is an understatement. Gaggles of famous and rich people (I'm not kidding; I've seen them on Instagram and Tik-Tok) are wrapped up in bubbles of drunkenness, some gathered around mountainous bowls of white powder on the coffee table, all speaking rapidly to one another like they're going to run out of words iftheydon'thurrythefuckupandjustsayevery thingtheyneedtosay.

Others are busy dry humping, tongues intertwined, not giving a shit. It's an Insta orgy in a magazine- and drool-worthy house.

"Do you know where Reggie is?" I ask a guy hugging a column. His denim short-shorts leave his butt cheeks hanging out like flappy chicken cutlets. It's a lot of look on one person, but he manages to pull it off.

"Eh, who?" he says, eyes swimming, before detaching himself and sauntering away.

How rude, and what the . . .

I wade through the human stew, sweat and breath and

cigarette smoke swirling around me, until I make it out to the pool. The music is so loud, I can't hear the lyrics of whatever's playing.

And there she is, that same black ponytail, skin overly bronzed, splashing around with flotsam made up of cheek-bones, nose jobs, and hair extensions. "Reggie," I shout. It takes at least six tries before some girl next to her grabs her by the shoulder and points to me.

Our eyes meet, and her smile cuts into a frown, the change lightning quick. She adds a knitting of brows, lips snarling, teeth bared. Reggie clambers out of the pool, surprising me with the same thing she had on the other day—black bra and miniskirt—and hops her way over, bellowing hot alcohol breath inches from my face. "What're you doing here?" she asks.

Not the response I was expecting. "You told me to come when I spoke to you fifteen minutes ago."

Reggie tries to stroke something on her shoulder, presum-ably a braid (it's only Sofia's favoritest move ever), until she realizes it's missing and grabs the ponytail on the top of her head instead. "That's where it's been all this while. Thought I'd gone bananas. Anyway, yes, S . . . S . . . S . . ."

"Why are you hissing?"

"S. Your name begins with an S. Is it Steve?" But a beach ball bonks her on the head, and she disappears into the bushes with the loudest "Motherfu—"

I gasp before rushing to the edge, sticking a hand out. "Reg-gie? Are you okay? Follow my voice."

Her head pops out, eyes glazed. "I don't know about you,

but I think I'm done with this circus of a clown show, aren't you?" She crawls out without a single scratch on her body, but it's obvious she's suffered a tiny bruising of the ego, even though that seems pretty hardy too. She turns to the crowd and booms, "Oy, all you bastards and freeloaders, shut it."

Every single body stiffens, laughter and music dying in a flat five seconds.

"Get the bloody hell out of my house. Now."

Tension builds, escalates as the crowd wonders if it's a joke. Nervous laughter rolls around.

"Seriously, get out before I call the police. And take some of that snow with you on the way out as consolation. Just leave me an ounce or two, you bloody leeches."

The crowd thins slowly. In between their labored departure, Reggie claps her hands repeatedly, demanding that they "move it along" and to "chop-chop." She continues to corral them from the pool area, then the stragglers inside, and a full fifteen minutes later, the whole place is just her and me.

A bit awkward, for sure.

"Welcome to the Hollywood Hills, Sayyed," she says, brandishing her arms at the glory of her huge mansion. "And a huge mess to clean up."

"You can call me Sy." The words slip from my mouth, but I'm staring out the whole wall of windows, down at the Los Angeles landscape. "Who are you? How do you have this much money?"

"I'm just your everyday drunk with a revolting inheritance. So do I call you Sayyed, then?" she asks, blinking furiously.

"Please call me Sy. Just Sy."

"Okay, little Sayyed. Soak it in. This can all be yours too."

I give up correcting her and just balk. "I could never afford a house like this."

"But you don't have to." She grins, and a twinkle escapes from one of her eyes.

The three wishes. "You're kidding about that, right? I mean, you've gotta be kidding about that. Tell me you're kidding about that, please? See, the question is so ridiculous, I have to ask you three times. Who in their right mind would believe in some stupid fairy tale?"

Reggie hobbles to a cabinet the size of my shower and opens the doors, exposing no less than a hundred bottles, multicolored and many-sized. "What is so difficult to believe? You make a wish, and I grant it. It's no fairy tale. Easy as pie. Great, now I'm hungry. Why am I craving chocolate and vodka? Never mind. Don't you want to see Farouk?"

"How do you know these things?"

She picks a clear bottle—the label says SMOOVE VODKA— and pours herself a tumbler's worth, hands it to me.

I leap back. "I don't drink."

She gets real close to me, like within an inch of my hair, and sniffs me. Once, twice. "Oh, so you're a liar? Why do you act like a sinless Mother Mary?"

I take another step back. "I am not, and I do not."

"Calm it, kid." She downs the whole tumbler in three gulps. "I know a prude when I smell one." She pours herself another tumblerful, but this time, she nurses it with conservative sips. "Don't stare at me like that, with those judgy eyes."

"I'm not."

"Sweetheart, you're the judgiest judgy judgerina there ever was."

I can only marvel at her liver. Does she even have one? I mean, what if she's not of this world? Wait, is she?

"So how can I help you tonight?" she asks, settling herself at the kitchen counter, chin propped on a fist, eyes glazing over.

"My father just kicked me out for being—"

"Oh, don't you dare start with a sob story," Reggie goes, arms fluttering. "You have a million dollars. You should be celebrating, living the dream. What's the dream anyway? I had a dream once; it was . . . something to do with helping people? Anyway, never mind, we're talking about you."

The dream? My dream? It was always to escape my father's wrath, which meant leaving home and going to college far enough to require me living on campus but near enough to visit when Umi wanted me to, because she was the only one who showered me with the love I always wanted. "What's your dream now?" I ask.

Her eyes take on a dull cast, as if she's digging up some long-ago memory. "For things to go back to the way they were. My life, especially." But her chin slips from her fist, and she almost slams her face into the counter until she steadies herself. "Oh, listen to me prattle away like an old lady who hasn't had enough spoonfuls of her syrupy medicine. So, on with you, then. What say we?"

I take off my backpack, the weight of it finally too much. "I know I have all the money I've ever dreamed of, but there's something else I need to be happy."

Her eyes brighten; her ponytail swishes. "Yes?"

I twist the hem of my T-shirt. "There's only one thing . . ."

She's practically gyrating with glee, or maybe she has to pee? "What is it? Go on."

What if something did happen to Farouk? It would explain why he hasn't responded to any of my texts and why his mom is so freaked out. *Oh my god. What if he was kidnapped?* Or . . . or . . . Is it possible for me to just wish him home? Is this hurricane of a girl really going to make it happen? If he comes back, then maybe we can repair what happened and try at it again. "Fine. Can you get my Farouk to come home?"

"Well, here we go," she says, hands clasped in front of her heaving bosom. "Say the magic words. Make the wish."

I take a deep breath, and the words tumble out. "I wish for Farouk to come home to me."

She yelps, waves her hands in the air, and says, "Absolutely not. I'm sorry, love. That just won't do at all."

Chapter Nineteen

I'm hopelessly confused, if there's such a thing. All I can say is, "Huh?"

Reggie fills her tumbler with more Smoove and swishes it around before taking deep chugs. "I'm fairly certain I said no. My ears heard me saying it, don't you? Ears? Hello?" She shrugs.

Fatigue creeps in, becoming best buddies with the ache making its home out of my whole body. I crash on the nearest ten-thousand-dollar-looking white leather couch, ouch'ing at my welts. I eye the bowl of powder or whatever it might actually be, afraid I might inhale some potentially toxic substance. "I heard you, and I don't mean to be rude, but you granted my first wish so easily and, like, almost instantly. The money was in my account a minute later. So please just bring Farouk back to me. That's all I really want. If you have to take back the million dollars, then do it. His mom is worried sick. Please."

Reggie shuts her left eye and scans me with her right, up and down. She slams her tumbler back, then chucks it aside, the noise clattering away. "That's not how wishes work, my dear boy. Compulsion is not the name of this game."

I wipe the tears away, feeling like such a fool for having all this hope and seeing it crushed. "Compulsion?"

She stumbles over and plops next to me. "Yes, compulsion. It's when . . . you know, like when Angelina Jolie told me she wanted to help the starving and the desolate, and I tried to force her into becoming a Playboy bunny, because that's just oodles more exciting, but it doesn't work—there was no way she was going to change her mind, and instead she became a UN ambassador. That's what compulsion is."

My head is throbbing really badly again. "So you're saying it's like being forced to do something against your will?"

"Precisely. What I'm trying to say is, there are rules to wishes, my poor boy."

"Please stop calling me boy. You're, like, my exact age."

"But I'm not."

"Aren't you?"

"Just trust me when I say I cannot do that." She squints at something in the window, suddenly alarmed at whatever she may have seen, and flicks her eyes back at me, swirling the irises slowly into focus. "Ah, it was just my reflection. Also, I can't bring someone back from the dead. Because that's just gross. Seriously, trust me. Corpses are usually covered in really unattractive things. Truly, they are just as gaunty and only slightly more icky than the ghost formerly known as Gwyneth Paltrow."

I'm too tired to even cringe at the visual. "But what exactly about my wish is compulsion?"

"I can't compel someone into doing what they can't or won't. I can't make Farouk come here. I can, however, take you to him."

"I have to go to him?"

"Of course, silly billy goat. Have you been living under a bridge? Just make the wish, and it shall be done."

Do I dare?

I get off the couch and walk to the window, staring at the big city I call home. There are so many people out there, and there are only a few I call family, and at this very moment, not a single one can help me. I have to help myself.

Farouk promised he'd take me traveling around the world. He promised so many things.

I don't understand how anyone can hurt someone they love.

His words echo in my mind.

✦ ✦ ✦ ✦ ✦

We were at Farouk's house, sharing his queen bed (his parents were surprisingly fine with their son and his boyfriend together like that), and we lay side by side facing each other.

"Ouch-a-ma-Tic-Tac."

The non-swear squeezed out of my lips with a wince. I was trying so hard to keep us hushed because I didn't want his mom to hear us. "I thought you said your kisses wouldn't hurt?"

He eyed me as his soft, plump red lips kissed a welt on my arm. "I never said they could heal your wounds."

"Then there's clearly some overselling there, and"—I flinched—"you know what, maybe I might have to take it all back. Maybe you do know what you're doing, Roukie."

Farouk laid a careful hand on my waist. "I don't understand how anyone can hurt someone they love."

I cupped his face and planted a kiss on his lips. "You don't know my dad. He has two emotions—angry and angrier. Umi and Sofia truly love me, which makes up for the lack of it from my sperm donor of a dad. But they cower to him."

He turned his head away from me, a frustrated sigh shaking his entire body. "I want to hug you, but I don't want to hurt you."

We stayed silent a second, until I spun around so my back was to him. I pulled his arm and wrapped it around me. Him big spoon, me little spoon. The pain hadn't dulled since the belting that morning—all for failing to take out the garbage—but the warmth of his touch was slowly regenerating me.

"Are you sure?" he asked.

I nodded.

"Sy . . . a story just popped into my head."

"What story?"

"About this man and woman who were so in love until she died. He wanted her back, so he went all the way to the Underworld to try and retrieve her."

"Uh . . . why're you telling me this?"

"Because, my dearest and handsomest Sy, I promise, forever and always, to be the one to rescue you from your hell."

⋆ ✦ ⋆ ✦ ⋆

Did I cry when he said that? Of course not.

Well, maybe just a little.

Actually, a lot. Because no one had ever wanted to rescue me before.

Could I do it for him now? Maybe just try to find him and convince him to come home? But can this girl even figure out where he is?

You know what? Fuck it.

I spin on my heels and say the words. "I wish for you to take me to Farouk."

Chapter Twenty

"Arrrrrre you innnnnnsane?"

I can't even get the words out properly because we're swerving this way and that, down the same windy street I hiked up, heavy metal blaring at some cardrum-decimating volume.

"Did you say something, darling? I can't hear you."

What makes things a million times worse is that she's on her damn phone, texting, swiping, Instagramming, swiping some more, liking, and doing all the unmentionable shit you shouldn't be doing when you're driving. "You're going to kill us," I say.

"Hush now. There's no reason to accuse me of such. I'm the best driver I know. Whoops, sorry, skunk."

At one point, she lifts both her hands, and at my death stare, she finally rolls her eyes and says, "Will you just unclench? It's self-driving, you big ding-dong."

By the way, we're not on a flying carpet with an amazing sound system. We're in a car. Specifically, a roaring red Lamborghini with a posh tan leather interior that might very soon be covered in chunks of my very volatile insides.

Under normal circumstances, I'd be too dazzled by riding in such a ridiculously expensive car, but with g-forces slamming me into the door, and then at her, and then the door again, many, many times, my brain cells are too discombobulated to do anything but hold on for dear life. The engine revs faster and faster, louder and louder, while she screams at the random person making the silly mistake of trying to cross the street. In the dark. At this time of night.

"Get out of the way, you tiresome twat." The silhouetted figure barely has the chance to tuck and roll before we rocket past them.

"You're going to kill someone!"

"Flattery gets you nowhere but down my blouse." She side-eyes me. "Say, you are buckled in, aren't you?"

Of course I am, but it's fast becoming a noose. "Mm-hmm."

"Good." We hit a straight path, and the car switches to a higher gear, and we zoom on down, arriving at the next turn at sixty miles per hour in 2.4 seconds.

"What did you program this for? A launch into the outer atmosphere?" I have no choice but to grab on to the seat belt, while also considering biting down on it. Because unlike some one-hit-wonder boy band from the 2000s, my breakfast might be making a successful comeback.

Is this how I die? Forget fearlessness. Once I get out of here, I plan to latch on to the pavement and not let go.

We finally exit the windiness that is Sunset Plaza Drive and into the heavy traffic of Sunset Boulevard. The steering wheel does its marvelous independent driving as Reggie introduces her symphony of constant honking while we creep along at a tenth of the speed we were just going seconds ago.

"Reggie, please stop. And the music . . . I swear my eardrums will burst."

She *ugh*s loudly, and then the sudden silence is so screamingly earth-shattering, I figure I must've definitely lost my hearing. There's just a dull ringing until she opens her mouth again. "We'll never get there in time."

"What? Where are we going? And can't you just, you know, fly us there?"

She snorts out a laugh that rocks her head, her ponytail swinging wildly. "Last time I flew was when I'd sucked a huge puff of the ganj—" And then her stare blanks out when she notices my curious look. "We'll give you a few years, lad, before those stories surface."

"No, I mean, aren't you, like, magical? Don't you have a . . . carpet?"

Another blank stare. "I have no idea what carpet you're talking about. If it's a euphemism, then I must say, the drapes don't—"

I raise both hands in surrender. "Please don't go there. For the love of everything left that is good in the rich-eat-poor world we live in, please do not make any references or jokes about your lady parts."

"There's nothing scary about the vagina, Sayyed. Say it with me—*vagina*."

A groan. "What does—?"

"Vagina. Say it."

"Vag . . . gina."

"Don't stutter. There's no space in there. Seriously, there isn't. Vagina."

"Vagina."

"There. Gay men are the worst when it comes to female genitalia. Seriously, you're all so terrified of it. Now listen to me. There are scarier things in life. For example, this journey you're about to take. If you can't handle all of my loveliness, then how are you going to handle being in a foreign country, with locals screaming at you to get out of their way or they'll throw you in the river? Do not buy in to fear, because you'll never get a step ahead if you do. And one more thing."

I'm still trying to understand her entire rant about fear. Do I really have what it takes to face Farouk?

There's a glint in her side-eye and a gleam in the teeth she bares. "Trust me when I tell you this: everyone lies. Even the most loyal of subjects. The closest of family members. The bestest of friends. I know this beyond a fact. You cannot trust anyone."

The look in her eyes makes me wonder: *Who was it who lied to her?*

Then it's gone. "Now hold on. This might get a little bumpy."

"No, please, no."

A few taps on her phone. And it's too late as we take off, my stomach once again glued to my back.

✦ ✦ ✦ ✦ ✦

We pull up to the curb at . . . Santa Monica Airport?

I unclick the seat belt, yank at the door handle, and kick my whole body out. I want to hug the dusty ground, but that's such a cliché. So all I can do is stand facing a giant column, dazed.

Luggage and limos and honks swirl all around me.

Reggie hops out, stilettos clacking a merry melody. "Don't just stand there, silly boy. They'll arrest you for ogling a column," she says, dragging me by the elbow and shoving my backpack in my face.

She throws a denim jacket over her pairing of a canary-yellow tube top and leggings, while clutching tight her tote—a looker with its unusual pink-and-green color blocking. She swishes us into the terminal, blowing air kisses and thanking anyone trying to tell her not to park her cherry-red Lamborghini at the curb. "Honestly, getting towed is practically valet parking," she says.

We make our way to the check-in counters, with their tiny lines of no more than two each. "Where's your passport?" Reggie asks.

I have no idea what we're doing, since I've never flown before. Baba's the only one who's ever had the privilege. I dig the empty book out of my backpack and hand it over.

"Watch and learn, kid," she says, then to the check-in agent, "Regina Watson and traveling companion."

The dimply, smiley guy has tightness in the corners of his eyes as he scans our passports.

Reggie flashes a grin and a wink to the passengers in the other lines. The glaze in her eyes seems to be wearing off. Is she looking for her next drink already? She downed the rest of the bottle of Smoove before we left her mansion.

A minute later, the agent slides our tickets and passports across the counter. "Your plane is waiting for you."

She saunters through the terminal with hardly a care for anyone around, and a minute later we're outside, where a line of tiny planes awaits. None of them is much bigger than a school bus, except they have wings.

And I'm just stunned. "Uh. Are these tiny things safe?"

She *tsk*s me with a side-eye while reapplying eyeliner. "I refuse to fly with cattle. Besides, I only treat my wishers in the best way possible, all right? So enjoy it while you can. Any form of travel or accommodation is included in the entire package. Am I generous? Tell me I'm generous, because it makes me positively giddy."

"All this for a sandwich? I . . . guess."

There's a downright questionable twinkle in her eye. "More than just a sandwich, silly boy."

Reggie beckons at me as she climbs a tiny stepladder into one of the planes.

But my feet are glued to the asphalt.

I've never had a this-is-it moment in my entire life. A moment one might call "the door of no return," because once I step through, it literally will be that. I won't be able to leave the plane, not without the FBI swarming in.

A female flight attendant hovers at the entrance. "Would you like to join us, sir?"

"Uh. Just one moment."

Umi. Sofia. I know they still love me. I'm not wrong about that. But they're all trapped in their own bubbles of devotion, and I can't live in theirs.

Dzakir is the only one who understands what I need to do.

One step forward, and something changes in me.

Because I'm finally about to take charge of my whole damn life.

Chapter Twenty-One

These seats are space pods. They actually look self-sustaining. If this plane falls out of the sky, I'm sure a parachute will self-deploy from under me. And if I'm left stranded on an island all alone, I bet I can figure out a way to generate electricity from my pod so I can remain entertained by the million buttons and the huge TV right in front of me. I mean, what is that—twenty inches?

Then the situation finally bonks me on the head . . . I'll be flying. First time ever. Oh, good god.

The flight attendant—her name is Phoebe—beams a wide smile. I take a seat. Wait . . . does this comfy chair actually . . . oh yes, it does collapse into an actual bed. It's so cloudlike that it actually takes some of the pain away from my welts.

Somewhere in the distance, a cork pops.

Oh. My. Good. Golly. "This looks pretty nice," I say.

Reggie sniffs while riffling through her oversize tote. "Isn't it?" she says. "I just can't do the cesspool that is"—she takes a second to swallow down a sudden bout of nausea—"an international airport. A private jet is truly a worthy investment. I mean, if I'm desperate, I might fly first class on a commercial airline, but Lady Luck smiles upon us, that miserable wench. Just don't tell her I said that."

I've seen plenty of insides of planes on TV and in movies, but this is . . . beyond anything. "So I don't have to pay you back for this?"

Reggie balks. "You never ask such things, dear boy. It's unbecoming of a gentle-lady. You don't ever have to worry about how rich I am or what a million dollars means to me. Because trust me, money means nothing. There are other things that are more important. Like your word. Now buckle up."

Can't imagine what it's like for a million dollars not to mean anything. Also because my word . . . or words . . . have zero value. Seriously. Not a single cent.

I make the mistake of looking out the window, at the tarmac and the people out there driving around carts packed with luggage. Oh shit, that ground's going to give way to nothing. Absolutely nothing but air and sea and mountains. And more air. And clouds.

The plane's not moving, but I can't help almost tearing out the armrests.

"What's wrong?" Reggie's brows are tight with concern. Or nonchalance. It's hard to tell. "Have you never flown before?"

I shake my head so hard, it almost unscrews from my neck. "We never could afford to fly as a family. Money was always a problem for us to do anything like that."

It's her turn to shake her head. "Well, it's not every day that I marvel at the miracle of poorhood. Poor. What a hardworking bunch you all are. So do not let your impecunious state rob you of the successes life can offer. Plenty of the penniless have made miraculous advancements with personality and seductive body language."

Change the subject, change the subject. Before she can act it out. "So we're going to London?"

Reggie raises a finger at me. "Correct. His last photos were taken in that town, and by all scientifically accurate measurements, he should most probably still be there. Do you feel like it's a clue? I feel like it's a clue. Once we land, I'll scour the Instas for more about him and his exact location. Might even call in some chums of mine for help. They know London pretty well, and we'll survey the streets and make sure we round him up and deliver you safely to his lap so you two can make up for whatever lost time you might need making up for. Does that make sense?"

The plane's taxiing, and some informational video blares on and on about me paying attention as she casually waves it away with an exclamation of how much she hates documentaries. I really should watch the whole thing, especially since it's my first time ever flying, and I really, really, really need to know where the inflatable vests and the emergency lights are, and how about that slide that transforms into a life raft, how cool is that, when my phone vibrates.

It's Sofia. And she's trying to FaceTime me. She never does that. Ever. So I answer. "What's going on? I can't really talk—"

She's sobbing.

"Sister, talk to me. Are you okay?"

She finally opens her mouth to speak. "Brother, you—"

But before she can say anything else, Phoebe, who's just handed Reggie an entire bottle of champagne, kneels next to me and says, "Sir, all phones must be in airplane mode for takeoff."

"But it's my sister, and she's—"

"Unfortunately, sir, it is a federal regulation. Please disconnect from the call."

Sofia's saying, "Where are you? Are you on a plane?"

"I have to go. I'll call you later." I have no choice but to hit the End button.

What did Sofia want? For me to go back? Did she convince Umi I was more important than Baba? Did he do something to them?

Except it's all a little too late, isn't it?

Chapter Twenty-Two

"Who was that?" Reggie asks.

"My sister. I haven't seen her cry in a long time." Intense pressure glues me to the seat, and there's a roar that sounds like the plane's being torn apart. What's happening?

"And? Do I even want to know?" she asks.

I want to tell Reggie the entire story, but she doesn't seem the kind to skinny-dip in emotions. "Family drama. Dad kicked me out for being gay, that sort of thing." Which launches me into a fifteen-minute recap of earlier events.

"Was that what you were trying to tell me earlier? Ah. We all have those moments. Now look outside," Reggie says.

I brave a glance. Whoa. Is that LA from up high? Pretty stunning and glittery. So this is what it feels like to finally fly. "Oh. You were trying to distract me. That's nice."

"Is that all you can say? *Nice?* Is that your favorite word? There are many others, you know." She pauses briefly before continuing. "Shall I venture a guess that you're close to your sister?"

"Sofia's always looked out for me. I mean, she's pretty serious about everything. When she found out about Farouk and me, she said, 'I'll always love you, and you're the best brother I can have, but I don't like the whole gay thing, because it's not the best climate to be that way.' She was mainly concerned about me getting bashed up."

Reggie looks like she's at a loss for words, which somehow feels worse than when she won't stop talking.

So I ramble on to fill the silence. "Anyway. I want to thank you for being so nice—or kind or whatever—to me. I can be a nervous wreck sometimes, and—"

She turns away from me the instant Phoebe arrives with more beverages.

"Wait. Did you finish that bottle of champagne before we—"

"This? What . . . this," she says, or slurps, "is iced tea with a hint of spike. Nothing you need to worry about, although you can drink to calm your nerves, you know. Even if you do keep it rather well hidden. And don't look at me like that."

I'm confused. "Like what?"

"Your thought bubble says you're judging me again. I can see it, gavel in one hand, arms akimbo. Anyhow, you really should go to sleep. Like the saying goes, *Off to the cupboard with you now, Chip. It's past your bedtime. Good night, love.*"

"Wait, isn't that from—?"

"I have absolutely no clue if it's from a movie where the girl

Stockholm Syndromes herself into falling in love with her captor, because again, that's what happens when you let men tell stories. Am I right? Wait a sec. You're a man? Boy? Manboy? Guess I'll just have to make sure your story is a real one. Not some bullshit fairy tale that—"

At this very second, I catch Reggie staring at the pilot as he steps out of the cockpit. Five-o'clock shadow, maybe late twenties, bulgy biceps. He pretty much is the definition of a lumberdaddy. Reggie sticks out her ample bosom and *hmm*s at him with a saucy wink, then maneuvers out of her seat and pod. She turns back to me. "How do they look?"

Speaking of thought bubbles, mine must be absolutely blank. "How do what look?"

Her excited eyes point at her excited chest. "These babies. Do they scream, *Tweak to enter my holy temple*? And by *holy*, I mean—"

"Yes, yes, it's a euphemism. I get it. Honestly, they look very . . . well maintained."

"Don't they, though?" she says with adoration, much like a mom admiring her newborn twin infants. "Anyway, off to the loo. And I am serious about the nap. We have a long, long day tomorrow. Think about Farouk. Farouk, Farouk, Farouk."

And she's gone, toward the lumberdaddy. In her wake are a dozen empty, travel-size gin bottle carcasses, all kind of stashed away in compartments and pockets but still very visible. Her seat looks like any LA back alley on a Sunday morning.

Guess I should try to sleep. Even though Sofia's pained face remains seared in my mind. What was my sister trying to tell me? I just hope everything turns out all right. She's the sturdiest person in my family. The one all common sense was distilled into. The one who is able to calm anyone and everyone down if they're making a fuss about the silliest things (that would usually be me).

What was bothering her so much?

Nope. Sleep's not going to work. My brain's just buzz-buzz-buzzing.

Reggie's not back yet, but I guess I'm allowed to explore this tiny thing?

I head toward the back of the plane and am surprised by a bar with a bartender—his name tag says Trent—filling a bucket of ice. As I make my approach, he smiles and asks, "Would you like a drink, sir?"

I don't know if it's my lightest fluff of a mustache that enhances the illusion of being years older than I am, but I'll take whatever I can get. Maybe it'll help me sleep. "Hmm, how about a gin?"

He furrows his brows. "Just gin?"

"And tonic." Good save. "Just to . . . uh, cut through all that, uh, gin, y'know."

"Of course. Just one minute."

I remember the first time I drank. I could only call it putrid because it tasted like a hobo's butthole. I am not kidding. I don't even know why anyone would drink it. Farouk tried taking the bottle of Bud Light away from me, of course, but only after he laughed at the face I made. I'd never thought I was capable of making anyone laugh from a simple, genuine expression, but he did. So I had to teach him a lesson for making fun of me by drinking some more. I downed the bottle in a record two minutes, and sadly, eight minutes later, I was pretty smashed. He laughed at me even more. And I drank some more. Because it also started feeling kinda good. I mean, let's not lie to ourselves.

The next morning was pretty much an eternal promise to never. Ever. Drink. Again. Because hangovers are the worst payback.

But I guess promises were meant to be broken, right, Farouk?

"Are you sure he's in London? I hear the city's pretty nervous after the protests the last few days," Brandon says. He's the bartender. Apparently we've been discussing all of the above out loud (instead of in my thoughts) over what? Three, four, maybe even a who's-counting number of gin and tonics.

"Yes. London. Never been, although I'm pretty excited. Wanna hear a secret? I hear people there speak English. Like, real English. How weird is that?"

Louis looks at me funny. His thought bubble—I feel like that's a term someone else has used very recently—says, *Maybe he shouldn't have any more because he looks pretty wasted.*

"Uh, I should go to sleep. My traveling companion told me I'm going to have a long day tomorrow. Goodbye Brady."

"Okay, Sy. Take care, buddy."

"I will. Thanks, Jasper."

My bartender friend takes my empty cup away. "Sleep well."

"You too, Austin."

Why is this plane moving? *Someone make it stop, please.* I think I just have to hold on to each seat pod and hopefully make my way back.

But who's this?

"Are you drunk?" a shrillness asks.

I never realized how high-pitched her voice is. Whose? Reggie's, and she's right here, helping me slink back to my seat pod, where I want to stay cocooned forever.

"How much have you had?" she asks.

But someone else decides to speak for me instead. Oh look, it's bartender Jeremy, and he's . . . What is he saying? That I've only had *one* gin and tonic?

A total and absolute lie. *Reggie, listen to me—I need to go to bed. Hey, can you hear me?*

"Why are you moving your face like you're having a seizure? Are you about to start drooling, Sy? Can you say something?" she asks.

Oh. I thought I was speaking. *Listen, I need to sleep. Like, stat. We have a long day tomorrow; I don't know how many more times I have to tell everyone on this plane, but . . . Yay, thanks for tucking me in, but we need to find Farouk.*

"There, there, you little waster of good gin. May you find peace in sleep. Amen."

Wait, no. I need you to help me find Farouk. Promise me you'll find Farouk, because . . .

This time, slumber claims me for real.

* * * * *

"It's not a proposal, so don't freak out. It's just a token of how much I love you."

The ring was weightless but cold in my palm. "Just? It's not *just* a token." I couldn't even describe the feelings. I don't know how I managed to speak. "You silly boy. I love it. And I love you."

We were at the Getty Center, up high above LA, gazing down at the smog-blanketed city. Thank goodness the beach was still somewhat sparkly. His large eyes captured the afternoon light, shining brilliantly. "Here. Let me put it on you."

It was too big for my skeletal fingers. So I tugged it onto my thumb, where it stayed.

We kissed hard after that. Because I just couldn't keep my hands off him.

But surprise, surprise. When he finally pulled away, I pulled out a ring of my own for him.

Yes, he did let me put it on him instantly. No questions. On his ring finger too. Which was kinda odd, but it was the only one that'd fit, considering his kielbasa fingers. I tried not to think too much about it, even if I did an internal somersault chuckle anyway.

And so our love was sealed from that day on.

Or so I thought.

★ ✦ ⋆ ✦ ★

When I open my eyes, peering through sticky eyelids, it's Reggie's face I see instead as she shoves a cup of water at me, saying, "Welcome to London. We have got to go."

Chapter Twenty-Three

Hamza stared at the creature and its glittering teeth, wondering how they could reflect so much light in a garden so dim, and how something the size of a five-year-old possessed so much strength as to fell him. The more he stared at it, the more he realized that the creature was filled with curiosity more than menace. It sniffed him, flicked its finger at his shirt, leaving behind a tarry trail. The creature smelled like nothing he could identify—a sort of sweet smokiness. Upon intense scrutiny, Hamza realized the creature was coated in a layer of what appeared to be crude oil. Still, he dared not move until he found out its intentions. And could ask the djinn for guidance.

The djinn shrugged in her shimmery silver robe and suggested that they should get to know the creature together.

The creature looked at this other being, then licked its lips and bounded off Hamza to stand erect in front of the djinn. It sniffed her once, twice, thrice, then cocked its head, as if asking why she was scentless.

The djinn laughed as she twirled her ponytail and explained that she was a creature of air and therefore possessed no physical body for odor to cling to.

The creature thought about this for a few breaths, then reached out, only to grasp at nothing. It cackled, but neither the djinn nor Hamza knew why, until it turned its attention back toward Hamza and throatily uttered that it had been watching him since before he entered the gates.

Hamza was so surprised that the creature had a voice, and spoke in his language, that he had no response.

The creature, impatient at the silence, asked why he had gone where no mortal had gone before.

Hamza finally found his tongue and explained his motivation. That he needed to be made whole once again, and could only do so by finding his other half and bringing her home.

The creature's cackle curdled Hamza's blood, and with one sudden motion, it lifted an oily black hand and splayed its palm wide open.

Hamza, back on his feet again, looked at the djinn, and the djinn looked at Hamza. They knew not what to do. The djinn swiped her silver robe aside and stooped to her haunches so she could speak to the creature face-to-face and asked what it wanted.

To which it replied, Only for beauty to shine through the darkness, for a comfortable passage on the roads ahead.

Hamza heard the clinking in his pockets as he shuffled his feet in place. He pulled out a gold coin, which elicited a look of confusion on the creature's face. It swung its hand and swiped the coin from Hamza. It bit into the coin and threw it aside, dissatisfied.

It pointed to the flute and to Hamza's lips.

Hamza could only assume that it wanted to hear a melody, so he played. It was a mournful tune, because that was all his soul could manage. And as he played, he watched the creature with curious eyes.

It seemed hypnotized, staring at something and at nothing in the distance. When satisfied, it shook itself free of its reverie and dashed deeper into the garden, which Hamza and the djinn now saw led into a dark forest with branches overhead that loomed like claws.

Hamza was curious about the creature. He asked the djinn if she knew what it was. She could only shrug and explain that she was not all-knowing like her creator, but she had heard of how torturous the road through the Underworld could be, and if the creature were to promise easier passage, then they might be at an advantage.

Hamza wondered what was in store for him as they took off once again on their journey.

Into the woods.

Chapter Twenty-Four

There's a noisy bird in my skull, pecking away at my brain. It's like garbage day, when the truck swings by, grabs the bin, upends the contents into its belly, and then there's a racket of compacting and squeezing and loudness. That's what my head feels like.

I'm literally—real use of that word here—being dragged through the gangway, with Reggie cursing like a truck-driving French sailor. "Can't believe I have to fly into Heathrow. What the heck are they doing at City Airport, scrubbing the floors with the bodies of dead billionaires? I'll make sure someone loses their head for this."

I'm quite sure I'm saying, *I don't want to go*, but who knows what tumbles out.

Reggie's literally—again, real use—huffing her way along, with me limping. "How is this even possible, you silly boy? You need to work yourself up to my level."

"I couldn't sleep. I swear, I tried. Promise me you'll never let me drink ever again."

"That isn't my job. I could've given you an Ambien but no, you chose to wander off twenty feet and get yourself into a drunken tizzy, you silly thing. Next time, let the pro show you how it's done. Now, wait here while I swim through this people goulash to withdraw some cashiola. I mean it—do not move."

But she's already lost my attention. It's not the hundreds of people around us or the announcements overhead but the news all over. Most of the monitors are stuck with commentaries on an ongoing protest. Even the newsstands scream with huge fonts:

London in Crisis

The Queen Mourns for Her Country

The Latest Clues on the Bombing Near the US Embassy

Uh. That's a twist. Didn't Umi mention that just recently? Really should keep up with the so-called current affairs.

It hacks at my insides, but I cringe when stuff like this happens, because the first thing anyone thinks is . . . Ugh, I don't even want to think it. Islamophobia is real. Is it as bad over here as it is back home?

"And she's arrived," Reggie says. "Are we ready to paint this town a deathly red?"

I can only flinch as I point to the screens. "You're being a little insensitive."

Reggie diverts her attention, her ponytail swatting me in

the face. "Relax, Londoners are the peaceful protester kind of bunch, but fine. Rewind. Are we ready to paint this town a boring cherry red? Yes?"

I'm about to ask where we're headed to until I realize there's something more important. My phone and texts.

I turn it on, and the thing won't stop dinging and vibrating for a good two minutes. Seven texts from Dzakir and ten from Sofia. Before I can even read a single one, it starts to ring. It's Umi, which isn't surprising. I'm struggling to juggle all of this when a uniformed officer gruffly pokes my chest and points at a sign that says, ALL MOBILE PHONES MUST BE TURNED OFF.

I do what I'm told.

Reggie's curious eyes rake my face as we reach the immigration line and inch our way along. "Mommy issues?"

"She's just really into checking up on me at all times, to make sure I'm safe. Plus, she probably has something to add to what Sofia was trying to say."

She sniffs. "That's obvious. She's also clearly obsessed with you. So what is the story there?"

I survey the landscape, the human caterpillar trudging along, up and down, back and forth, through the immigration line, wondering when it'll be our turn. "It's a pretty sensitive topic."

Reggie balks as she twirls her ponytail. "Try me. I daresay, my soul can be rather soft and plushy."

Is that even possible? "I'm actually the middle child of the family. My older brother died before he was born, which made my mom very protective of Sofia and me. It gets pretty old real quick, but I kind of just go along with it. I mean, it seems to make her happy."

"You've piqued my interest. What happened?"

A wave of nausea swirls around in my stomach. Can I confide in her? "My mom was super pregnant and it was past her due date and still the baby wouldn't come, which got everyone worried, so my parents went to the hospital to induce labor, but they couldn't find a heartbeat. When they finally got him out, they found the umbilical cord wrapped around his neck."

I picture Umi's smile every time she looks at Sofia and me. It's always the happiest of smiles, but anyone can see it, that tiny tinge of sorrow in her eyes. "Anyway, even though it wasn't her fault, my mom blamed herself for it. Said she should've done more to make sure he would've survived, especially since the doctors said the baby died barely a few days before that. My mom has never shown a lot of emotion when she talks about it, but she also reminds us daily that we need to be careful with everything we do, since we just won't know when something tragic will happen. It's why she panics so easily. That's the whole story. Sorry if it's a downer, but you wanted to know."

Reggie slaps a hand on her heart. "Gosh. The feels. How do you regular people deal with it? A long time ago, I watched as a man made the most heartbreaking decision he ever had to make, and I said, *Not for me, dearie.* And do you know the best ingredient for *I don't give a bloody knuckle about any of that drama?*" There's a sprinkle of serious in her voice until she says, "Alcohol. Copious amounts. If there was a sea made entirely of tequila, you could find me resorting there, year-round. Come now. We exit, pursued by a bear. Through this sea of people and their—major heave incoming—*children*."

I have zero idea what she's saying, but there it is again. That look. So she drinks to forget. Forget what? I'm also noticing her rambling seems to amp up when things are getting real in the conversation.

Has she gone through a whole lot of trauma? Guess that makes it difficult for her to dig deep into her emotions?

But then there's also the conflicting part inside me, the one that only God could've implanted me with. Being gay is not something I chose; I just am, and that's something I've read many times would be a test of my faith. It sucks to hear people say I came out of the gates with a severe deficiency. It's like the Kentucky Derby, where everyone else is a thoroughbred, seeds of the greatest stallions in the world, and I'm a damn seal, flapping my flippers for ten minutes to get a measly hundred yards from the starting line.

I fan myself with my passport as we reach the front of the line. Reggie goes first, smiling as she fishes hers out of her pink-and-green tote.

The officer asks Reggie a few questions, and she flaps her denim jacket open, presumably to flash her ampleness at him, but he chucks her passport on the counter and waves her through. She grumbles off toward the escalator, which a sign says leads down to baggage claim and the exit.

It's my turn, but my phone's going off again. *Argh. Umi, why do you have to call right now?* I must look like a fool as I try to stop the vibration and hand over my passport at the same time, so of course I drop both and have to scramble to the floor to pick them up before I slap both on the counter.

Swear to god this headache is not helping one bit.

He checks out my photo, then me, does a tiny squint, then says, "Sayyed Nizam?"

"Who?"

His eyes are dull stones. "You're Sayyed Nizam?"

"Oh, yes. That's me." Why is it so hot? No one seems to be feeling the way I do.

"Why do you look so nervous?" he asks.

"What? Me? Nervous? No, sir, I'm just a little . . . hungover."

"This passport looks fresh. No stamps. Is this your first time to the United Kingdom?"

"Yes, sir. I've never flown before."

"Never flown before? And yet you chose the UK. Why?" His mustache frowns.

"Because . . . I'm looking for someone."

"Someone? Who is it?"

"A friend."

"A friend?" His unibrow hikes up almost an inch. "I bet. How long will you be staying?"

"Uh . . . I don't know. A few days maybe?"

"You're looking for someone, and you're staying *a few days?*" At this point, he gingerly lays my passport on the counter at his end as if it's filled with dusty white powder, interlocks his fingers, and rests his chin on it. "And where are you staying?"

"I don't know. Sorry, Officer, is there a problem?"

"We'll know the answer to that shortly, won't we? Where's your return ticket?"

Uh . . . Reggie might have it? "It's over there with . . ." Where the heck did she go? She was just there a minute ago.

What. The. Flying. Fuck.

"Come with me, Mr. Nizam."

I can only nod because suddenly it feels like my brain is sloshing around in my tummy along with all that alcohol, because I now understand what Farouk was trying to tell me.

Chapter Twenty-Five

You don't get it," Farouk said. "My parents will never loosen their grip on me. I'm their only child, so it's pretty much their way. All the way. But, like, they think it's so easy."

It was around five months after we met; I was lying next to him on the bed, and I planted my hand on his chest. "What can you do?"

"Nothing. I'm freaking powerless." Farouk jumped out of bed and paced by his window. "Pakistani kid expected to be a surgeon. In this country? They get called names all the time, and they act like nothing's wrong with it."

"Wait, what do you mean?"

Farouk stopped, stared out at the blue sky. "Do you know that they've had actual patients who've refused treatment simply because they took a look at my mom's or dad's name tag and realized they were Muslim? It still happens. Even in this stupid town."

Farouk had grown . . . "distant" wasn't the right word. I guess maybe morose? I thought it was due to the pressure he felt to perform. Get all the A's, get into a fancy university, and follow in his parents' choice of profession.

We'd talked about it, and there was no way I could afford going to USC to be by his side. I couldn't even afford to go to UCLA. My only option was Santa Monica College. And I hated that that was it for me, but at least we'd find a way to be together. We'd started to look at apartments, but something was definitely not right on his end. He couldn't agree on anything.

And then he just collapsed back onto his bed. Sat there with his back to the wall, a tree stump, quiet and unmoving. We tried to play video games, but I kept kicking his ass at *Smash Bros.*, so I knew he wasn't concentrating.

After an hour of trying, it finally happened. He broke down.

It was the weight of so many burdens on his shoulders—me included. Until he finally looked up at me and said, "At least I have my passport. Maybe I just need to go away and not worry about me being me. Somewhere."

I didn't think much of it, other than him taking off for a month to travel or whatever. A clearing-of-the-mind thing.

If only I'd realized what he was actually considering back then.

Chapter Twenty-Six

After interrogating me for a half hour with the same barrage of questions over and over—including how I got my fresh-smelling new phone—the powers-that-be-the-UK-immigration-service deposit me in a room with a few dozen other people. I can't help but feel very much herded. As I scan the faces, it's obvious a single common thread corrals us.

Our earth-toned skins.

There are people here who appear Middle Eastern, South Asian, a couple of women in hijabs and burkas. Funny how in situations like this, people would say it doesn't look like racial profiling, and it doesn't smell like racial profiling, even though it stinks of racial profiling. No use beating around the bush when the bush is just a bare stump at this point.

The stilted interaction I had with the officer dings me on the head. I acted like the most suspicious fool on the whole planet. What kind of ridiculous answers were those? Granted, they were all honest, but they made zero sense. There was that mention of the bombing on the news. No surprise then that they're freaking out about randos, especially us Muslims, causing trouble after entering their country.

So how suckerrific is this?

And that Reggie. Did she really just abandon me? They've taken away my phone, and all I can do is sit and smile. It's a pretty fucked-up situation, and I need out.

"Are you alone, son?" someone says with an English accent.

It's the man to my right, whose wife cradles their sleeping baby. He kinda resembles Baba, but without the bristling mustache, which makes him look a thousand times kinder.

"I'm with a friend, but she went ahead because she got the okay, and I didn't."

"Let me guess. You're Muslim?"

"How'd you guess?" Pretty sure I don't have it stamped on my forehead.

He nods as if I make the most sense. "Single Muslim men traveling alone are the most highly profiled all over the world. Did you know that is a fact?" His smile is kind and sympathetic.

"I didn't . . . didn't know that." How silly of me. Maybe coming on this trip was the worst idea after all.

"It's even worse now—today—with this elevated threat level. So just tell them the honest truth. Look at us. My wife and I and our little daughter—we were all born and raised here. I'm an astrophysicist, and she's a mechanical engineer, yet because of the religion we practice, we're forced to endure this now. Somehow, I don't think it helps that the incident happened by your embassy."

Honestly, I don't get the implications. "It's so unfair."

"It is, isn't it? In their eyes, we are all but one and the same. A sad, pathetic lot. I'd like to invite them over to our house, for us to show true Islamic hospitality."

"Kill them with kindness?"

"Yes. That's the most appropriate saying. Why not? Maybe they can begin to understand that we love peace as much as they do."

"I wish it were that easy to change someone's—"

A door swings open, and an officer steps out. "Sayyed Nizam? Follow me."

"Lucky you, skipping the line," the man says. "Maybe it's a positive thing. Good luck, son. May Allah show mercy on you." He holds out a hand, and I shake it.

The officer takes me through a series of doors and finally unlocks one labeled Search Room. In it is a table and . . . not much else. "I've pretty much told you everything, sir," I say. "I don't know what else I can say to convince you."

"We'll see about that," he says as he slaps on a pair of latex gloves. "Now, I need you to strip for me."

My mind goes utterly clean-slate blank. "I'm sorry?"

"Take off all your clothes and place them on this table right here. When you're done, turn around and face that wall over there and spread your legs. Let's see if you're hiding anything."

Chapter Twenty-Seven

I . . . I . . . What?"

"This is a strip search," he says. "If you do not comply, I shall have your clothes forcibly removed."

"Forcibly? Like, rip them off me? But, Officer, can you just explain to me why you're doing . . . why I'm being put through this? If you want to know the truth, then fine, I'm here to find my boyfriend."

"I thought you'd told me the truth."

"Yes, but this is like an . . . addendum or a footnote. I'm in London searching for my missing boyfriend."

"Missing boyfriend? In London? Sounds like absolute—"

"His name's Farouk Hameed, and we met a year ago, and he took off three months ago on this study-teaching thing, and he hasn't been in contact with anyone who knows him for the last month. I'm not lying. His photo is on my phone. Just unlock it and see."

He laughs. A hale, hearty laugh, before his gaze turns cold. "Utter and absolute bullshit. Now take off your clothes."

"But I'm underaged."

"Take. Off. Your. Clothes."

I also don't want anyone to see the bruises on my naked body. "Please don't. It's unfair that you're doing this just because of my name and religion." Recalling what the man in the holding room said, I blurt out, "Us single Muslim men are the most highly profiled individuals in the world. And . . . and . . ." And that's all I've got. *Way to go, Sy—you sure know how to fight for your freedom.*

The knock on the door echoes, and the officer hurries over to swing it open. A female officer with a plastic bag of what appears to be my belongings, along with my backpack, whispers in his ear. His chilling stare at me melts into confusion as he whispers back, "How can that be? Who sent that order?"

Her eyes widen, and he backs down. "Understood." He grabs all my belongings and flings them at me; they land on the table with many clangs.

Ack. My phone. "Is everything okay, Officer?"

"You're free to go. Take your things." He holds the door open.

If anyone were to see my face this very instant, they would see only blank confusion. It's all I can muster right now. Did I just win?

Because it feels like I just did.

I zip out of the interrogation department—with huge imaginary middle fingers aloft—through hallways, and end up at baggage claim. There, leaning against a column by herself is my obviously inebriated companion who abandoned me.

"There you are, chicken," Reggie says as she watches my approach, hugging her green-and-pink tote bag. "Took you a while. Did something happen? I came down here to look for a bar, but nothing's open this early, which is a shame, because jet laggers like moi are constantly looking for a refreshment."

"Why'd you leave me alone? They took me into some interrogation room because I was traveling by myself and didn't have a return ticket or accommodations. I couldn't give them any answer. You could've done that for me."

"What?" she says, sniffing the air with annoyance. "They did what to you?"

"I just told you what they did to me."

"Despicable. Abhorrent. Disgusting. Revolting. Positively maniacal."

"Are you just spitting out random words?"

She blinks the annoyance away and stares at a group of tourists in the distance. There's one in particular—a bearded man at the very back whistling a shrill tune—who's seemed to catch her attention. And it's almost as if she recognizes him but shakes it off. "Were you expecting something else? Law enforcement is totally ridiculous, full of rules made up by powerful white people against those with brown skin like us. But I called some people to help find out where you were, and they got you out of it, so I guess we're over it. Shirley Temple?"

"Please don't call me Shirley."

"It's an alcohol-free drink, you pointless waste of gay. And I was asking if you wanted one. Anyway, off to Londontown we go. Get ready, because we are going to let her rip." She pushes me toward the exit—where it says PUBLIC TRANSPORTATION.

"I've never understood what that saying meant," I say.

"I think it's when you booze it up so much that you tear something in your liver or colon or, you know, when you get the—"

Chapter Twenty-Eight

I can't stop staring out the window, at the landscape. Tall buildings. Streets packed with cars and people. It's all so honkingly loud.

Although everyone seems more formal here, all covered up and plenty of suits, compared to the shorts and short skirts back home in LA.

I hear it's because London is always chilly?

We've been in this black cab fifteen whole minutes, and what's not helping is the throbbing in my head. I'm still annoyed at her, but I guess she really can pull strings to get me out of any trouble. I mean, that was a pretty swift exit from UK immigration. "You said you knew where we have to go?"

Our taxi comes to an abrupt stop, and Reggie scans the outside. "Here we are. Let's go, love. Driver, sir, here's a gob-smackingly indecent amount of pounds I'm thrusting into your hand. Do wait for us. It won't take more than a minute." She grabs her tote and jumps out before I can say a word.

I'm by her side a minute later, staring at the sign. "Cod Save the Queen? Oh. The fish-and-chips shop in Farouk's photo?"

"Precisely. I tried calling them before we left Los Angeles. Some guy answered and, can you believe the nerve, asked me for my number? I mean, give a girl a chance to breathe before—"

"Are you sure he wasn't asking you for your number so he could take your order?"

She bites down on her lip, then shakes her head. "Off we go. Interrogation time."

We step into the eatery with a ding of the doorbell. The place could use a bit more lighting and a tiny investment in the worn booth seats. The fresh smell of cod or haddock fry hangs in the air, and I have no doubt it'll stick to my clothes.

"What can I help you with?" the cashier asks, a tinge of Arabic in his accent.

My eyes meet the man's, and my heart skips a beat. It's the same older guy—he may be Middle Eastern?—Farouk had his arm wrapped around in his Instagram. Excitement fuels my feet as I rush to the counter. "I'm sorry to bother you, sir, but I'm here about Farouk?"

The man's eyes light up, but he hesitates. "What Farouk? I don't know anyone by that name."

Reggie steps up next to me and thrusts her phone rudely into the man's face. "This Farouk. Shall I remind you again?"

The man lets out a heavy sigh, then points to one of the

booths. "I knew this would happen. Have a seat." He shouts out to one of his workers in the back, who simply nods at him.

My mind's reeling. What secret is this man about to reveal? We take our places, sliding into some really squeaky vinyl booth seats, Reggie taking a whole minute to get herself situated.

The man slips in next to me. "Who are you?"

I stammer out a, "W-we're his friends from Los Angeles. We just want to know what happened to him."

The man sighs again, like he knows he's been caught at something. "Look, I hired him knowing he didn't have papers to work, because he was a good kid. He went to this school nearby."

"So he was working for you, and . . ."

"He was the best employee I've ever had. Worked so hard, and everyone just loved him. I wanted to keep him working for me for life." The man digs his elbows into the table, leans forward. "But then he said he had to go. London was too expensive for him, and he had found a better opportunity. He said he'd let me know where he ended up."

"And he didn't?" Reggie asks.

The man shakes his head. "I tried calling him, but his number . . . it wouldn't go through, you know?"

"That's it?"

He shakes his head again. "I'm sorry, my friend. If you hear from him, let him know Ali wants his help again." He continues with a whisper. "This new guy burns everything."

The man gets up to return behind the counter, and my heart sinks. "That's it. Dead end. What now?"

Reggie winks at me. "Not quite. We have one more lead. Off we go."

* + * * *

We're back in the taxi, and some dark cloud has settled over my head. This is not going the way I was hoping. And another person unable to get through to Roukie . . . what happened to him?

But Reggie continues her optimism as she shoves her phone into my face. "Ah, yes. By all counts, there's an ALDI and a Lafferty's at this corner here on this map, which might be the same one in his photo. See, I figure we can track him down from that point on. Ask around. Sniff my good old bloodhound nose here and there. There's nothing I can't smell, you know. For example, I know you haven't showered in a day."

I reek, that's true, and there's not much I can do about it now. "How the heck are we going to find anything that shows where he's gone? It's been a month—the trail's probably gone cold, even for a bloodhound."

She crosses her eyes, flares her nostrils, and sticks out her tongue. "Is this not the face of someone you can trust?"

I don't know how, but that one simple act actually coughs a laugh out of me. "Thanks for that. I reeeeally needed it."

"Needed what?" Her eyes are still crossed and nostrils still flared. "This? You needed a dose of this? I can give it to you all day long, darling boy." She wipes the expression off her face and glances out the window.

"I really should shower, though."

"We'll check into a hotel once we figure out where your lovely fiancé's at."

"He's not my fiancé."

"What, then? Lover? Paramour? Boyfriend?"

"Ex-boyfriend is fine. Anyway, my umi and . . . baba will never approve of a gay union."

"Baba? Is that a sheep?" Reggie asks with genuine curiosity. "Your mother married a sheep?"

"No. He's my father."

"Why Baba? Strange nickname," she says, coiling her ponytail with one finger.

"It's what we've always called him, or were instructed to, I guess. Funny how you have no choice in calling your parents whatever you're supposed to. *Call me Umi and call me Baba*, and children just do what they're told."

Reggie nods. "You are right. Children are just tiny little suckling things that suck the life out of you. They expect parents to do everything for them, don't they? Take care of them. Be there for them. Never die on them." She stops, wrinkles her nose, her gaze heading somewhere out the window and into the distance. "They're cute and all, and then they start crying, and you just want to stuff them down the toilet or— What? Am I being too frank? Oh, relax that frowny face of yours. Anyway, back to you."

"I love Umi and Sofia, but Baba, he exists on a totally different level in my brain. He's just someone who's there and makes things more difficult, making me really think twice about saying or doing anything to not offend him, because his smacks are free and many. I honestly try not to think anything about him. It's hard, though, because he's always around, but he goes to Mumbai twice a year to visit his other wife and kids for at least a month, and that's when I get to relax and kick back and whatever, you know? You think babies are a damper? My father's even worse."

"Why?"

"He's just strict about . . . anything and everything. Umi's afraid I'm going to get hurt by a falling leaf, but Baba, if something doesn't go his way, then I'm in trouble. And I might get a beating out of it. Hasn't been fun being his oh-so-gay son; you can trust me on that. Anyway . . . Oh, shit. Umi's calls and Sofia's texts."

In the commotion of everything that's been happening, I've forgotten to check my phone.

There's a nagging something about ridiculous roaming charges, but I do have a million dollars. And Sofia was pretty upset.

Whoa. What an alarming number of texts. Like, a lot. Even more than when we landed.

> *Dzakir:* Where are you?
>
> *Dzakir:* Why aren't you answering?
>
> *Dzakir:* Why is your phone not ringing? Goes straight to voice mail? Your sister's looking for you. Call her.

Sofia doesn't really get along with Dzakir, so it must be pretty serious if she reached out to him.

I text him back real quick to tell him everything's okay . . . ish. And then I go to Sofia's messages.

My heart sinks at her texts. Not at what's happening, not at why she's trying to get ahold of me, but at how both she and Umi are doing.

"What's this here? Your aura is a sudden shade of purple, which I think means you're spiritually constipated," Reggie says.

"I . . . I don't know what to do."

"What is it?" Her voice is suddenly soft, her eyes warm. "Maybe I can help."

"Sofia says just after I left, my dad fell over, dropped to the ground. He had a heart attack."

She jerks back instantly. "Taking that offer of help back, but ouch. Those can be painful, I know."

"Anyway, both my sister and my mom are at the hospital, waiting for him in the ICU. He's about to have surgery."

"And what's the problem?"

I can't be sure if it's me saying this or someone else who's taken over my whole body, but it feels like the truth. "To be totally honest, I don't know if I care."

Chapter Twenty-Nine

I gave up wanting to try and love Baba by the time I was five. I'd so desperately wanted him to see how amazing I was, even though I knew something was different with me; I think he knew it too.

Baba had belted the screaming shits out of me when he came home early one day and found me all dolled up in Umi's makeup and stuffed into my sister's tiny dress. I tried to scapegoat Sofia for it, but it was too late. I saw the change in him. His young boy, the one he had placed so much faith in, was not who he'd expected. I was a disappointment. A disgrace. An aberration according to the whisperings among his friends. The beatings got more and more frequent, as if he were trying to rid me of whatever evil I'd been inflicted with—maybe even the sin of my stillborn elder brother's death.

Beyond that, there was also the subject of his outright infidelity. His childhood friend in India had died, and he'd taken off for a whole month to tend to the funeral arrangements. But guess what he did instead?

That's right. He got married to his dead friend's wife, and the kid was suddenly his.

So Baba had another wife. Which Umi, the dutiful wife she was, could not argue against.

Altogether very, utterly mind-boggling, because we hardly got by, and for him to suddenly have another family to support?

Ooh, but I did make the mistake of asking why, if he was allowed to have multiple wives, couldn't Umi have two husbands? For another man to support our floundering family with an extra income.

Oh, my brazen mouth. How it got slapped silly and silent.

Anyway, he said it was an act of pity and compassion. The widow was poor and destitute, unable to care for herself and the kid, and had no other relatives to care for her.

But he had a daughter of his own with her after. Again, I was like, *Huh?*

I learned that you don't have to love anyone you grew up with, even your father, especially if he couldn't show you the love you needed in return. Couldn't help you to grow up strong and confident enough to face the world. What I wanted most, knowing that, was to get out and be away from him.

Because a tree could still grow high and mighty all alone in a field of nothing.

I don't have the energy to explain it in so many words to Reggie, but I owe her something. "My father is just a difficult man to love."

Reggie tries to answer, but she has to raise her voice, because it's getting hard to hear anything in the cab, thanks to the crowds around us. "What? Just trifle and a shove? That sounds like a Lewis Carroll rhyme. Anyway, what is going on here?"

"It's the protest, miss," says our driver, who's practiced mostly silence until now. "We're almost there, though. Just across the bridge."

Reggie surveys the crowd. "Such fun. I do hate large groups of people, but the energy courses through me like grasping a dozen electric eels. Ugh, so many pubs nearby, but I fear nothing will be spelunking down my throat anytime soon. Anyway, it's obvious your baba is an old-fashioned man, so out of touch with his feelings. Don't sweat it, little pariah—or Mariah, whichever you prefer—because there's one man who loves you and that is Farouk Hameed, international man of mystery. All we have to do is find him and make things right again. Can we do that? Of course we can do that. It's the wish you made, and I shall grant it."

I probably shouldn't say this, but . . . "What's with you and all the drinking? Is there something . . . you want to discuss?"

Reggie grimaces, tugs at her ponytail. "You know, dear, sweet, innocent boy who's only lived a fraction of what I've gone through, it should be clear by now that I drink because I enjoy it. Is that not obvious?"

What's obvious is her shifty eyes. "I'm not known to be a good advice giver, but I promise not to tell, if you ever decide to spill the truth."

She turns to me with eyebrows tight. "Let's just say your

upbringing can really mess you up. I mean, you can agree with that, right? My parents—I mean, they were rich. Filthier than rich. And they gave me everything. Whatever I wanted. But they died and left me all alone. So there's that."

"Oh. I'm sorry."

But she waves her hands in the air. "I'm rich. What's to be sorry about? Money is happy, and happy is getting what you want. I mean, seriously, that's the one thing almost everyone wants. But you know what's funny about a man coming into money? He suddenly becomes a paranoid person, distrustful of everyone, and is just ever so selfish. Seen it many, many, many times. It's usually the first thing anyone wishes for. Kind of like what happened with you. Wishing for a million dollars. See what I mean?"

"Wait, that's not fair. I didn't—"

Her stare becomes a stony one. "Whatever you do, don't let money change you. Because it'll change everyone around you, and that's something you can't control. If you refuse to trust anything I say, then just trust that one thing." Her voice is heavy with a seriousness I've never heard before.

"Pretty sure I won't change. I don't even know if I'll need the money. I mean . . . I'm sure it'll help, but I want to be my own self-made person."

Reggie's dead stare is a chilling one. "You are a jolly kid. I'll give you that."

To which I can only cross my eyes and flare my nostrils, just like she did earlier. "And I have loads more jolly to give you."

She actually snorts out loud as she pulls a bottle of brown

liquid out of her purse. "Maybe your next wish should be for that look to freeze forever on your face. It actually brings me joy." And as if she's changed her mind, tucks the bottle back in. "Anyway, I don't think we're going to get any farther in this traffic, and what's with these people? Hold on, Sayyed— Excuse me, monsieur? You can let us out now. Keep the change." She stuffs a generous stack of colorful notes bearing the queen's face through the tiny opening in the partition and yanks the door handle open. She plops herself out with a whisk of pink-and-green tote.

I quickly do the same, mindful of my backpack in the crowd. There are a lot of things about Reggie I don't understand, and at the rate we're going, I have no hope of ever unraveling it all.

There must be hundreds of people marching alongside and around us—chanting and buzzing—mostly headed in one direction. Some hold up signs that say, END ISLAMOPHOBIA NOW! and FUCK INTOLERANCE!

"Wow. This is my first protest, and it's a lot of people." I say.

"We're a few blocks from where we need to be, so away we go, I say. Onward, and in that general direction."

As I stare at the thousands of people rubbing shoulders, the only thing I can think is, *How are we going to get through this?*

Chapter Thirty

I have no idea where we are. I can't even see the street names. We're surrounded by buildings that claw at the sky, looking as generic as the ones back home. The chill is pretty mean, though, so I dig a light jacket out of my backpack and throw it on before I start brr'ing to death.

But we're definitely in a park. And it seems like we're next to a river.

There are men, women, and children of all ages, races, and colors—pretty much feels like everyone?—and they're all united, shaking the ground, as they recite rallying cry after rallying cry in support of something. I still have no clue what they're protesting about? My heart sinks because it doesn't take long to find out.

Just another block up, a different group of protesters. More of a homogenous variety. Most appear to be skinheads, with a smattering of Union Jacks and incendiary banners and posters.

It seems like they're specifically blaming brown people for . . . everything. But the chief cause of the bombing? Islam. A meh of a shrug seems very much justified.

A line of police barricades one from the other, but it's clear the uniformed, standing out with their neon-yellow vests, are tolerating the segregated groups. They're letting them hurl roaring insults at each other.

Reggie and I get dragged into the crowd, and we try to inch closer, but it's worse than sardines. The crowd is too dense. She thrusts her phone in my face again and points at the location of the bookstore, which is across the bridge, which seems impossible to get to from where we are.

Unless my six-foot-three Farouk sticks his head out over this ocean of people, I'll never find him.

"It'd be a miracle if he's here. Do you see anything that can help us?" I ask.

Reggie tiptoes every few steps, then huffs her frustration. "Let me see what I can see. Nope, no Farouk. There are a lot of people—ouch, manners please, young lass—and it's rather overwhelming, but no one as tall as he is. A few shops, though. I'm just looking at my phone and the GPS, and okay, right behind those police people, there's supposed to be an ALDI, which is a supermarket, kind of like your 7-Eleven, I guess? Everything looks so tiny from over here, but I see the matching colors of the logo, I guess? Oh, wait, weren't we looking for that? And an electronics store, a tiny little clothing store, and the Lafferty's Used Books is right there."

But Reggie can only smile as she starts to hyperventilate,

before screaming, "Help! Someone! I can't breathe. Please help me through. I need to get through." And those few words are our secret pass code. She bulldozes her way through the parting crowd, dragging my arm. Minutes, and a trail of curses, later, we're at the front of the line, where a dozen police officers scan the two of us suspiciously.

"Well?" Reggie says. "Do you see it?"

"I'm looking." It's too far to see anything across the river. "How do we get past all this?"

And there's no way to get across the bridge in front of us, since the police have set up a barricade.

"So crossing the river is not happening. They're blocking us, as if to contain us. We need to figure another way through or around it, and I can try to squeeze through the gaps between those officers. I mean, I've managed to make do in the past, if you know what I'm saying," she says with a wink.

If I had any trace of food in me, it'd come up. "Let's get out of here. It's pointless. We need an actual plan."

We backtrack, away from the crowd. The progressive side seems to have the better, wittier comebacks. I guess empathy is a measure of intelligence?

Minutes and several blocks later, we find ourselves stomping away from all the emotions. I didn't expect London to be this rowdy, but I guess politics get people riled up.

Reggie spins on her heels. "This way."

Fifty steps or so later, we're at the entrance to The Lady's Lamb. I think it's a pub/bar/restaurant based on the menu board outside.

I've never been in a pub before, and it's not quite what I expected. A little dim—no idea why they can't turn on the lights; even the windows are tinted—and a little musty. Stools at the bar, rows of bottles behind the counter. There's already a handful of people in here, sipping pints of foam-topped golden and dark beverages.

Reggie says, "You need to eat," as we slide into a booth. "And I'll keep watch with my beady eagle eyes for anything that might be of assistance on our mission. You say bookstore, I say how far."

"We know how far it is. We were just there."

The waitress stops by to take our order.

"Oh, hello there, miss," Reggie says. "Nice weather you've got here, and love the vest. Menu's on the wall over there? Great. Yes, I'd like a tumbler of your most expensive vodka. No tumbler, huh? How about a pint glass? None of that either? All right then, let's do six shots from six different vodkas. And what would you like, Sayyed?"

The chicken tenders sound good. The waitress asks if I'd like a pint of anything with that, and I vigorously shake my head. "Just a Diet Coke, please."

Reggie looks at me like I've got parasitic worms streaming out of my ears; then she looks at the waitress. "Sorry, love. He's had a rough night, so you must excuse him. Apparently, he's regressed into being a five-year-old." Once the girl disappears, Reggie continues. "So we need to get to the bookstore. How do we do that?"

"I don't know. Honestly, I can't really think until I get a

bite. I don't even remember the last time I ate." Actually, I do. Umi's leftovers, which I might never get to taste ever again.

"Okay then, so we wait."

What ensues is the most awkward silence ever as we sit there facing each other, with not a single attempt at making small talk. She's on her phone and I'm charging mine, since it's on the verge of actual death.

More texts from Dzakir and Sofia. More missed calls. Updates on Baba—he's still in surgery. But I can't be distracted.

Because we have to start planning.

Chapter Thirty-One

Farouk left for Pakistan with his family for two weeks. It was some vacation thing they'd planned.

I couldn't contact him the entire time because he'd decided to leave his cell phone behind, which I couldn't understand. Plus, I had to force some unselfishness on my part, since he was there to hang out with distant relatives.

He'd looked forward to the trip, for clarity of mind, because his new obsession was politics. It was tough watching him obsess over the latest developments as reported by Rachel Maddow, when I was still obsessed with a regular intake of boba and cyberstalking my favorite TikTokers.

I mean, I even started to understand the differences between the left and right wings. *Shudder.*

Three days after he flew off, I started to get loopy. Half a month was a long time to be apart from the boy I loved, and I didn't think it was a surprise when I began to experience the five stages of grief.

There was definitely a ton of denial in the beginning. Did he really go away? Did I imagine him in my life? No, he must've never existed.

Then anger. Boy, that was a tough one. I was mad at Farouk for leaving, and I got mad at the slightest thing. Like, if a shoelace came undone. I'd stomp on it, blaming it for ruining my life.

Then there came the bargaining. Please please please. Just bring him back. This started as early as the third day he was gone.

Then depression set in. I must've chugged a gallon of Diet Coke a day to drown the dozen almonds that'd sneak into my tummy. Ugh.

And finally, acceptance. Farouk was just never going to come back to me.

But fear remained the greatest motivator of grief: that we'd grow apart. That what we had would wither instead of blossoming into something that could bloom until the end of days. I was afraid that all the love I had would be trapped under a mountain of snow and soil and newfound awakenings and realizations.

So I called around and, finally, at an old bookstore, I found a copy of the story he'd talked about. I even paid extra to etch an inscription that I thought was appropriate and decided to hand deliver it the night he got back.

After a fifteen-minute bus ride, I rang the doorbell and

waited. The door creaked open, and his mom's smile beamed through. "Sayyed, of course you'd be the first to greet Farouk home. He's upstairs . . . Oh, wait, here he is."

Farouk was a changed boy. He'd shaved his head before he left, but his curls had started to grow out again. And that cheeky grin remained the same. "Sy, it's been so long. I'm sure you've got so many things to talk about. Let's go play games in my room. We brought home a ton of dates. You like them, right?"

Yuck, no. "Mm, yum. Of course I do. Love those dried fruits so much."

His mom frowned at us. "You boys and your Nintendo. Make sure to come down for dinner in an hour."

My heart was close to exploding; I followed him without question.

One thing hadn't changed. Our kiss.

That whole time away brought a feverish fervor to the moment our lips met again in the privacy of his room.

"I've missed you, Sy," he whispered. "You may have to hold me back or I'll just eat you up whole."

I could only shove my gift at him, because I was definitely getting excited too.

"For me?" He grabbed the package and slid it onto his desk.

And then we kissed some more. For the whole hour until his mom called us down.

Until my lips almost fell off.

Chapter Thirty-Two

Our food arrives—vodka is food to Reggie, apparently—and we down it all in two minutes.

Although just minutes ago, I did excuse myself to run to the restroom, where I snuck away to the waitress, to reduce Reggie's order from a half dozen to a single shot. Thought it'd be a worthy experiment. If it would work at all.

It's funny how Reggie eyes the single shot that arrives as if something's wrong with it—with a tiny mumbling of "huh"—then slams it back without question.

I munch on chicken tender after chicken tender, side-eyeing her without judgment. I convince myself it's for her own sake. So she can think clearly as we execute our mission.

Through the haze of my pigging out, pubbers trickle their way in, including two men with skin as brown as mine. I can't help but notice that their T-shirts are stained with red as they take the booth to our right. One of them has a yellow bandanna around his neck, and the other has a full-on healthy beard.

Something about the greasiness of what I just ate makes me miss Umi's turmeric fried chicken again.

Bellies full, Reggie sits back as we discuss ideas to get to the bookstore.

1. Run up to the cops and flash them. That always gets attention.
2. Sneak all the way around and try to find an entry that way.
3. Pretend we're with the good side, and once we get close, we'll switch allegiance to the bad side and then slide on through the barrier. Oh, but that's not going to be possible. Everyone's going to be distracted by my beauty.
4. Swim along the river and creep up to the bookstore?

Not difficult to guess which suggestions are mine and which are Reggie's.

"You two planning something bad?" a gruff voice says.

My eyes go wide as I turn to look at the man with the yellow bandanna around his neck.

Reggie has *uh-oh* scrawled on her face as we exchange a glance that spells total guilt. "Nothing," she says. "What's it to you? And what's with your T-shirts?"

"Tomato sauce. Anyway, thought we could help," the other

guy, the one with the beard, says. "I'm Vishnu. This is Saleem."

Saleem gives us a wicked smile as he sips his pint, tugging at his yellow bandanna. "You look like you're up to no good. My question is, are you going to let us in on this?"

I do that nervous gulp thing because my throat is suddenly deserty dry. "I-in on what?"

"Come sit with us," Saleem says with a grin. "Today is a special day."

"Oh? Why's that?" Reggie asks.

"Because through all the commotion going on out there, we celebrated our marriage," Vishnu says.

My partner in future crime throws her hands in the air. "Of course you did. Why the bloody hell not. I'm Reggie, and this is Sy. And we shall take you up on your invite."

We shall?

There's a second of silence as we slide into their booth.

"American, huh?" Vishnu says.

I wish there was some tonic of friendliness I could consume to— Oh, I think some people call that alcohol. "Yes. I am . . . we're here . . . to find someone."

"Was that what you were planning? To find this someone? Through the muck outside?" Saleem asks as he unties his bandanna, slips it into his pocket.

Reggie and I both nod.

"Good luck with that," Vishnu says. "This protest is going to last awhile."

"What exactly are they protesting?" I ask.

Vishnu and Saleem exchange a quick glance at each other.

"*We* are sick of how we're treated. It's getting harder and harder to be brown-skinned in this country, especially after the whole Brexit thing and all," Vishnu says. "And now with this explosion. It's suddenly gone into upheaval."

"Brexit?" I ask.

Saleem sighs. "Yeah, the referendum to leave the EU a few years ago. Shows how frightened these people are of us and foreigners. We're constantly being vilified. But even further than that, there's major infighting. Vishnu is Indian and Hindu, and I'm Pakistani-Muslim, and even our own people find issues with that. If it's not our skin color, then it's religion. It's almost impossible to unite everyone against the common enemy."

I am still a clueless little sheeplet when it comes to world matters, obviously, so a blank look is all I can offer.

Reggie's wearing the same expression as I am.

"The enemy is the right wing, yeah," Vishnu says. "Those people who want our country to go back to the way it was. Homogeneous and . . ." Vishnu drops to a whisper. "Very pale."

Reggie gasps. "How dare they. Utterly despicable. Do they want the black plague as well?"

Vishnu grabs Saleem's hand and says, "Back to the protest. See, the bombing happened by your embassy. And the escalation happened so quickly. Some of the right-wing commentators in the US picked it up and fanned the flames, and their vile commentaries have spread to some of the conservative vloggers here,

which . . . has really infected the minds of the sheeple who follow along with their lack of critical thinking. And they want
none of us."

"We're lucky that London is a pretty diverse, accepting,
cosmopolitan town," Saleem says as he runs a hand through
Vishnu's lush beard. "But the rest of the country is still pretty
backward, and we still get looks. That protest of white nationalists out there is because they think we're the root of all problems, and right now, it's anyone Muslim. But that's why we're
here. Because we don't ever intend to back down from anything, especially when it feels like our life together is at stake."

Vishnu nods with a grin. "So we got all our friends to come
join us. Gay? Hindu? Muslim? Brown-skinned? Ticking all
the boxes. It was the biggest fuck-you we could think of, to
celebrate our union together here, in front of them. To show
them that you can't take us away. And . . . then we got pelted by
bloody tomatoes."

Vishnu gives Saleem's hand a pat, and they share a brief
kiss, their eyes lingering on each other for a second longer than
maybe I should be witnessing.

I feel something inside me melting, watching them. The
bond they have together is clearly woven with steely threads of
joy and affection and all the good things two people in love can
share.

I mean, if they can have it, why can't I? Is it so hard for me
to try and fight for the boy I love? Umi always talks about how
Indians and Pakistanis try to get along, but look at these two.
It's like . . . a sign.

"Well, enough with the boring talk about politics. So who is it you're looking for again?"

I have no clue how to put it delicately. "We are looking for my . . . ex-boyfriend, who I think . . . is missing."

Their jaws drop.

Then Vishnu says, "You're looking for your ex? All the way from America? Now, that's tragic. Tell us all about it."

Before I can stop her, Reggie doesn't just spill all the freaking beans, she starts handing them out to anyone who's willing to listen.

"So you need to get to the bookstore," Vishnu says. "Why? What's so special about it?"

Reggie looks at me. "Huh. Never thought to ask you that, Sayyed, my dear boy. Why *do* we have to go there?"

I mean . . . they know practically *everything* already. "I think he might have . . . I don't know . . . Maybe it's all a little too impossible."

Three pairs of eyebrows knit into confused knots, in real time.

"The bookstore was one of his last photos on Instagram, and I'm hoping . . ." What? That someone there may have a clue to his disappearance?

Saleem wears a look of sheer concentration. "Okaaaaaay. So this bookstore is on the other side of the barricade? But we have to get around it?"

They look at each other, then back at us. And then the two of them say, in perfect unison: "We can help!"

Oh. That's a little unexpected. How have we suddenly

managed to earn the assistance of these two guys? Two guys with oodles of their own problems to trudge through willing to help two random strangers in need?

"What fine, upstanding gays you are," Reggie says. "So far we've failed to come up with a bulletproof plan, one that'll shoot us through to our end goal."

"Let's get on with it, then," Vishnu says as he and Saleem chug the remnants of their drinks.

When we step out of the pub, Reggie's eyes latch on to something.

There's a group of construction workers, with a bearded, dark-skinned man whistling a merry tune as he lugs a wheel-barrow out to a truck especially catching her eye.

"What's wrong? Don't tell me you need to take a quick break to let them watch you?" I ask.

She bites her lip. There's something about the change in her demeanor. "Nothing. It's not that at all. Let's just totter along."

Saleem says, "We just need to get changed real quick, if that's all right?"

I'm anxious to get to the bookstore, but I'm not about to tell these two guys willing to help us out that they can't go home and change out of clothes that make it look like they've just murdered someone together.

Twenty minutes later, we're outside a stout two-story brown building. Even though I really want to get going, I'm super curious to see how the adult versions of Farouk and me live their lives together. Because we could be them.

Vishnu unlocks the door and ushers us in. "It's simple;

neither of us has an eye for decorating. But our flat's pretty comfortable. We're happy to call it home."

Saleem rushes down the hallway and disappears through a door in the back.

Puffs of honey and lemon wrap around me, warming me up. I've only just met them, but I can tell how happy they must be living together here. It's positively glowing with joy. It's just the cutest place, with not-so-subtle touches of their partnership, like the semiabstract paintings of two nude guys on the walls.

There are photos of them everywhere: of their travels, with family and friends. There's one that surprises me. Two boys, probably younger than I am. "How long have you known each other?"

Saleem returns with two fresh black T-shirts.

"Ummmmm . . . ," Vishnu says with a quick glance at his partner. "Since secondary school. High school for you American lot. How old were we, Sal?"

"Fifteen. Twenty bloody years ago. Can you imagine?"

Reggie narrows her eyes. "I can barely tell," she says, her voice suddenly all silky.

Ew, girl.

Anyway. "That's a long time." I'm starting to feel that melting feeling again. This time, mixed in with . . . longing. Hope.

"We've had our ups and downs," Saleem says. "But I've always thought if I wanted to get along with someone a hundred percent, I should just clone myself."

"And where's the fun in that?" Vishnu says with a laugh, his eyes softening. "How old are you again, Sayyed?"

My cheeks heat up, getting real toasty. "Seventeen."

They exchange a glance. Vishnu lays a hand on my shoulder. "I think it's great that you want to find . . . Farouk, is it? But . . . look. It's okay if you're not meant to be together. All right? You can try to force it, but what's not meant to be will figure a way to squirm out of your grasp."

Everything inside me is fighting against what he says. I can't help but want what they have. They made it. Why can't we? I want to be with someone for so long, it may as well be for eternity. I want to have arguments with him and make up after that with as many kisses as possible. I want to just sit around our apartment—like these two probably do—and watch TV or cuddle or make pancakes together for breakfast before we go to class.

Saleem disappears into the kitchen and returns with a paper bag. "Shall we?"

No clue what's in it, but I say a very firm, "Yes."

We leave their flat and make our way back; they fill us in on their plan. Vishnu and Saleem sure know the area well, and I think they've formulated something that may work. We're going to sneak all the way around and find a way through with only a few officers. Reggie has volunteered to distract them with something—I don't know, her charming personality, maybe?—so we can slip past them.

We'll all meet back at The Lady's Lamb. And we've exchanged numbers just in case something goes awry.

Plans aren't always flawless, but in our current sad situation, we don't have the luxury of a backup. Meaning it's one and done.

For the next hour, we circle the area, trying to find the easiest and remotest chance of a way through. It's late afternoon, and the crowd by the park is getting thicker and rowdier with whistles and bullhorns, and the police have sent in reinforcements. They must suspect things will get dangerous anytime now, which I don't doubt, considering the white nationalists are at the front of it all.

But all the bridges have been barricaded off.

It feels too hopeless. We're at the rear of the chanting crowd as they continue to put pressure on the assholes still standing their ground with their vile posters and banners.

"Sayyed, can you smell that?" Vishnu asks.

"Ew, no. I don't want to."

Saleem laughs, sharing a look with Vishnu. "That is the smell of our *moment*. You have to forgive me if things go south very quickly, which means, you two must get out of here as soon as you can." He reaches into the paper bag and pulls out a—

Ripe, baseball-size tomato.

"What're you going to do with that thing?" I ask.

Vishnu wears a sickening grin. "We haven't a clue. It's very heavy, though. Thoughts?"

"What?" I say. "Why do you two look like you're about to do something terrible?"

"Sayyed," Vishnu says. "Think about it. It's us against a very volatile, easily angered group of not-very-smart white supremacists. The tiniest thing—as tiny as this tomato here—can set them off. Giving us the very thing we need."

A light bulb goes off. "A distraction." We just need to get across the bridge to the other side.

"It's up to you," Saleem says. "Because we each have a little revolution in us. And you're doing it for love."

My gaze skates over the throng of people, some distracted, some watching us and our interaction, while Vishnu and Saleem wait for me to decide.

Reggie is strangely quiet, just eyeing the tomato.

I grab the ripe fruit, which bruises easily against my fingers. Am I really going to do this?

It looks like a doable distance. Less than fifty feet. I'm pretty sure I have enough arm strength for that.

It's weighing me down by the second. Don't think I can hold it for much longer.

So it's all up to me. The kid from LA. The one with the strangest purpose of all. Guess this is it.

Their apartment comes to mind. Along with the photos. Their life together. The life I want.

I rear my arm back and throw it as high and as far as I can.

It tumbles in the air. The lazy arc seems to take forever, and within the space of those five seconds, the sudden thought of going to jail pierces my brain. *AM I A FREAKING CRIMINAL NOW? WHAT IF I HURT SOMEONE? WHAT IF SOMEONE DIES FROM MY RECKLESS ACTION?*

Uh-bloody-oh.

My heart drops into my shoe as the tomato sails over one

of the officers and bonks a white skinhead. Red liquid bursts out all over his face.

Saleem and Vishnu yell out this crazy whoop, then grab both Reggie and me by the arms, dragging us out of the roaring crowd. "Here's your chance, so take it. You have to go now," Vishnu says.

Saleem gives us the sweetest smile as he pulls out his bandanna to tie around the lower half of his face. "Good luck finding your boy. Come visit us anytime."

Before we know it, panic surges through the crowd, roiling above and around us, people screaming, shouting curses, sirens wailing, loudspeakers loudspeaking, elbows jostling against one another.

And through it all, Reggie says, "Well, well, well. Who would've thought it possible. That Sayyed Nizam could single-handed-throwingly start a riot in London."

Chapter Thirty-Three

Adrenaline boils inside me. The only person I can truly trust, the one I'm desperately running with, is the last person I'd ever expect to have my back. I don't even know what's happening behind us as we escape the uproar—and I definitely hope Vishnu and Saleem make it out okay—but Reggie's hugging her pink-and-green tote tight, her denim jacket flapping away, both of us fighting for breath. It's pretty obvious neither of us is fit enough to survive if we're caught.

More police SUVs siren past us as we slow down.

"That worked marvelously, didn't it?" Reggie says with a wince and a hand clutching her side. "Boy, your new friends packed a jolly good punch with them."

I can't help but glance over my shoulder every five seconds. "So it worked, you think?"

She scans the signs on the street, then points left. "I told you we needed a distraction."

"A distraction is flashing your boobs at a police officer. That was large-scale mayhem."

"Mayhem. I like that. Maybe I'll make it my middle name. Reggie Mayhem Watson."

"*Argh.* Now the police are probably looking for us, and I'm in a foreign land, and I'm going to get arrested once they ID me as the one who started all this, and I really don't want to go to jail."

Reggie rolls her eyes. "The Oscars called. They want to give you the lifetime achievement drama-queen award. Listen, you eenie meenie whiny mo. Nothing's going to happen to you or me. No one saw us, and we can easily point the finger elsewhere. Temporary insanity or something. I hear that works very well in American courtroom dramas."

"That's not real life, and we're not in America! We're in the UK. Or Great Britain, or the United Kingdom of Great Britain? Whatever! Listen, Reggie. I can't get in trouble. This is too much. I thought all we needed to do was find Farouk, and then we could take him home with us."

"Precisely. That's precisely what we're going to do, or as they say in France—précisément. Or is that exactement?" She continues to navigate the street, always keeping the river to our left.

"I can't believe I did that. Why did I do that? There's, like, so much energy coursing through me, like my veins are on fire or something. Is that why you aren't afraid of anything? Because you like living on the edge?"

We're down to a smooth stroll. "What's the point of living if you don't drink enough, eat enough, cause some racial tension enough?" Reggie asks. "This life is dull if you just sit by the sidelines, waiting for others to play the game, and all you do is cheer for them once they score a goal. Why not take a chance and see what can happen if you let go of some of that fear? Why not strip and run naked across the field for everyone to see? I learned long ago that you won't get anything playing it safe."

"Let go of my fear?" I scoff. "I don't think it's wrong to be afraid of going to prison. Like, will I be shanked dead the first week I get there? Will I have to eat . . . what's that goopy dish . . . gruel? For the rest of my life?"

"I heard you loud and clear the first few hours of your wah-wah'ing. Now, look. We'll just keep going like this. I've guaranteed you're going to find Farouk. What comes with that guarantee is your safety, which I am personally handling. Not every one of my previous wishers got me to go along with them on their journey."

"What do you mean, *previous wishers*?"

She shrugs. "Most people just wished to be rich and powerful, rubbish like that. No one's ever wanted what you've wanted, so I'm here to make sure nothing bad's going to happen to you. And to get you out of sticky situations, if we ever get into them. Because it's obvious you need all the help you can get, and who better to lend assistance than me, the world-renowned traveler known as Reggie Watson?"

"How can you say that? You don't know what's going to happen."

"I don't. But I'm really good at staying out of trouble. If

you've noticed, I drink a lot, and no one's ever questioned my sobriety—or appearance of. I don't do the hiccupping or slurring or lazy-eyeing thing . . . much. Very functional here. And when you're with me, you're under my protection."

I feel sick. "If something happens to me, you're going to have to face my umi's wrath." And Sofia's. And Dzakir's. But . . . that's pretty much it. Three people. Maybe. Three people who might worry about me. They may even be the only ones to attend my funeral.

I've started a riot in London, put myself directly in danger, and if something happens, I can't even count on a full hand the number of people who will care.

Deep breath. I'm building more. That's why I'm here. For Farouk. Still not a full hand, though.

I'm just following along as she navigates on her phone, and the next two bridges we get to are also barricaded off, with a dozen police on either end. So we keep trudging onward, and I'm so completely lost—seriously, the names are astounding, like what's an "Elephant and Castle"?—until we get to a stout brick town house right in front of another bridge, where another barricade's set up, no surprise. "This one's only got one poor guy. The rest have been pulled to the riot," Reggie says.

She's right. One lonesome male police officer guarding a bridge, too distracted by his walkie-talkie to even understand the ruckus ten minutes away.

Which is exactly what we've been hoping for. "You distract him," I say, huddling my backpack close, "and I'll sneak past him somehow."

"All right, then, love. How about a kiss for good luck?"

I wince, very visibly, and she backs off, disturbed.

"I'll pretend I'm not hurt in the least bit," she says. She gives me a thumbs-up along with a wink, then marches onward, pretending to be lost in her phone, unsure of the street or her senses.

I creep forward on my haunches, hiding behind cars, until I know she's snared him.

It looks like charades from here: the officer forces Reggie to return the way she came from, but Reggie flutters her hands and pretends to speak some Nordic language—"hurdy meerkat goober angstrom beard papa" is what she screams back, which may be pure nonsense.

Now's my only chance. With his back to me, I sneak forward and past the two of them, through the low-rising barricade. When I'm only ten feet away, I hear:

"Stop! And don't go any farther."

I spin on my heels in slow motion and stand up to face him.

The officer's got his baton out, waving it at me. "What're you two planning? Do not even think of moving from that spot. Now, walk slowly toward—"

And he wilts to the ground.

Reggie's tote swings back to her side, and she scoffs at the horror on my face. "What? Oh, he'll live. I didn't hit him in the head that hard. No harm or foul whatsoever."

"People have died from being punched in the head, Reggie. This is serious stuff."

She sniffs. "He looks like he's breathing. His chest is rising, falling, rising, falling, rising—anyway, let's go. He's going to wake up in minutes." And she takes off again.

I'm falling behind. That's two crimes we've committed in a single hour. How much more trouble am I going to get into by the time I get Farouk back?

Then I'm flooded with the strangest feeling ever, spreading throughout my insides, like a warm cup of chai. That all-too-familiar adrenaline with a tinge of excitement. Can it be, am I actually enjoying myself?

We stick our heads around a low-lying building for a quick peek. There's still a ton of commotion at the first bridge we were at by the park. But it's too far to watch all the intense shit happen in real time.

Reggie's on her phone, though. ". . . And it's really real. Punches thrown, police pounding on protesters with batons, tear gas smoking the crowd. Aren't you glad we're nowhere close?"

We're on the other side of the gigantic river—she called it the Thames?—and we crawl back toward the other side of the park, leaving behind a trail like a sideways horseshoe, watching the riot happen in real time at the park. But the closer we get, the more my blood pressure rises. Just need to complete our task before my heart bursts out of my chest.

"Look, Sayyed, my boy. I think we're safe as long as we dash in and out, understand? No dillydallying, no stopping to smell the roses. We just need to get there, find what we need to find, and bound on out like bunny rabbits hooked on speed. Are you ready to do this?"

The bookstore is two hundred feet away, in the neighborhood right across from the first bridge. Here's to hoping none of the cops turn around to look behind them on the bridge and see our approach.

I nod, taking a deep breath to try and chase away the fear, but nope. Still there. "Ready when you are."

Reggie swings her tote around, rests her hands on her knees. "On my mark. Go!"

And I take off, my footsteps lost in the screams just across the bridge. But I'm close. Thirty yards. Twenty. Ten.

Then a right. And here we are. Twist the knob. "It's locked! What do we—?"

Reggie's nowhere. Oh wait, her head's floating back there, her entire body hidden around the corner, the bridge right behind her as she blinks at me repeatedly. "Just go," she shouts. "Go make your way in already."

Someone's going to see me here. Must do something. I scan the storefront window. Takes me only a second to see the book, and realize that it truly is what I think it is.

And suddenly, the adrenaline flowing through me is making me feel not so great.

I can't believe it. The gift I gave him. It meant everything to me, and it should've meant everything to him, too, because it was a symbol of everything we were together.

And he sold the damn thing. Which doesn't make sense, because he came from money, and he had money on him.

How much could he have even gotten for it? Doesn't matter. Ugh. I can feel all the emotion, all the hope and want and *pain* of rejection rising up in me. The crowd is a distant roar in my ears as my heartbeat races. My fists ache from clenching so hard, fingernails digging into flesh.

There's only one thing I can do. That I *have* to do.

My third crime of the hour.

I rear back, and with a swing, my elbow shatters the window into a million pieces, the crunch of glass deafening. The next thing I hear is a voice shouting at me. And it's not Reggie's.

Uh-oh. Not a second to waste. I reach in, grasp my fingers around the book—the same gilt-edged hardcover. I turn to the dedication page, and there it is. My own writing.

My Roukie. He really was here.

"Hey!"

I take off. Behind me, a pair of officers makes their approach from within the neighborhood, headed for me and the bridge.

Reggie's eyes are rounder than I've ever seen them as I return toward her, screaming at the top of my lungs. "Run, Reggie! Run!"

Chapter Thirty-Four

Sayyed! Stop . . . I can't breathe."

I yank Reggie's arm as we retrace our steps back to the bridge we snuck through, past the officer she knocked out, who is now sitting up, dazed. It'll only take a second before he notices us, so I will more power into my legs and keep going.

But I'm one step ahead when I hear another shrill cry. I turn to see—

Reggie stuck in place. Her leg held tight by the fallen officer. His eyes are all super murdery this time.

Uh-oh. So I scramble back a few steps. "Please let her go."

"No," he says, trying to get to his feet, but he plops down instead. "I have no doubt the both of you are looters, looking as guilty as you do. Criminals. I shall not let you go."

"But we're not. I just needed to get this." My hasty hands thrust the book in his face.

He refuses to see it for its truth. "I knew I was right. Now stand still."

Reggie's got her purse held high, but before she can do it again—

I slam the book down on the officer's hand, severing the hold he has on her.

He yelps.

Reggie leaps toward me, sticks her tongue out back at him. "That's what you get." Then to me, "Did you actually just save me, your damsel with the ankle that was in much distress? I have never been prouder of you, my son."

My first instinct is to beg for her to not call me *son*, since we're obviously not related, but that can wait. Because we need to outrun them all. "Do. Not. Stop," I pant. "If we don't get out of here, we'll be arrested for sure."

We spin through the alleys and, in some strange twist of fate, end up back at the front steps of The Lady's Lamb. We burst through the front door and throw ourselves into the same booth that must've been sitting empty since we left.

All we can manage is heavy breathing and a couple of nervous chuckles.

The waitress and bartender eye us, then the three officers streaming past the tinted windows, before they return to wiping the counter and hanging up dry wineglasses.

Reggie sucks in huge gulps of air, her bosom heaving, and suddenly I realize she's laughing. The heaves transform into absolute mania as she bangs the table.

"That was literally the most fun I've had in a yonkers amount of years," she says, laughing away. "Oh, you dirty devil, you are the bearer of the most unanticipated joyride ever."

My body's still curled into a ball, the top of my head peeking just above the windowsill, my eyes on the street—a dozen other uniformed men run around corralling people, but none I recognize or who might recognize me. I pull out my phone and send Vishnu and Saleem a group text:

Me: We're safe by the way! Got what we came for!

Along with a photo of the book.

When I'm sure—really sure, like let's-wait-one-more-minute kind of sure—I finally flip through the opening pages. Until I again see my own handwriting:

> *To my dearest Farouk.*
> *If the need ever arises, I'll walk through*
> *the same fires of Hell to save you too.*
> *Yours, Sy.*

Reggie's about to ask some ridiculous question as she eyes me but thinks better of it.

So . . . I have the book I gave him. And a casual flip through produces nothing. No clue to whatever happened to him or where he went after. How am I going to find him? Where do I even start? There are some scribbly lines, but nothing that makes sense.

But why did he leave it or sell it? It's not like it was worth much. Was Farouk in so much trouble that he needed the few extra pounds to get by?

And even worse than that . . . it was my damn gift to him! Who sells off a gift? My blood's simmering, nearing a boil, the more I think about it. But I'm also like . . . trying so hard to hold on. Because he cherished the book. I know he read it multiple times. He loved it.

Do I have the right to be angry with him about leaving it? "Now what?"

Reggie grabs it with both hands, flips it 180 degrees, then squints at the cover. "Orfus and Yoo-ree-dais. Looks boring."

"It's *Orpheus and Eurydice.*"

"You do you, I say." She turns it over and slams her head back, pretending to snore. "There's no synopsis? What a crock of—"

"It was my gift to Farouk. Read the inscription."

Reggie flicks her ponytail and thumbs through the opening pages. Then flips through the first chapters, scans a few lines. "What's most confounding is the lack of pictures. Who bothers with this nonsense?"

Would Farouk do something like maybe . . . underline some words that will lead me to find him? But he didn't know I was coming, so why would he leave clues? I grab the book and flip through, paper whispering at my fingertips, until I get to the last page. There's something penciled in that I missed the first time through. "*Mustafa.* Followed by a long string of digits. Is it a phone number?" I spin the book so she can read it. Have I wasted my time?

Reggie pulls out her phone. "Let's see what happens, shall we?" She punches it in and . . . it rings.

"What the heck are you doing?" I ask.

"Shush."

On speaker a second later, a raspy, brusque male voice rings out. He sounds like he gargles with barbed wire. "Hello?"

Reggie winks at me. "Hello, is this Mustafa?"

"Yes, who's this?"

"My name's Reggie, and I was just wondering if you know someone named Farouk?"

"Farouk? How do you know him? You know what, forget it. Don't ever call this number again."

The line cuts out. Reggie tries calling again, but it goes straight to voice mail.

Whoa. What's that about?

"I know. I'm wondering what that's about too," Reggie says with a tightening of the eyes, but she's already tap-tap-tapping on her phone.

"Stop reading my mind. Maybe . . . it was a travel agent or something?"

Reggie laughs. "Oh, darling. It's all about apps these days. Travel agent? Your parents teach you the strangest things." She continues tapping until her eyes light up. "Well, look at that."

"Look at what?"

"I don't think we're done with the traveling part of this adventure yet. This is but a stepping stone to our next destination. We have to leave London immediately. Come, gather your wit and your things."

"I have nothing to gather. My backpack's right here."

She flings a stack of bills as thick as my thumb onto the table. For what? I don't know, since we haven't even ordered.

Braving a quick peek out the front door, I see a black cab approaching. Reggie darts out with me behind, and we hop into the back seat. "Back to Heathrow we go."

"Why? Why are we going back there?"

"Because, my dearest. We are going to Istanbul."

Chapter Thirty-Five

Reggie's round eyes can't contain her glee. "See the country code? That's Turkey. And the area code and whatever codes around it, that seems to be Istanbul. Now, I do have a way to triangulate this Mustafa's exact location. So even if he's not answering, we can track him down and make him answer us. Oh, I'm a tinge more excited than a Tasmanian devil that's just been accepted to ballet school."

"Triangulate his location? Do you have someone in the CIA or NSA or something to help you?"

She narrows her eyes at me. "Yessssss . . . all of those things. And when we find him, we will get all the information we need."

"How do you plan to make him tell us where Farouk is?"

"I've made the hardiest of men reveal the most sensitive of information with my beguiling charm and a little hip sway. Body language hasn't failed me yet."

"Um . . . okay . . ."

She hands me the copy of *Orpheus and Eurydice.* "For your safekeeping. Hope there are no termites in there. They can be such a bother to eradicate. I have no idea how something can love paper—"

Reggie drones on and on while I slink away into my thoughts. *Who is Mustafa? And why's he so touchy about Farouk?* Whatever it is, I can only hope he'll have the answers. "Istanbul is pretty safe, right?" I ask.

Reggie scratches at the root of her ponytail. "What does safety have to do with termites being related to ants?"

"I mean, I hear London is a safe town. How about Istanbul?"

"That's a horrible accusation. We were just in a riot in this town. What makes you think it's safe?" She riffles through her pink-and-green tote and pulls out that same bottle with the brown liquid.

Maybe a distraction can help? "Oh wow, that building looks like a pickle."

She points the bottle at it. "Ah yes. The Pickle Building. So called because it looks like a giant penis. Can you guess how many women architects were involved in the design? None."

Reggie launches into the history of the building, and as she keeps talking with her hands pointing this way and that, I keep nodding, and at one point, the bottle disappears from her hand and ends up back in her purse. She doesn't even notice my mysterious sleight of hand.

"Oy. Where the heck is this driver taking us? One sec, Sayyed. Oy, miss. Stop giving us a free tour and get on it."

"Lots of checkpoints, miss," our driver says with an Irish accent. "Trying to avoid them. Look, here's one."

We come to a rolling stop, and then to a standstill, at a barricade. There's about a half dozen yellow-vested officers waving everyone down. When we finally get to our turn, though, panic sets in. It can't possibly be.

The cop we accosted twice earlier. Right here, with a purpling eye socket to match a possibly bruised ego. And he'll see us in seconds.

"What . . . what do . . . ?" The most useless words escape my mouth.

"Yikes." Reggie looks like she's about to munch her ponytail to its roots. "If there's ever a more appropriate word the Americans invented for truly bile-worthy situations such as these, then 'yikes' it is."

"I'm too young to go to jail. I thought you'd—Don't pinch me. *You* keep *your* voice down. I thought you'd save me from any harm."

"I made no such promise. That's just utter ridiculosity."

Too late. Our windows roll down automatically.

"You two, show your faces," the policeman says.

Slowly, so slowly, we turn.

The officer's eyes take us both in. I volunteer a weak smile, and Reggie flashes her sparkly whites before saying, "Well, howdy there, partner. Maybe you can let us scooch on by without a hee-hawing us into tardiness? Thank ya, gen'l'men."

The man stares at us. And then . . . and then he pulls himself away and says, "Drive on."

Our Irish driver rolls up the windows as she stares at us with curiosity. I look at Reggie.

What just happened?

Chapter Thirty-Six

We get to Heathrow Airport, and Reggie shoos us through all the lines.

"Argh. Please just listen to me. After everything"—I lower my voice to a hoarse whisper—"I really don't think my heart can handle much more excitement."

"Coming through! Private jetters, thank you," Reggie says to everyone in line, nudging disgruntled passengers, ponytail whipping faces, phone aloft in one hand. We make it to the front of the security line practically breathless, and both of us walk through the metal detectors without a hitch.

We stroll down the gangway, and Phoebe welcomes us back on board, ushering us to our seats.

Then the text comes in.

Vishnu: Good luck, brave boy! Invitation is open for you

and Farouk whenever. Bring Reggie along too. You two
are loads of fun together!

Along with a selfie of the two of them positively drenched
in even more tomato juice but wrapped in each other's arms
outside their flat.

So glad they're okay. "That was kinda painless, huh?" I say.
"A little too painless, don't you think?"

But Reggie's already lost to the bubbling champagne.

Guess she needed a refreshment after such an exhilarating
afternoon.

The door slams shut, and there's an announcement of some
cross-checking going on as I squeeze into my seat pod.

I hope that this is it, that I'll finally find Farouk in Istanbul.
I *need* to find him. Farouk is the family I choose. It was my fault
that I lost him. This time, I'm ready to fight.

"If I had a penny for every time you lose yourself in your
thoughts, I'd get about a shilling, which is pretty darn good.
And stay away from the bartender in the back. You are forbidden," Reggie says.

I catch her eyeing me, really inspecting me. "Remember
what I said earlier? About not having the stamina for this?"

She takes a deep gulp of her drink, nodding away. "I recall
you mentioning what a pussy you are."

"I never said I—"

"Listen. I'm here to tell you—and I rarely say stuff like this,
because, ugh, vomit—it's clear to me there's more to you than

you ever thought. A hidden side with so much potential for surprise, and so relentlessly fearless, you will one day learn what it's like to finally let go."

"Let go of what?"

"Not let go *of*. Let go *and*."

"Let go and what?"

"Let go and . . . you're just going to have to figure that out on your own."

The plane takes off. My neck whiplashes at the screen that's just turned on in front of me. It's almost impossible to tell, but the BBC has a screenshot of Reggie and me, a little blurry for sure, but it's us. Those are our clothes, my backpack, her pink-and-green tote. "We're on the damn news."

Reggie squints at it, then waves it off. "Don't you worry about a thing, little puppet. Mama Reggie will take care of ya." She holds her glass up, downs it in a shot, and waves it around for Phoebe to take notice. "Your wishes grant you safe passage aboard Air Reggie. We greatly pride ourselves on our motto: Here's to Your Greatest Escape—Even if I Have to Lose an Ankle Myself for It."

The caption says . . . apparently we're looters amid an ongoing riot. I mean, no one can actually tell those two little blobs are us, and that police officer did—accidentally—let us go. Probably got bigger fish sticks to fry. The coverage shifts to footage of the riot. Of people getting hurt.

I was the catalyst. True, there were ridiculous racists there, but I don't know what to make of it. I don't believe in violence—I absolutely and positively abhor it—so why am I now the one dealing it out?

So. Many. Thoughts. And none of them quelling any of the unrest inside me.

Oh. Twist.

The authorities are saying they've found explosive materials in one of the white nationalists' homes, along with a manifesto to set off a civil war after having set off the car bomb by the embassy. A whole line of volatile dominoes just waiting to be flicked over.

I can only snort.

"What?" Reggie asks.

"Don't you hate it when you're instantly blamed for something bad, even though there was not even the slightest chance you did it? Because . . . I don't know . . . you were miles away?"

Her eyes glaze over. "You need to explain."

I'm not sure I can. Or want to. "Sometimes, I wonder if being brown-skinned instantly puts the target on my back for a crime I did not commit. Like if I was walking down the street next to a white boy, and the police rolled up, pretty sure I'd be the one they'd detain and question."

She looks like she's about to start filing her nails. "Except you did do the crime. In this case."

"Not the point. Although it does feel good to break the rules a bit and get away with it. Gosh, is this what those . . . white-collar criminals feel every time they steal money from us poor people? I can get addicted to this power." A sulk threatens its way to my lips. "Anyway, what're we going to do once we get to Istanbul?"

"Patience, my delectable turkey sandwich. No need to get constipatey about things. We'll get there when we get there, and then things will unfold before our very eyes."

"You know nothing like that's going to happen, don't you? So what should I know about Istanbul?"

"Well, there are a few amazing landmarks you should gaze your eyes on. There's the Blue Mosque. It's huge. And blue. Very, very blue. And then there's the Ayasofya, which used to be a cathedral but was converted into a mosque by some very questionable interior decorators. You'll see. Wood has never looked so good against marble," she says, rolling her eyes so hard, they look like they may freeze in place. "But enough about the days of yore. Let's talk the book. Why's it so important? Have we talked about this already? Let me know if we have. My memory is sometimes as clear as a scratched-up magnifying glass. Sometimes I see things up close, but the picture's a little cloudy."

I grab my backpack and pull it out. Its edges are smooth gold, which made it stand out like it did. "It's about this guy who falls in love with this girl, and she dies, and he decides to rescue her from Hell."

Reggie halts mid-gulp. "Wait a bloody barnacle second. That sounds extremely familiar. Come again?"

"It's what I just said."

She absentmindedly twirls her ponytail. "What happens at the end?"

"He plays his flute, and the . . . I don't know . . . Hades, I guess . . . falls in love with his music and lets her leave with him. With one very simple rule."

Her eyes are narrower than slits. "Go on."

"His wife will follow him, but he must walk all the way out, through the exit, and not turn once to look at her."

Reggie mumbles something under her breath that sounds like "not quite what I remember" as she rubs her temples. "Keep going."

"The guy's so excited, and he's just steps away from getting what he wants when he makes the mistake of turning around, and even though she is only a few feet away, she is whisked back to the depths of Hell. Because of a broken promise."

"It figures, doesn't it? Men just can't listen to instructions. Serves him right. Cheers to that." She downs the rest of her drink and wags a finger at me. "By the way, that bullshit of a tale doesn't even come close to the truth. Who the heck wrote it? Plato? He sure was the biggest, most well-draped liar in all of history."

"No, it wasn't Plato, and how do you know it's all a lie?"

"Remember my trust face?" She crosses her eyes, flares her nostrils, and sticks out her tongue. "This is the face that a lot of people have come to realize means only the most absolutest of believe-in-mes. All my previous wishers know that this look is not to be trifled with. It's spelled the end to wars. The beginning of romances. The . . . avowal of eternal friendship that ends up breaking your heart."

As the ridiculous face falls, she cuts me a look. For the

briefest of seconds, I can't tell what I see in her eyes. But it's like . . . she really does know. I dare to consider she may actually be telling the truth, that she's lived through thousands of years, hiding in plain sight, swaying along with the merry folks of the world as she downs drink after drink, but I quash that thought immediately.

Because she's most likely some heiress with high levels of boredom. And there's no such thing as genies.

Chapter Thirty-Seven

As Hamza and the djinn feared, the road to the Underworld was paved with treachery, but the djinn did remind him of his half-living nature, that the lord of the Underworld could not easily claim him, even if he wanted to.

Soon they entered a forest full of flapping creatures that shot poison-tipped arrows. The first would've pierced his heart if it hadn't been for the oily creature that continued to protect him with every tune he played. Its flying kick landed Hamza on his side at the very second the arrow whizzed past him. It sneered at the creatures overhead as a dozen of its comrades loosed even more arrows. The creature dragged Hamza into the hollow trunk of a diseased tree and, countless heart-beats later, signaled his safety.

The djinn watched with wonder at the creature's tenacity.

Hamza regarded the creature with curiosity, wondering why it helped him. Why it hid him. Why it saved him.

The creature pointed to the flute again and said, Play. Hamza knew then that, even in that foul place, the oily black creature with the glimmering teeth was keeping its promise to secure him a more comfortable journey.

He brought his flute to his lips and played, and the creature marveled again before disappearing once more.

So it was that, for every new peril that Hamza was to face, he had to pay for safe passage with a melody. Serpents as long as Salamat's wells were deep, hut-size scorpions by the thousands, many-fanged and hundred-legged spiders—all of these were nimbly overcome by the sprightly, child-size creature.

The djinn laughed at every one of the creature's antics, confiding in Hamza that their journey was infinitely more eventful because of it.

They were three days in when Hamza, the soles of his feet cracked and bleeding from not stopping for rest the entire walk, arrived upon the throne of the lord of the Underworld in the deepest cavern.

The lord was as tall as the ceiling, with a gray face petrified from dry age. A crown of skulls perched atop his head and a perpetual grin spread wide, as if he knew he would rule over the entire world someday.

As Hamza approached, he saw the love of his life seated on the floor, leaning against the throne, her gaze upon the realm's owner, her master. Hamza's heart drowned in the warmth of joy, knowing he was within reach of Delima's smooth, earthy skin and the kind heart that had showered him with love.

The djinn raised a hand, warned him of the potential for failure, that he should steady himself.

Hamza called out her name, and both Delima and the lord turned their heads. She gasped at seeing her fiancé's appearance in the

Underworld, for she had assumed the woven threads of his life had been severed too soon, like hers. But the lord, who was intimate with the inhabitants of his domain, shook his head, announcing Hamza was a stranger there.

Delima, confused, strode up to Hamza and laid a careful hand on his cheek, to affirm his physical presence next to her, and convinced, wrapped herself around him, streams of tears flowing down her cheeks. The pair sealed their love with a kiss.

When they finally tore themselves apart from each other, Hamza introduced the djinn to Delima, explaining how the djinn had granted his wishes and empowered his journey. He made no mention of the child-creature, for fear the lord might punish it for providing assistance on a mere human's journey to reclaim what rightfully belonged to the Underworld.

Hamza asked Delima why she was there and not in Heaven.

Delima glanced at the figure on the throne and reminded Hamza of all the crimes he had forgiven her for, but which the lord had never forgotten.

The lord on his throne rested his chin on an ashy fist. His laugh boomed throughout the cavern, and when he was done, Hamza summoned his courage and declared his intentions—to bring his beloved home. Hamza stood ready, for he was but a puny man, about to do battle with the emperor of the Underworld. He steadied himself, and Delima released his hand.

Her words were small. Smaller than the beetles that scurried across the ground. Hamza thought he had misheard.

Delima repeated herself, and this time, the words speared his heart, soul, his entire being. She did not wish to go back to the world of the humans.

He demanded, begged to know why. Why did she not want him to take her home?

She was happy there.

And with those words, she left his side, returning to the foot of the lord's throne.

The lord interjected, claiming that Delima's soul was more at ease down there, without the human eyes of judgment that were everywhere up above. In the Underworld, everyone was free to do as they pleased, and no one would dare frown upon them. He expressed his condolences to Hamza, who'd wasted all his time in a task that would bear no fruit.

Hamza took a step forward, his outreached hand mere inches from his love, but a distance that could never be bridged. He decided to play, and play his flute he did.

The lord of the Underworld, who showed rare moments of sympathy, was struck by the notes in the air, all tinged with sadness. Because of the adoration for the beauty of his melody, the lord granted Hamza safe passage out of the Underworld.

The djinn bowed before the lord and grabbed Hamza by the arm, pulling him to return to the surface where he belonged, but Hamza shook his arm free, declaring that he was ready to use his third wish to save Delima.

The lord jumped out of his seat at such insolence.

The djinn expressed her disapproval, because if he were to try and retrieve Delima without the girl's approval or desire, it would amount to compulsion, and her love would always be out of reach.

His loved one would have to remain a lost cause.

But the lord swiped his stout gray arm at Hamza, and to the man's surprise, the oily child-creature leaped out of the dark bushes it had been hiding in to yank Hamza back. It spat at Hamza, cursing him for his foolishness against such an impossible foe.

The lord, with all his frustration apparent, rescinded Hamza's safe protections across his lands, and our hero was left with one wish and only the hope of finding his way home.

As they departed the cavern, and with Hamza holding aloft one last longing look at Delima, the djinn asked how he wanted to proceed.

Hamza looked at the child-creature and thanked it for saving his life again. To the djinn, he said he hadn't the faintest idea how he should go on.

Chapter Thirty-Eight

Wake up, sir. Reggie. We're almost there."

Must've fallen asleep. How tired was I? The flight was supposed to be only four hours, but stealing books, starting riots, and knocking out cops really take a lot out of you.

It's dark out.

Reggie's so still in her seat/bed/cocoon, snoring, that I have to shake her arm till my shoulder hurts.

She finally slams herself upright, saying, "Come hit me right there, Tom Holland Cavill Reynolds." When she sees my face, her cheeks redden, but not before her eyes widen. "Oh my god. This is the worst. Get Phoebe right now. Stat. I mean *now*. Sayyed, what're you still doing here? Go grab her."

"Okay, okay." I scramble, hitting what I think is the right button on the armrest, until I hear the ding. "What's wrong, though?"

"I'm sober," she says with eyes closed, as if praying.

Seconds later, our flight attendant appears in the aisle.

"Oh, thank goodness. I need a drink. Give me anything," Reggie says with alarm.

"What would you like?"

"I don't care. Does this look like I care? Get me three mini bottles of tequila or rum or vodka or, ew, whiskey, right now, and I promise you I'll down them in a minute. I don't even need the tray tables lowered."

The three bottles plop in Reggie's lap seconds later, and she really does down them all in less than a minute. Before a look of absolute bliss settles in.

The plane lands, and we disembark without a hitch. More new texts and voice mails ping from my phone, and I can't stop the dread from settling in. Because clearly Sofia and Umi are worried about me. But I have no choice now—I need to keep onward. I've made my promise to Farouk, whether he knows it or not, and I'm going to find him.

Reggie rushes me through the private-jet terminal, but this time I'm holding tight to her pink-and-green tote—she's not escaping from me again, leaving me stranded. But here, no one seems to think either of us is anything suspicious.

A half hour later, she's got money changed, and we find ourselves at the taxi stand.

At nine at night. "Where the heck do we go?" I ask as I scan for transportation options at the terminal.

Reggie's on her phone, rat-tat-tatting away, swiping, and

when she's done, she hurries me to the front of the line, where she salutes a cab driver, a grizzled man with the sweetest smile, then points her phone at him. "Take us here, please."

He nods, and we slide on in the back. Thick wafts of jasmine stab my nostrils. "Woo. That's a lot of flowers. Where are we headed?"

"The finest hotel in this town. What? Did you think we were headed out to the land over yonder instantly? I'm still waiting for my contact to get back to me on the exact location." She concludes the rant with a rude brushing of my face with her ponytail.

"What does this contact of yours do?"

"Um . . . telecommunications. That's what he does. All he needs is to triangulate the cell phone towers. Anyway, we may as well have some fun while we wait for further details, do some research on this town that'll hopefully lend us a fresh pair of eyes, which will lead us to your amazing, wonderful Farouk. Got that? Good. Why is everything so dark out there? Sir? Sir, do you know where one can procure a bottle of some world-renowned tequila?"

The driver flicks a hand by his mouth, then his ears. Universal for *No English.*

"Well, that was a waste of three calories," Reggie says.

✦ ✦ ✦ ✦ ✦

The hotel's skeleton crew greets us, and I have to admit it must've been a real palace at one point. Elegance to the heavens, with marble everywhere. There's ornate, and then there's *ornate.* This is *ornate* ornate. Like ridiculornate. Monumentornate. Anyway.

Our two-bedroom suite is beyond. The bed, the wallpaper, the bathrooms. I mean, they're all magazine-worthy. I know Reggie's the purveyor of everything fancy, but it makes me wonder. "I think I've asked you before, but you evaded the question. Exactly how did you get so rich?" I ask as I plug in my dead phone to charge.

We're in my room when she body slams the king-size bed (and I do the same on the other side) and twirls her ponytail. "Oh, dearest pumpkin. You are just dying to know, aren't you? Simple, really. My parents had money. They died, and I got everything."

"How'd they get it?"

"Oh, nothing you'd understand. Trade stuff. Something to do with aquifers, I think? Listen, if you want to make it in this world, you have to understand your worth. What are you really good at?"

I haven't had time to really think about the direction of my life since I got kicked out. "Don't know. I feel like . . . I know this is tough to say, but I can't help feeling like my mom held me back from really becoming my own person."

Reggie rolls her eyes. "So you're blaming someone else for your own deficiencies? Figures. Remember what I said about men? You are one such example, mein freund. Male privilege much?"

I sit up straight, hug one of the 150 pillows that crowd the bed. "No, I don't want to blame my umi for anything wrong with me. I'm just saying, see, she's afraid for my sister and me for so many reasons. Just today, she's called a hundred times, and Sofia's texted about the same amount. I mean, when you've got that kind of safety net, it stops you from . . . really falling. Do you know what I mean?"

Reggie's stopped twirling her hair, and her eyes turn glassy. "You've got the analogy all wrong."

I leave her statement hanging. Surely she's got more to say?

She stares past me, at the wall to my back. "I'm the one with all the safety nets. Money. Properties. Jets. All of them designed to *catch* me before I land. See, I'm already falling, and I'll keep falling, again and again. But you're the one with all the people—mom, sister, friend. They're the ones who'll *stop* you from falling."

What the heck? Is she actually making sense for once? "Why do you say you're falling? You seem pretty . . . grounded?"

She rests her head on a pillow, grabs another to hug real tight. "This may seem funny to you, but 'grounded' is the last word I'd use to describe me. If you can't already tell. I'm always doing so much, running here and there, with strangers or whatever—"

"Helping us?"

She makes a face. "I don't know if it's helping, but someone once told me that there's no such thing as altruism. Because helping others makes you feel good, which isn't entirely self-less, then, is it? So me granting wishes . . . it's not the good thing you probably think it is."

I don't quite understand what she's trying to say. Maybe I'm just tired. But a curious thought comes to me. "Have you ever seen *Aladdin*?"

"No. What is it?" She's starting to look super bored.

"Seriously? It's about this kid who meets a genie and gets three wishes, but in the end, he wishes the genie free." I take a deep breath and ask the question that's been making me feel all sorts of cringey. "Um . . . Reggie. Are you . . . a real genie? Are you waiting for me to set you free?"

Reggie's laughter shakes my very core, because it's the realest, most concrete thing I've heard coming from her. But there's also a tinge of something wistful in her eyes she can't hide. As if she's been longing for something other than freedom. "Oh, honeybun. I'm freer than an AmEx Centurion Black card. Seriously, there's nothing like free money, right? So don't you worry about me."

My voice softens, so I don't lose the momentum I've gained. "There's got to be something you want. I don't believe for a second that you have everything."

Reggie massages the back of her neck, as if a knot has just formed. "I've learned that I can try to give anyone all sorts of happy and wowwee, but eventually it wears out. Everything loses its shiny over time, and everyone just moves on. And I have to do the same."

I can't help feeling that she's lonely. That this is her sport, and helping people is just something she does to fuel her days.

She goes on. "Anyway, I've been free since the day I was left alone on this planet, when my parents died. No need to unshackle these nonexistent shackles on my wrists. So there's no more to be said about me. Now, I am curious about what your third wish would be."

"Oh. Haven't thought about that. I guess I'll wish for you to take Farouk and me home instantly. Or, I guess, the fastest, safest route home."

"Well, once I finish granting your second wish, then I'll get started on the third. Deal?"

"Isn't that how wishes work?"

"How else would they?" she asks while punching buttons on the remote haphazardly.

But something else bothers me. Something else I feel like I have to say. "What would you wish for? If you had wishes?"

Her eyes widen slowly, until they're almost round. "Me? Wishes? If I had wishes? That's just silly. I can get everything I've ever wanted. With a snap of my fingers."

"Seriously, though. If you could have just one thing you never could have. What would it be?"

She drags herself off the bed and walks over to the window, her back to me. "Don't you think sometimes it'd be easier if you didn't have anything? That, in that moment, you are in possession of the inviolable belief that someone can love you for who you truly are? And not what you might possess?"

I can't help but watch as the whole of Reggie slumps a fraction of an inch. "I honestly don't know if it's easier to not have anything," I say.

She gazes out the window a minute longer before flinging the remote onto the bed. "Enough of this chitchat. Are you ready?"

"What? Ready for what?"

She twirls around, brandishing a brand-new bottle of something, then takes a long chug out of it. When she finally pulls her lips away, she says, "We're going sightseeing. Maybe even get you to forget about lover boy for a quick minute. Come on." She chucks the half-empty bottle aside.

I probably should have seen that coming. I wonder if she's ever told the truth to anyone. If she's ever really opened up.

Guess it won't be to me.

Chapter Thirty-Nine

"Where are we?" I ask.

The taxi has brought us to some super-crowded part of town where it seems like every single person is out for the evening. It's a large spot nestled in a group of buildings, and right smack-dab in the center is a monument of . . . something?

"This, my dear chickadee, is Taksim Square. Quite a sight, isn't it?" she says, arms open wide.

It truly is. The people sure know how to enjoy themselves. There's a street bazaar where vendors are set up, and the smells coming from them . . . I can only swoon. It's as if spices are worshipped here, as they mingle and dance and kiss in the air. Some I've never even had the privilege of inviting into my soul before. Can't remember the last time I had a truly satisfying meal—I've really done my body no good since the breakup—will tonight be it?

My eyes feast on baklava, and my stomach grumbles at

rotisseried meats, but the one thing that commands my absolute attention is this see-through cabinet piled with wet, soggy, steamed meat burgers. "What is that?"

"Looks like actual food. Not too familiar, though. Here, go get it." Reggie hands me a wad of hundred lira bills. "Shouldn't cost more than that."

My eyes blink at the cash—not quite sure how much all of that is—before I run over and get two of the Islak burgers—that's what they're called—and hand one to her, along with the plenty of change left over.

She waves away the cash, looks at the burger, at me, then back at it again with a curling of the lips. "Revolting." Before pulling out a mini bottle, untwisting the cap. "I'm good for a while after the sandwich you voluntarily gave me. Besides, I've got my own meal right here."

She downs it while I take a bite of the burger and stuff the money in my front pocket.

And my head explodes. Not literally, but almost. Because this is just the most perfectest, absolutely scrum-yumptiously delicious thing I've ever had. It may seriously rival Umi's chicken korma.

The first one's gone. Just like that. Vanished in mere seconds.

I don't plan on wasting the other. That, too, disappears as quickly as the first. I have also not seen Reggie's eyes that wide before. "What? Do I have something on my face?"

Reggie wipes a smear of sauce from the edges of my lips. "Nope. I just didn't think you had that kind of talent. To make something so big disappear through such a small hole."

"Ew." Of course she'd go there.

Her eyes go back to normal as we return to the bustling square and walk down a street lined with more food shops. Breaking up with Farouk killed my appetite for so long. Is the thought of seeing him so exciting to me that I'm actually craving food again? Or am I . . . slightly happier? Can't be. Better hush that thought, because nothing's for sure yet. I don't even know what tomorrow morning's going to bring.

We step into cafés so I can try out stewed lamb shanks, so many kinds of deliciously cooked rice, more meaty sandwiches, and jugs of lip-puckeringly tart cherry juice.

Reggie looks on with growing disgust and sloppying drunkenness.

When we head back to the hotel, I can only plop myself onto the bed with a groan of, "I think I ate too much."

"That's the problem with you *young people*. Never satisfied, always looking for more."

What? There's something there . . . something I should follow up on . . . about my *young*ness, which means she's the one with the *old*ness . . . but I'm so tired . . .

The TV flickers on, and my heart skips as I hear a familiar song. *Pum-puh-puh-pummm!*

Reggie squeals in her highest pitch possible. "Look at that! *Aladdin.* Weren't you just talking about this? What're the chances they'd play this kids' cartoon so late at night?"

There's something unexplainable about the coincidence.

But I don't push it. Not tonight.

Chapter Forty

A loud ping drags me out of sleep as bright rays of morning sun spear my eyeballs. "Is that a gong?"

Reggie's in her bathrobe, tapping at her phone. "No, darling, much better, though. We've got a location. My contact pulled through. And a face! What a handsome one too."

I blink at the photo on her phone. And kind of wake up a bit more. The guy is . . . a stunner for sure. That nose, so sharp it looks like it cuts cheese with ease. "That's Mustafa? Uh, he's young, isn't he? He sounded much older."

Minutes later, I step out of the shower, grateful for having caught up on my sleep, but also wondering what Mustafa has to do with Farouk.

What luxury, to have a clean body and clean teeth again. And to get out of the T-shirt-and-basketball-shorts combo. For Istanbul, it's jean shorts and an Ariana Grande T-shirt. Sometimes, I think I can gay quite well.

My phone is fully charged, and I'm ready. But there's no avoiding the messages now.

> *Dzakir:* Where the flickity foot pedal are you?
> *Dzakir:* I promise to never get angry with you ever again. Is that what you want to hear?
> *Dzakir:* Don't think I won't spank you for giving me the silent treatment. I won't be taking no for an answer, missy.

I text him back real quick that I've just been hanging out with Reggie. Which isn't a lie.

A few from my sister:

> *Sofia:* Brother, where art thou? Please talk to me. I'll be nice to you for a whole week if you just call.
> *Sofia:* Brother, I'm at the hospital with Umi and Baba every day. Why aren't you here?
> *Sofia:* Can you just call me already, insufferable brother of mine? I love you.

From my ever-loving umi, one of many voice mails:

Sayyed, my dear son. I'm sorry I couldn't fight for you, and I hope someday you will understand. I don't know where you are, but I can't stop worrying. Please come back. Just come back. I promise to make everything right.

As much as my heart tears to pieces for her, I can't speak to Umi this very minute, because I'll be an absolute sobby mess if

I do. There are several aches inside me—one's for Farouk and one's for Umi and neither will go away easily. I'm just waiting for the right time.

My fingers hover over the phone. Hesitating. I should at least tell them I'm okay.

But Reggie blares out the loudest *"I'm thirrrrrrrrsssssttttt-tyyyyyy!"* that echoes through the whole suite.

And my phone almost plops out of my hand as I stumble from the room.

There she is, waiting by the door. She's got the same pink-and-green tote, but I'm appreciating today's red jumpsuit. Pretty tame.

Before setting off, we make a quick stop at the hotel café that's open for breakfast, so Reggie can—in her own words—"get a couple shots of breakfast vodka but without the tomato mix and celery because Bloody Marys look like pureed kidneys or something worse."

And a light croissant sandwich for me.

As our taxi pulls up, Reggie says, "And away we go, our magic Ottomanic flying carpet. Well, not really, but you get the idea."

★ ✦ ✦ ✦ ★

The streets are packed with cars, and throngs of people surround us. It's early, but the city thrums with life. I can feel it as we drive along a river—the Bosphorus—and spend an entire minute crossing a bridge. Ferries and small boats and ships dot the horizon. Our windows are down, inviting salty air and the merry squawk of seagulls.

We finally approach a gigantic pink building with a magnificent dome and minarets that hang from the clouds. Our cab driver lets us off, and here we stand, in front of the most majestic structure I have ever seen in my life.

"This is the last known pinged location. And that is the famed Ayasofya," Reggie says.

It's seriously monumental, but what's just as surprising is the blue building across the street.

"That's the Blue Mosque. It's pretty famous, if you can't tell," Reggie says. "Why do I feel like I've told you all this already?"

We make our way to the pink building and spend a half hour circling it. Reggie's about to pay for our tickets so we can inspect the inside until my ear hooks on to something familiar.

"What is it?" Reggie asks.

I swing my backpack around. "Do you hear?"

Reggie stares at the sky, then, with a wink and a smile, says, "Looks like this trip isn't such a waste after all."

I can only stare at the teen passing us by, the one leading a group of tourists toward the entrance of the museum, right where we stand.

Because the voice is the exact same barbed-wire voice we heard on the phone.

And it's him. The guy in the photo.

Mustafa.

Chapter Forty-One

I told you my contact would do his magic," Reggie says with a nudge to my side. "It's almost a miracle, but not quite. He's a rather tasty one, isn't he? It's no wonder those tourists stare at him more than the Ayasofya itself."

I want to shrivel into the ground or behind the nearest tree. "Please, for the love of everything that you hold sacred—tequila, vodka, rum, whatever—do not lick your lips while giving him the hungry eye. Just don't."

The smartly dressed teen is close enough for me to hear his English, tinged with that familiar accent, as he discusses the building that claws at the sky.

"They sure are erect, all right," Reggie says. "What? Oh, don't give me that look. I'm talking about the minarets."

I elbow her in the rib, and she yelps out a "What'd you do that for?" which draws everyone's attention, but thankfully not the handsome subject of our investigation.

Mustafa ushers the group into the building while Reggie and I follow through the ticket counter. A minute later, the tour group has adopted two unexpected freeloaders, but not really, since we're more interested in him than learning about the history of this place.

Reggie decides to expound on *her* version of "history." "Sy, do you see what I mean when I said marble and wood? I don't even know how anyone could think such tragicness could even remotely be matchy-matchy? Did the conquerors not have gay interior designers?"

I can't stop taking in the sights, though. There's just so much to see everywhere. Plus the gigantic *Allah* and *Muhammad* inscriptions in Arabic propped up high. "I think it's kinda cool, though. I honestly have no opinion on the wood-versus-marble debate. The only word I can think of to describe this whole place is 'grand.' It's just all soooooo . . . grandtastic."

"You know what's not clashy-clashy? You and Farouk. I can't wait to see you two in action once you're back together. Even though you were the one who did him wrong. Wait, was that the moral of this story?" Reggie tugs her ponytail like she might a string of pearls around her neck.

Was I the one who did Farouk wrong? When he was the one who left me?

Were we two boys who were as clashy-clashy as the marble and wood in here, at least according to Reggie?

The handsome teen—he can't be much older than I am—continues his trek around the insides of the museum, detailing significant etchings and murals and wall coverings. He makes it sound like the Muslims were quite the conquerors back then, which I had no clue about.

I don't know how long it'll be before he notices us, so I pull Reggie next to the stairs, and we let the group go on ahead. "Let's just hang out by the entrance—seems like it's also the only exit. We'll just corner him when he leaves."

She gives me a salute, and we make our way there, where we look like the welcoming committee for new arrivals.

Barely five minutes later . . .

"Act natural. Romeo's coming this way." Reggie flounces her ponytail around to some strange internal beat, looking every bit the opposite of natural.

I slink to a column and hide in its shadows, hoping to jump at our target when the moment is right. But before I can reach out to grab his attention, he glances at his watch, pops in a pair of wireless earbuds, and sprints out of the building.

"Where's he going?" I ask.

We watch in alarm as he disappears from us, getting farther and farther away.

"Wait, sir. Mustafa, stop!" Reggie screams.

But the guy probably has his music on super loud.

This is it. It's my only lead. "Reggie, we have to go."

She nods, and we run, hoping we can catch up. It's funny watching Reggie skip and almost-run, because her boobage look like they're about to give her black eyes.

We almost lose him after he turns a corner, only to see him in line to board a train.

We're still about thirty yards away but closing in fast.

Reggie wheezes so hard, her lungs might pop out. "Get . . . going. Slow . . . the . . . train . . . down . . ."

I'm dragging her by the arm, and we're still five seconds away, but he's already boarded. Damn, he's fast. "Reggie, you can make it. Come on."

"I will. Just . . . give me a second." She's speed walking now, clutching her sides, sweat popping out in the most unmentionable of places. "I'll . . . get . . . there. Oof. Thought running around in London . . . yesterday . . . would've been it."

I let go of her arm, to rush to board the train and tell the conductor to wait for her, when I hear the shrill screech behind me.

"My bag. Sayyed, that guy has my bag!"

I turn to see Reggie without her beloved pink-and-green tote, taking off after some guy in a leather jacket. The door's dinging away, on the verge of closing, and I have no idea what to do.

The conductor's screaming at me in a language I don't understand, and I'm stuck.

If I let Mustafa go, there's no guarantee we'll find him again. Who knows if Reggie's contact can track his phone a second time, especially if he switches it off like he did yesterday?

If I let Reggie go, how the heck will I find my way around to meeting her again if the thief has her phone and all her money, and she never gets to retrieve it?

I have only seconds to make my decision.

Chapter Forty-Two

Reggie's gone. Disappeared. Somewhere into the depths of Istanbul, chasing some thief who's running off with her tote. And here I am. Alone.

Chasing after some guy I know nothing about.

I say a little prayer and pay the fare with leftover cash Reggie had given me last night, my grip on the handrail so tight while eyeing the guy, trying not to attract attention. He's all the way at the very back. Probably not a good place to chat him up about Farouk, but I don't want him to freak out if he realizes I've been following him.

The train is super packed with laughter and chatter and lots of determined faces rushing to work or the shops, so there's no way for me to reach him and start with the questions anyway, although is that really a good idea for me in a foreign land all by myself?

But maybe it's luck that I'm invisible most of the time—no

one really notices some scrawny brown kid making his way through the world. There are some advantages to being me, I guess.

He gets off just a few stops later at a station called Aksaray, and I tail him through the streets, past vibrant shops, including one with the stickiest, syrupiest, nuttiest-looking baklava and another that totally reeks of cheese. All this chasing is starting to get my underworked lungs a little winded, and he's just too fast, but I force my feet to keep on going. Keep on going. I'd make a very bad spy; my tread is very un-stealthy. It's pretty much a stomp.

My target makes his final destination through a nondescript wooden slab of a door.

Finally catching my damn breath, I tiptoe forward and, not sensing anything diabolical about the establishment, step on through.

Aksaray Turkish Hamam—says the sign by the entrance.

I've heard of these. They're like bathhouses where you get scrubbed down and someone squeezes soap bubbles onto your back. *Might be fun.* I try to convince myself as I venture on in. Besides, it's reconnaissance to get closer to the guy while he gets his treatment, unless Farouk might be hiding inside somewhere?

Oh. What if Farouk works here?

The fluty lilt of Mediterranean instruments accompanies my entrance, along with a bouquet of aromatherapy oils and incense. The lady behind the counter's sales pitch is so good and hypnotizing that in a mere three minutes, I'm sold. I mean, who doesn't need the ultimate package, which includes massage, facial, and foot scrub? My neck does feel a little sore after all that traveling.

She asks if I need anything before we get started.

Yes, please. Mustafa. If it's not too much of a bother.

She hands me a key and ushers me to a room. I swing my backpack off and strip down to . . . Oh, I'm supposed to be naked under this cloth thing hanging on the rack. I see.

But what about the welts on my body? Thank goodness they're starting to fade.

Wrapping this fabric around my waist is a little tricky, but I manage. I slip on a pair of flip-flops and, after a mini personal pep talk, off I go.

Only to be face-to-face with him, his deep brown eyes drilling me, lips so curvy and swollen.

Just. So. Dreamy.

"Uh . . ." is all I can say.

And he has those bulgy biceps under that super-tight, almost uncomfortable-looking T-shirt.

"Hello, sir. My name is Mustafa. This way, please."

I cough out a "sure" and follow his lead into a steam room. "My first time."

"You will enjoy, I promise."

What a very powerful weapon. He can use that raspy voice against anyone to get what he wants.

"I will leave you here for fifteen minutes. Please lie down and relax. I'll come back, and we will start." He eyes my bruises. "I promise I'll be gentle."

It's just me, no one else around, and my heart thumps faster and faster, because as exciting as it is to be one step closer, I've also seen gangster movies where someone's relaxing in a steam room just like this and some hit man tries to knock them out or twist their neck. So I crawl to one corner and watch all sides and all entrances.

How the heck does anyone relax in here? What else can I do but twist my thumb ring.

My blood pressure has spiked to the ceiling when Mustafa finally returns. I'm in even bigger trouble because he's shirtless, and I can't help but melt into a hot, steamy puddle on the floor.

Wait—what's that gleaming thing hanging from around his neck?

No freaking way. It can't be.

Mustafa leads me into another chamber with octagonal walls and a raised octagonal marble central table that can easily fit a dozen people on it. "Please lie down on your back."

It is at this point that my embarrassment starts to show because, hey, I am a (hopefully) virile boy with . . . needs and desires, having to cover my downstairs region. "Mind if I lie on my stomach?"

"If it works for you, of course. On the edge, please."

If he tells me to lick the tiles, I'll do it, but I must resist. *Farouk, Farouk, Farouk.* "How long have you been doing this?"

Mustafa splashes warm water over my entire body, head to toe. "Two years. I had to study hard. You are from America?"

"Yes, I am." I try to get a glimpse of the pendant hanging from his neck. "You're from here."

"Of course. I know someone from America too. He gave me this necklace you keep looking at."

I sit up straight, my manhood deflating in an instant. "Can I see it?" I inch forward, his chest so close, I can feel the radiant heat. His pecs are so defined, and there's a little musk to his scent, which I think is an aphrodisiac and—

Eyes straight. At the piece of gold. It's the only thing that exists. Nothing else.

The book locket, smaller than a matchbox. I reach out to grab it, to read the inscription on the back, and Mustafa doesn't stop me, only saying, "You've been following me. Why?"

There it is. With the inscription on the back:

A Koran for Sayyed.

The gift from Umi. "How did you get my locket?"

His eyes turn hard and cold. "Yours? This is yours? You are Sayyed?"

I don't need to nod or say mm-hmm or do anything at all.

Because he sees it in my face. "So you are the one, the mystery boy Farouk had to let go of so he could find true happiness."

Ouch. "How do you know Farouk?" I am suddenly afraid of the answer.

Mustafa inches toward me. "You don't need to worry about that."

"Please. I just need to know how you know Farouk."

There's a shift in the steamy room as Mustafa takes a step back, a glower blazing from his eyes. "You should not be asking that question. Weren't you the one who refused to leave with him? Let him cross the world all alone?"

"What . . . what? How do you know that?" Fear grips my throat, hoping the answer doesn't strangle me. "Who are you?"

"I was the one who comforted him. I was there for him when his heart was broken, and I made him well again. You have no right to be here."

I have a choice to make at this very moment. Do I prove my worth to Farouk against this well-built teen and maybe lose, with a concussion as a consolation prize? Or do I run out, with a very limp tail between my legs, giving up the chance of ever finding the love of my life?

Chapter Forty-Three

It was a starlit night, full moon in the sky, and a packed Griffith Observatory. Spotlights shining, swarming busloads of tourists invading. Every parking spot taken for a whole mile down the road.

Farouk had convinced me we could hike all the way up there from the flatlands of Los Angeles, and he'd promised it'd be worth it. I had hmm'd and I-don't-know'd because I'm not a fan of sweat—it's just icky—but I went along with his strange suggestion anyway.

He'd lied.

It was a million times more than worthy of being worth it. It was breathtaking, phenomenal, wondrous, seeing all those bright lights and the grid the city was constructed on. I stood there—after a good ten minutes of gasping and panting—staring out over the railing, when he leaned into my back, wrapped his arms around me, nuzzled my neck, and said, "I present to you, your city."

Magnetic? Electric? Combustible? Irresistible? It was all of those things and more. But most of all was the feeling of being enveloped in his cocoon of safety.

And that was only our first date.

A week later, we took the bus all the way up to Malibu for our second date.

This time, he had convinced me to bring a change of clothing and again, I had hmm'd and I don't know'd because that meant I might actually need to change my clothes, which also meant it might involve doing a mud run or something more athletic than hiking. Altogether no-no's for me.

It was dusk—again—as we walked along the beach, with warm sand in between our toes, salt air tingling my nostrils. We held hands in the near dark and stole kisses from each other on every body part we could see—shoulders, palms, cheeks, lips, etc.

Until he stripped and threw everything down to the sand.

I loved watching Farouk naked. My mind would never stop reeling at witnessing his lithe swimmer's body, the skin so flawlessly brown, the new growth of hair on that chest. I wouldn't be surprised if I had hearts for eyes every time I looked at him.

Then he told me to join him.

Join him? In what?

He started explaining. How there was no feeling as free as swimming in the ocean naked.

Aaaiiieee. That was precisely the squeal I made when he suggested something so ludicrous. But I toughened up my soft shell and hmm'd and I-don't-know'd a bit more, plus a little shuffling in place, until I was like, *Fuck it.*

I did it. Sprinted into the water with a splash and leaped right out with an unholy howl over what felt like ice freezing me to the spine. Farouk dragged me into his arms and held me close, keeping me warm, slowly leading me back into the ocean, which he claimed was in the warm sixties, and I got lost in his eyes for hours.

H-O-U-R-S.

The waning moon might've grinned as it witnessed two virginal boys sloshing around, then lying in the sand, the quiet darkness cloaking them from the rest of the world.

I had never felt more alive.

Our third date, in the space of just as many weeks, was when he insisted I remained blindfolded until we reached our destination.

The bus ride was fine, and he played some Ariana and classic Mariah on our shared earphones to keep me occupied, since I couldn't see anything but black. Behind the blindfold, I was still pretty sure people were staring at me the entire time. I'd also learned by then that his long neck was a safe haven for my tiny face. Multiple buses later, we got off at our stop. All I could hear was the rumbling of tracks and screams of pure terror. I thought he was taking me to a Halloween House of Horror, even though it was August, but everything made sense when he ripped off the blindfold.

We were at Disneyland. And he had planned for us to be there the entire day.

And what a magical day it was.

I didn't know if I was afraid of heights or if my heart could take being up so high and then plunging what looked like seventy-five floors down, but damn those kiddie coasters—they dug out actual screams from deep within the caverns of my untrained lungs. From Space Mountain to Indiana Jones Adventure, from turkey legs to funnel cakes, Farouk showed me the best time ever.

From first date to third.

As we rode the many buses back home that evening, I knew I was madly in love. I would do whatever I could to be happy with this boy for the rest of my life.

Chapter Forty-Four

*F*uck *that asshole Farouk.*

That's my first thought as I eject myself from the hamam, after embarrassingly having to walk my naked body away from Mustafa. I hope I will turn the corner and bump into my ex so I can drag his ass into the nearest restroom and flush his apologetic face down the toilet.

I mean, my silence left Farouk to make his own decision to leave the country, but still. It's only been three months. Could he not have waited before finding some hussy to comfort him?

Furious. Mad. Angry. Devastated. Confused. So many different words to describe how I feel. Expletives, pejoratives, synonyms, antonyms—I want to fling them all at the boy even if I stumble upon his grave, because he may as well be dead at this point.

Okay, fine. I don't wish him dead.

What the heck did I get myself into? And where the hell am

I going? Just keep walking. Just keep walking. I'm drunk on adrenaline, and it feels great.

Whatever. Whatever. Whatever.

Here I am. Alone in Istanbul. And where the heck is Reggie? Because maybe I should just go home. Convince Umi to leave Baba—even though he's probably recovering from surgery, which would make us pretty heartless. Could I try to live with Baba's presence in my life and force him to accept me?

The thumb ring feels awfully heavy right now.

What should I do with it?

People mill about, going to work, or school, or to shop, and it's not even noon yet. Can they see the steam pouring out of my ears, the smoke leaking out of my nostrils? Oh, if they only knew what I've gone through.

Down this cobbled street, and another, through a really narrow alley. The char of toasted bread and Turkish coffee hang in the air. But none of it matters.

I'm lost.

I switch to rage; it's the only thing preventing me from panicking. I want to scream at someone. But what can I do until Reggie decides to save me from chomping on all my fingers out of fury?

I'm pacing a street corner when something catches my eye. It's a man, reaching out to a stray dog.

At first, he looks like he's just holding an open hand for it, but no, he's feeding it water. And the dog . . . it's lapping it up. There's lots of coaxing and smiling and plenty of gentleness, and many tries later, the creature lets the kind man pet it on its head.

Muslims and dogs aren't supposed to be friendly—but look at these two.

I guess his heart is so big, he's willing to bear the price of such a sin.

A tiny amount of rage melts off as I sneak away from them. I walk past cafés serving more of those steamed burgers that smell like ketchup, storekeepers hawking their latest burka fashions, and lively bicycle stores until I turn another corner, where a woman stands guard against a folding table with a variety of bread on it. Her eyes flicker over me, and I can't imagine what's written on my face, but she beckons at me and hands me a slice.

Ooh! Free sample!

Although it must be a ploy, says my doubtful self. She must want something.

A girl no older than ten, in a shabby T-shirt and raggedy shorts, dirt speckling every inch of her face, joins my side. The lady takes one look and hands an even bigger slice to the small thing.

Funny how life works. While my entire being is in conflict, here the universe gives me extraordinary, completely unselfish acts.

I turn to the girl and, after one final twirl from my fingers, hand the ring to her. Confusion flashes on her face, but she grabs the ring anyway. She can throw it into the Bosphorus for all I care, because I don't need it anymore.

She's all smiles as she takes off, and I can't help but follow to see where she goes.

The girl seems to be familiar with the shops as she continues her afternoon journey as a gatherer. In the span of ten minutes, she's added two packs of orange juice, an apple, and an imperfect blue scarf to her collection.

Back in LA, the homeless are invisible. No one acknowledges their presence; I have hardly ever seen anyone give anything to them.

Because it's just easier to navigate with one eye closed.

When her arms are full, she weaves her way through the streets with even more purpose. Past shoppers who give her no mind, down quiet streets littered with even more stray dogs, ending up at a back alley no one would ever think of going through if they have no reason to do so.

That's when I see them. The young mother in tattered clothes, propped against a wall, with an infant clamped around a nipple as she assesses the day's donations. She runs a hand through her daughter's hair and hand-feeds the girl most of the bread, sparing little for herself. They share a warm smile as they work on the apple and sip orange juice together.

The girl drapes the scarf around her mother to conceal the breastfeeding.

I finally decide to walk away. Guilt stabs me in the side. With what little they had, I probably shouldn't have taken away their right to privacy.

There is kindness everywhere. Everywhere I least expect. In the middle of my hopelessness, all I see . . . is hope.

What else have I missed walking with one eye closed?

Nothing looks the tiniest bit familiar as I wander the streets. It feels like slugs are sliming their way around the bottom of my tummy, but strangely, after what I witnessed, it doesn't feel as bad as my first stint at near-homelessness back in LA. Can't say I'm numb to the experience, but I'm just realizing it could be much, much worse.

So I walk. And walk. And walk. Past gardens, more food stands than I can count, and throngs of tourists exploring the town. I'm not in the mood to talk to anyone right now.

If I lose enough of myself, maybe I'll be able to find me?

Ha. So not counting on it.

I finally get to the river—which I assume to be the Bosphorus—and then I see everything in the lowering sun. It's almost like I'm at the edge of the world, peering at what it has to offer. The many buildings now cast in failing light. The glittering water flowing with countless diamonds. And the melody of the adhan from all the imams in the many mosques across the city, as the call to prayer rolls over us all.

Is this actual bliss?

I figure I should head in the direction of the Ayasofya—I mean, that was where we started out. Even though it's about the size of my thumbnail from way over here. Which means I've got a whole lot of steppin' to get started on.

My poor feet. I don't last long. It's just too much to expect after a whole day of walking and being hungry. Although for some strange reason I don't even want to bother deciphering right now, I just don't feel like eating. Not even those tasty ketchupy Islak burgers I've seen so many times in the last few hours.

Well. Maybe there's some fried chicken somewhere.

I don't think it helps that when the sun sets in a few hours, it will take away the last of this dying light, which means I may get even more lost. But it's okay. All I need is a bench.

I find a wooden one in a small park where a smattering of kids is busy playing soccer in the tiniest field and a group of elderly men sits around discussing what looks to be something totally serious.

Finally getting to rest my screaming feet is just so *ahhhh-hhhhh*. I hear foot massages can feel pretty damn heavenly, and I would sell half my soul to get one right now. Even for ten minutes. The bench doesn't look super comfy—boy do I miss that bed I slept in last night—but maybe this will do me good.

I've got one bar of battery left on my phone. I should try and call Reggie.

The laughter from the kids nearby makes me look up. I think of the girl. Of family. All the missed notifications on my phone eating away at me.

There are more important people to contact first.

Dzakir answers the FaceTime almost instantly. "Where the blippity bleep are you?"

"Hey, D. I'm . . . Don't worry, please. Everything's fine."

"Are you sure? You promised to update me whenever you could. Oh my god. Seriously. Where are you?"

I want to hug him so tight. I've missed my BFF, like, intensely and wish he had gone on this trip with me, sass and all. "Um . . . Istanbul."

"What? Like . . . Turkey?"

"Uh . . . yup. I'm in Turkey."

Panic and shock wash over his face. "What the heck, Sy? How'd you end up there?"

"Oh god. It's a long story. But I'll explain it all when I get home. I promise, promise, promise. Listen. My phone's dying, and I need to call my mother. But I just wanted you to know I'm fine."

He chews on his lower lip. "You better be. Call me back whenever. I mean it."

"Love you, D."

Our chat ends. Umi's turn now.

My heart races.

"Sayyed? Is that really you, my poor son?" Nerves clip Umi's voice. "How are you?"

I exhale a semi-pregnant sigh. "I'm . . . okay."

"Your baba has come out of surgery, but he's still unconscious. I don't know what to do."

A muffled noise and Sofia takes over. "Brother, stop whatever it is you're doing and just come to us."

"But why, sister? What am I going back to? You and Umi have no power to go against Baba. He will still rule the house when he gets out of the hospital."

"You don't know that. Maybe he'll have a change of heart."

Changing his heart because of a heart attack is not likely. I can only grunt. "Do you not know Baba?"

Silence.

"I want you to be strong, okay?" I say. "Remember what I told you just before I left. And make sure Umi eats."

"I've been trying to, but all she wants to do is sit by Baba's bedside and pray. For him and for you."

"Get her a smoothie or something. And stick the straw in her mouth. She'll drink that."

"Things will go back to normal once you come home."

I doubt that. And I don't want Baba's normal. "I'm finding my home. I have to go now."

"Your home is here! Wait, why does it look like dawn or dusk where you are? What can you possibly be—?"

But there's some muffled noise again, and Umi's sweet voice pipes in. "Please, Sayyed. Do this for me. Just let me hold your face again."

"Umi, you need to let me go. Please. This is hard enough for me. You have no idea what it's been like."

"I know. I've never wanted to fail you as a mother, and I'm hoping you can forgive me and that you'll let me fight for you someday."

Someday. That's the problem. But I can't say another word, because my phone squawks one final beep and croaks a dying, vibrating shudder, and that's it. I'm truly alone.

I lay horizontal on the bench, so many parts of my body aching, psychologically banged up from chasing some boy. And just fall into a trance as I watch everything around me for what feels like hours.

Insert deep, heavy, grunty sigh here.

Damn, that rising full moon is bright. I wonder, with all its gravitational pull, if it can evaporate away some of the tears drowning me inside. Because as much as I want to let it all out, I just can't. There's still so much rage in me.

Why can't my family see how beautiful it is for two boys to be in love? Why can't the world see? Why must everything work against us? Why can't they understand that two Muslim boys who want to be in love should be allowed to love? And why can't Farouk understand that he shouldn't have left me to try and find himself, when I could have been his home until the freaking end of time?

Why am I here for someone? For *someone else*.

I traveled across the world to find a boy, and I don't even know if it's all going to be worth it. I need clarity. From all these confusing questions tumbling around inside me. But how do I get it?

⋆ ✦ ⋆ ✦ ⋆

A rooster crows, piercing my sleep. How long have I been out? Because the sky is still dark.

And then it happens. The call to prayer. Loudspeakered somewhere from a mosque nearby. The voice so sweet and lulling, it makes me want to shut my eyes again and drift away.

I must've fallen asleep very quickly. I guess no one thought anything of some random boy on a bench. What a safe town. I have no doubt if this were LA, my body would've been quartered into a dozen-ish pieces by now.

Oh. My. Back.

I don't think it's ever been this creaky. Casa de Sayyed is a rickety haunted mansion. I have to, in sloth time, bring myself up to a sitting position and lean against the bench back. Even the simple act of twisting my tight neck is like trying to swim against a riptide.

Did I actually sleep for ten whole hours?

But I've got to get going.

For what, though?

Reggie? I hope she got her purse back and her phone.

Time to get a-walking. Twenty minutes later, light streaks of azure trail the sky while wisps of clouds fade away. It's starting to get brighter, and I'm getting closer. I know it.

I just don't know what it is I'm getting closer to.

Being on my own has . . . actually, not been too bad. I never in a million years thought I'd be able to spend the night without a roof over my head. Without anyone. Or a plan.

I stroll past two men in front of a rug store, smoking, enjoying a chat while sipping some chai. Do they see this foreign brown boy who's suddenly grown a ridiculously stubborn streak? Or the slow drag of his achy feet that have never walked more than a mile in a twenty-four-hour period? There is something to be said for seeing countless faces that look . . . similar to mine. Being among my people. Back in the land of the free, I never actually felt . . . free. Knowing I had to sometimes keep my religion under wraps. I don't think it helps that so many people choose to brand us in the worst way possible.

It's always people against people. Why? To prove that we are better than the next person?

But Istanbul. Being here, wading through all this history, and roaming among the amazing crowds, filled with people who can't seem to stop smiling at each other and at me, I don't feel that way at all.

It's just so . . . calming. It almost lulls me into believing this is home. Even after hours of walking around.

I don't understand why it's so hard to believe we are good people. That *I* am good people.

Although my dad didn't think that way about me.

My stomach growls.

It's finally time to start figuring out where I am.

So . . . where am I?

Chapter Forty-Five

Nothing like a philosophical question to truly leave me stuck in place and time.

That's when the sign finds me:

BLUE MOSQUE—1 KM

Fifteen more minutes of slow-walking later, I see it.

The magnificent blue building is on a piece of land as large as the Ayasofya's, its dome just as large but with an additional two minarets for a total of six. Signs point to requirements for entry: NO SHOES. LOWER BODY MUST BE COVERED. WOMEN MUST WEAR HEAD COVERING. QUIET.

A small part of me whispers: *Enter and burn alive, you homo.*

It's super packed this afternoon, and I only just realize it's Friday—a pretty special day for prayers. They even seem to have set up spillover outside the mosque, rolling out lines of prayer mats for everyone to squeeze in.

Inching through the crowd, I slip my shoes off and into a

disposable plastic bag one of the guards hands over. Because I'm in shorts, he also hands me a bright blue cloth, which drapes down to my ankles.

I can't remember the last time I prayed. I head over to the washing area to perform the ablution and clumsily rinse the body parts that require cleansing.

Entering the mosque proper, my soft soles graze against plush blue carpet laced with red flowers. The sights all around astound me. I don't think I've ever seen anything as beautiful in my life. Delicate calligraphy adorns the intricate tiles. High-rising domes are propped on massive columns that must have drained the blood, sweat, and tears from tens of thousands of men. My heart soars at the magnificence of it all. And I feel . . . small.

I haven't the slightest clue what to do next.

I've arrived just in time for the sermon, which I assume will be in Turkish. So I edge into a tiny spot next to a smiling man and say "Assalamu'alaikum," as he replies with a handshake and a "Wa'alaikumsalam."

The imam switches to English on the speakers. Well, that's a surprise. Maybe there are a few internationals here, like me.

"To all my friends, thank you for gathering here on this Friday. What a week it has been. We can only recite a quick prayer for the city of London as they recover from the riots. Glad we are that no one was hurt. But I must admit, my body tensed when it was reported. Because my first thought was, please don't let it be one who'd been misguided by a false follower of our beautiful religion.

"For our religion is one of peace. Not of hatred, or jealousy, or strife. Bear patience for those who need help. And for those who seek to do us harm, let them strike first. Never, ever raise your hand before theirs.

"For someone possessing more than you, congratulate them. Be grateful for what you have. The air to breathe. The food you can bring to the table. The family and friends who surround you.

"We will be tested every day. Every single day. And how we respond to those tests sets up the constitution of our beings. Understand what a strong will can grant you against any weakness. And most of the battle is already won.

"Do not give in to temptation, for it is easy. Choose to resist instead, and you'll learn what it feels like to be a mountain. Sturdy and unmoving against the strongest gales.

"We don't know what's going to happen tomorrow. But we must be prepared for evil in all its forms. Their subjects are wreaking havoc in many parts of the world, and we can only hope our good brothers and sisters will join us in our fight against them.

"And finally, let's not forget that sometimes we have to lose ourselves to find our way. But for those who are lost and remain lost, let us do our best to find them and bring them home. Now, let us pray."

For those who are lost and remain lost, let us do our best to find them and bring them home.

Why am I here? What am I doing halfway across the world?

Is it only to find Farouk? To bring him home? Like the imam said, am I purposely trying to lose myself, to find my way?

No, that can't be it. How am I *that* lost?

We gather to our feet and squeeze in even tighter, so that others can join the masses.

And for the first time in close to a year, I raise my hands in supplication to God. With those gathered around me, I say, "Allah hu-akbar."

When the prayer concludes minutes later, I remain seated, basking in the beauty of all that a kingdom could produce. Surrounded by love and peace.

I know I am not alone.

My heart cracks. Splinters open. And what comes out is not blood but conviction.

And somehow, this lost boy knows what he must do.

✦ ✦ ✦ ✦ ✦

Outside the Blue Mosque, I ask the first stranger I see, a stunning woman in a beautiful blue hijab, if she knows a Ciragan Palace, only to get a headshake in return. I ask about ten random locals before a slim, bearded man finally shakes his head and hands over his phone, gesturing for me to type it out, which I do.

Then the realization sets in on his face. Oh, how my American tongue butchers and chops up any foreign word. I've been saying "See-Rah-Gone," and his correction is that the C is a soft "ch" and the "G" is totally silent. The result? "Ciragan" is a simple "Cheer-On."

He points out the directions in as much English as he can muster, and it doesn't sound too bad. He does say thirty minutes, which makes my toes curl, wrapping themselves around newborn callouses. Oy.

And so the trek continues. Down streets, around corners, and up hills.

A little dusty and a lot worn out, I nearly crawl my way through the lobby. At the door to the room, I knock. I hope she's here.

A knock. Another.

The door opens. And I could break down that very instant.

"There you are, chicken. I could smell you from a mile away. You're a bloody slacker, aren't you? I bet your night was half as fun as mine was," Reggie says.

I shut the door behind me. "I'm so sorry. I should have gone with you instead of staying on that stupid train. Are you okay?"

"Let me tell you," Reggie says, downing a glass of what appears to be tomato juice but which smells like the sea, "my purse is a thief magnet. I mean, just look at that wide-open maw, inviting anyone to dip their hands in to steal my limited-edition pantyhose, those hungry savages."

So much intense relief floods through me that it makes me do the most alien thing I've ever done.

I wrap my arms around her so tight, she actually starts to wheeze. "I prayed for you, you know. For you to reappear," I say. "And you didn't. So I had to do my best to find you. Can we please not lose each other again?"

"No one's ever prayed for me before. It's almost like you're an actual . . ." There's a raw moment of something real in her eyes, but she waves it off.

"An actual what?" My curiosity is piqued.

"An actual carer. You know. Someone who cares." She downs the rest of her drink. "Anyway, I told you I'm not going to leave you. Unlike that ex of yours. Speaking of, did we get anywhere with chasing that hunk of prime-cut model meat?"

I fall onto the bed, wrapping myself in the delicious comforter. Nothing like basking on a cloud. "You first. How'd you get your tote back?"

Reggie smacks herself on the forehead. "It's just like me to attract so much drama. You saw that man snatch my purse and me take off after him, didn't you? Oh, we went through some horrid twists and turns, until he rounded a bend, and bam! Straight into a wall. Nose all bloody kind of bam. He was positively dazed. Didn't take me no time at all to sit on his pained face and smack the living daylights out of him. He'd broken my phone with the collision, and that got me mad. But he was seeing more than stars—planets and constellations and all."

"Constellations are stars."

"Are they? Well, look at you. Anyway, I got everything back, and you see, I had to make a quick stop at a restaurant, bar, café something, for, you know, a replenishment of lost bodily fluids, and one long night later, I swear, I was literally about to text you this very second right after the concierge bought me my new phone, when I got the ping, and here you are. But it's no coincidence, is it? Or is it? Anyway, what about you? What happened?"

I recount the torrid tale of my meeting with Mustafa.

She balks. "That's positively dreadful. How could one really hot man be attracted to another really hot man? The math just doesn't add up, does it? I tell you what, I say we march up to him, right this very instant, and feed him a knuckle sandwich. Bet he won't forget that anytime soon."

I don't know how to throw a punch, much less land one, and besides, Mustafa is twice my size. "I need to freshen up first, but I have an even better idea."

Chapter Forty-Six

Psst. It's been days. What're we doing staring at that hamam? Didn't you take a bath this morning? Although you do smell like the seven oceans."

I smack Reggie on the shoulder. "Stop your sass. It's only been an hour. And that is where Mustafa works."

We're in the café across the street. "You'd think there'd be some soundtrack playing overhead as we wait, but nope. Nothing. No 'Kung Fu Fighting' or 'Rocky' or RuPaul's 'Drag Race' opening jingle or anything of the sort. You'd think after a gazillion years of fulfilling wishes, I'd be given music for even a sashay."

As if in response, the café's music switches from unfamiliar Turkish to Christina Aguilera's "Fighter." A classic.

"A gazillion years, huh? How do you look so young?"

"Virgin blood, my dear. It's what I bathe in."

She says it so deadpan, I can't help but inch away from her.

Reggie laughs. "Oh, gosh. I really should clarify myself sometimes. Virgin crickets. Takes an awful lot of them to produce one drop of their blood, but thank goodness I am a gazillionaire."

"Gazillion is not a real number."

"I vote for it to be. A gazillion times." The waiter tries to take our order, but Reggie waves him off.

"So I know you've promised me you'll help grant my wish in every way possible, but . . . in your history of granting wishes, have any of them backfired? Say . . . did someone not get what they wished for?"

Reggie scratches her chin. "Now that you mention it, here's the funny thing. Almost everyone's excited about getting their wishes granted and fulfilled and what have you . . . but I don't think I recall anyone ever making a third wish. Fancy that?"

"What do you mean, they never made their third wish?"

She shrugs. "Some of them just didn't want it. They were done after the second. But want to hear something even hilariouser? Some of those bastards actually died before they got there."

My heart is in my throat. "They died?"

"They do, or did. But I think it was just from old age or boredom. They got the riches, they got the girl or guy or the whole harem, and then that was it. It was all they ever wanted, and they just moved along, went kerplonk with smiles on their faces. Certainly happy endings."

I watch her. And decide to try again. "What about you? What do you want?"

Reggie gasps. "Me? I just want to see you happy, little chicklet. It'll bring me so much joy."

"You're avoiding the question."

"Didn't we do this already? When you asked me what I'd dreamed and wished for?"

"Dreaming and wishing and wanting are different."

"What do I want?" It's as if she's never thought of the question as she pulls a metal flask out of her left armpit, takes a swig from it. "I want . . . to not have to work so hard. My bones are starting to get weary."

"What do you mean, *work*? You're just flying around, having a good time. Aren't you?"

"I still have to go along with you and make sure your wishes come true. That's still work, the last time I checked." Another swig from her flask, which starts to bubble of emptiness.

"But you don't have to do any of this. You can just change your mind and leave and go along your way and holiday in the Maldives or . . . just do you."

She balks at that. "What a ridiculous suggestion. Then what's the point of life? And all the riches I have?"

And then it hits me. "Are you telling me . . . you're *actually* a nice person?"

She smacks me on the lips. "Don't you dare accuse me of such nonsense again. Anyway, look." She hushes me, points to our familiar target exiting the hamam. "What now?" she asks, fanning out Turkish liras onto the table and tossing the empty flask into her tote.

No clue how much she just left for the café, but I'm out the door, marching across the street.

Mustafa freezes in his tracks. "You again. What do you want?" he asks.

"I need to know what happened to Farouk."

He looks at me, then at Reggie, doubt painting his entire face. "Is this your bodyguard?"

Reggie frowns while I nod.

Mustafa crosses his arms and just stands there, chewing on a thought. "He told me about what happened when he asked you to join him on his trip. You didn't even ask him where he was going. He told me about your selfish ultimatum—stay or go. Of course he decided to do what was best for him."

I bite my tongue. Everything he says is true. He must see that on my face; I'm not here to fight him. I just need to find Farouk. Regardless of what he's done, what I've done, I need to make amends. And find out if there's still a future for us? Somehow?

"We chatted online for a few weeks while he was in London," Mustafa says, "working in some fish-and-chips shop. He was studying to become a teacher; did you even know that? Against my better instincts, I told this random guy I'd never met to come to Istanbul, because I knew Arabic, and it would help him where he wanted to eventually teach. So a month ago, he came here and stayed with me for two weeks."

A sliver of something stabs my heart deep. But there's real

pain etched on his face, and I can only wonder if it mirrors mine. Looks like Farouk did a number on him too. Which means . . .

"He's not here?"

Mustafa shakes his head. He reaches for the gold chain and lifts it off his neck, bundling it in his palm. "Do you know why he gave me this locket?"

Reggie and I stare back in silence.

"He insisted I take it in exchange for my help. What a fool I was. He left two weeks ago. Went to Marrakech to teach at an English school—the Monte Carlo Language School." He thrusts the locket at me. "Take this. I don't want to see you or think about him ever again."

I grab the chain and locket from him. It weighs down my hand more than I remember. "Thank you for—"

But he's already gone, his back to me, walking silently away.

The locket is cool even if it's the subject of so much anger and confusion. "This was a gift from my mom. It's large enough to hold the tiny Koran she gave me, but that's stowed away . . . somewhere else." I almost spit out "at home" until I realize I have to make a new one. A new home.

Reggie's lost in her thoughts, her stare fixed on a bearded man sitting outside the café, scrolling on the screen of an iPad. He looks lost in concentration as he whistles a tune.

But Reggie won't tear her eyes away.

"What's going on with you?" I ask.

She grabs her ponytail and chews on the end, not hearing a word I've said.

I slip the chain over my head and tap her on the arm. "Reggie, did you hear what Mustafa said?"

Her blank face says everything. "Oh, right. What an absolute prat, huh? Falling for a stranger after knowing him a few weeks? Who does a thing like that?"

"We need to go to Marrakech."

"Just wait an Yves Saint Laurent minute. Why are we chasing after him again when it's clear he's moved on? And why aren't you angry?"

"Because I think . . . this is my fault. That he's missing. Maybe in trouble. Was it because I let him go, that I wasn't there for him when I promised I would be, that I didn't have the strength to force him to stay? But he's my family. So did I do him wrong?"

Reggie scrunches her face, then blows out a fake sneeze infused with a dash of, "Denial."

"Will you help me or not?" I ask.

She pulls out her phone, and her fingers fly all over the screen. "Oh, by the holiest hand of Chris Hemsworth. Have I failed you yet?" She hails the next cab she sees, and we slide on in, making our way back to the airport.

To search for a boy who may not want to be found. But a boy to whom I need to make amends.

Chapter Forty-Seven

"Can you lighten up a little? It's your birthday. Eighteen should be a nicer color on you," I said.

Farouk stuck his fork in his slice of picanha to placate me. We were at his favorite restaurant—Fogo de Chão in Beverly Hills. I'd saved up for a whole three months knowing this special day was coming up.

"Food doesn't taste the same anymore," he said, eyes dull. "How can you keep eating?"

"Like this." I knifed my lamb, stabbed it, and chomped, chewing exaggeratedly, topping it off with a slow swallow so he could see my Adam's apple bob. "So easy, you can do it too."

"I'm serious. How can anyone . . . all these people around us . . . continue to celebrate their birthdays, weddings, anniversaries, when other people are hurting? Middle America is losing jobs. The Middle East is in turmoil, on the brink of war.

The rich are getting richer by the day. The poor can't figure out how to put food on the table—"

"You mentioned Middle America losing jobs, which I think leads to not being able to put food on the table. Kinda redundant there, boyfriend."

He laid his fork on his plate. "Why aren't you taking me seriously?"

Farouk had continued to have bouts of moroseness—he'd let his own lack of control about his personal life spiral into not having control over all of the world's problems—and I'd usually been great at handling them. "Of course I'm taking you seriously, but if I let every single issue weigh me down, then I'll be the most depressed person ever to live. Oh, no. I wasn't talking about you. I think you're slowly figuring things out, and it's going to take a while, but I want you to know I'll always be here for you."

"I doubt it," he mumbled.

"What? Do you seriously doubt a promise Sy Nizam makes to you? Have you ever known me to give you my word and stomp my heel on it? Never."

"So you're saying, and I guess you've always said this, but I just want to make it doubly, triply sure, that if I were to ever call for you in my time of need, that you will be there for me?"

I laid the cutlery on my plate. "You know all those old-timey sayings? Like, hell or high water? Between a rock and a hard place? In the deepest hellhole on this planet? I'll go through all of those to make sure I'm there for you."

A curl of his beautiful hair fell on his forehead as his grin lit up the entire restaurant, shooing away the ever-creeping darkness in my heart. "Sy, I'm sorry if I seem different, but you always know how to bring me back."

"Because your skull is chock-full of silly ideas like I'll leave you if you stop walking me to the bus stop." I reach into my jacket and grasp at the locket. "Now, hold out your hand, because this is the best birthday present I can think of. I doubt you've ever seen something like it before."

Curiosity and surprise mingled on his face as he stared at the trinket I slipped into his hand. "Gold? What is it?"

"My mom gave it to me. It's an heirloom from her grandpa. It used to store the tiniest Koran, which I don't think you need, and now, the locket's yours. Probably the most expensive thing I've ever owned."

His eyes glistened as hc unlatched the miniature clasp. "There's nothing in it."

"Correct. Fill it with whatever you want. You can find a tiny book of your own and store it in there, for when you feel like paging through it with a magnifying glass."

He made a silly face. "Well, thank you."

The tiny glint of gold looked unassuming. No one would ever suspect it was capable of harboring any number of secrets.

And I was too naive to suspect Farouk would ever hide anything from me.

Like wanting to leave everything and everyone he knew behind.

Chapter Forty-Eight

The road back to the land of the living wasn't without its peril, but Hamza and the djinn agreed it was monumentally easier with the oily creature leading the way. The return journey took no less time than the same three days inward, and once again, they arrived at the Underworld's gate.

Hamza stared at the footsteps he'd left behind, leading to Delima. He asked the djinn how he could be happy without her.

The djinn thought long and hard and pointed out that he should find joy from within, so he could live a life without ever looking back.

Hamza didn't know how to achieve that, straining to avert his gaze from the road back into the Underworld. The gate stood before him and, at its very precipice, the oily creature peered out, its head cocked to one side. Hamza asked why it was interested in the outside.

The child-creature explained that imps were never allowed to step into the land of the living. That imps did not belong out there.

The djinn listened to their exchange and tried to offer a sympathetic response but found herself wordless.

The imp got as close as it could, knowing that it couldn't go any farther. It shuffled in place with nervousness, until finally it settled with shoulders slumped in defeat.

Hamza asked why it wanted to go out there, when its home was safer.

The imp shrugged and said it had lived in the Underworld all its life and never met someone as kind as him, doing what he did for love. Its entire life's purpose had been to inflict misery upon the Underworld's occupants, until it came across Hamza. It knew he didn't belong there. Its first instinct, as always, was to make Hamza's journey an arduous one, but the imp held back as it learned of his quest.

Maybe it was also the music he'd played, which made it feel. *For the imp had never "felt" before.*

Hamza laughed—for the first time since Delima's passing—expressing how untrue the imp's opinion was. He explained his selfish nature—traveling all this way to claim what he thought belonged to him because he didn't think he'd have the ability to feel ever again without her.

He also said that "feeling" was a curse unto itself.

The imp considered this and shook its head, ridiculing Hamza for taking the quality of his constitution and character for granted. It knew a good man when it saw one, because it had never met one before.

Hamza lowered himself to his knees to face the imp and its glittering teeth. He planted a kiss on its dark, oily forehead and thanked it for believing in him, when he didn't have the gall to believe in himself.

Then he turned to the djinn and told her he was ready for his final wish.

Chapter Forty-Nine

What a restless flight it ends up being.

I spend the whole night walking back and forth on the plane, talking to Trent the bartender and Phoebe the flight attendant, asking them what they're doing with their lives. I don't think they were ready for someone to analyze and question all the life choices they've made.

Obviously, I'm a little loopy. Is this wooziness from all the wavering toying around with the conviction I thought I had?

The sun is setting by the time we land in Marrakech. Reggie takes a look at me and declares, "You need some good old orange juice. What they call here 'Portugal juice.'"

"They call oranges Portugal? They named a fruit after a whole country?"

Reggie, who's switched to a somber but simple getup of black blouse and jeans, nods violently. "It's either that or Spain. Or Finland. I guess we can just try until they understand."

"Can I ask you a question?"

The plane comes to a jerking stop as Reggie readies her pink-and-green tote and its contents. "I'm all ears."

"I'm not saying I want to change my mind or anything . . . but theoretically, what if I choose not to make my third wish, after we find Farouk? I mean, I've troubled you enough already."

Reggie's hard stare drills through me. "Is that what you want? To rescind and nullify your third wish?" Her voice gets louder and louder. "You can't take it back, you know, once you unwish it. It is a legally binding contract." She pauses before her expression turns oddly sincere. "Now, I don't know what kind of convincing you need, but I feel like you should see this to the very end, don't you?"

I don't think she's ever been this upset. Also, what's the big deal with not finishing all her wishes? It's not like her life depends on it. "Right. You're right."

"Thought you'd say that." And she's back to her merry, ginny, vodka-ish self. "It may be absolute fiddle-faddle, but something tells me it's going to rain today."

Even though there's not a cloud in the sky.

⋆ ⋆ ⋆ ⋆ ⋆

We speed-walk through the terminal, and I catch some news report on a screen of an attack that happened in a town a few hundred kilometers away some time ago. I hope it's not too bad and that those bad people don't make their way here. Because I don't know if I can handle things getting a little too scary.

But as we head to the taxi stand, my phone rings.

Uh-oh. I stare at the number a minute. I have to answer this. "Assalamualaikum . . . Auntie?"

Reggie looks at me with bewilderment, her eyes going all squinty.

"Sayyed. Your sister just called to tell me about your father. She wanted me to tell you to go back home."

Ugh. That sister of mine. How did she even get Farouk's mom's number? I will wring her neck. "Auntie, please understand how sorry I am for what happened. I'm trying to fix it."

"I just . . . I wanted to say sorry for . . . being so angry with you. I was too harsh to you."

I kind of gasp. "No, Auntie. You know I'm the sorry one. It's because of me that Farouk left."

"What? No." There's a sigh. "I should not have said that. He left because of us. He wasn't happy, and we couldn't see it. We were pressuring him too much. It was not your fault. I just miss him so much. I wish there was a way for me to find him."

"Ah . . ." I don't know how to respond to that. "Actually . . . I'm trying to do just that. Find Farouk."

A second of silence. "What do you mean? The police couldn't find any useful information, and—"

"I'm in Morocco right now. I found out he was teaching in an English school here, and . . . I'm getting close."

Even more silence. Then sobs. "How did you . . . ? You're too young . . . I don't even know what to say. It's dangerous for a young boy like you to be out there."

I glance at Reggie, who's haggling with a taxi driver, both of them with arms lifted to the sky, voices raising by several decibels with each passing second. "I'm with a friend. She's taking care of me." I'm surprised by how true the words sound once they're out of my mouth.

"Sayyed, your mother must be worried about you. No matter. My husband and I will be taking the next flight out there. And we will bring you and Farouk home. So keep us updated, please."

"Ah . . . I'm taking good care of myself. But Farouk is more important. Please, Auntie. Don't worry for now. I'll try to get back to you once I find him."

"You are brave. Braver than I thought you were."

There's that word again. Is that a joke? Brave? Am I actually brave?

✦ ✦ ✦ ✦ ✦

The road to Marrakech is a dry one, with lots of sand-colored buildings on either side. My heart's starting to resemble a desert too. So is my hope. Drying up faster than I ever expected.

But the city is as vibrant as Istanbul was, if not more. There's just something about being around people here that makes my heart soar even the tiniest bit. It almost feels like I belong.

Maybe I can understand why Farouk wants to be here.

"Marrakech. The city of a million old movies," Reggie says, pretending to puff a cigar with one hand and coiling her ponytail with the other. "I mean, if I were a Hollywood producer, I'd film everything here. *Star Wars. Captain Planet. Titanic.*"

"*Titanic?*"

"Sounds like a blockbuster, doesn't it?"

Honestly, I'd love to have an all-out romantic movie of my own with Farouk. That would be the dreamiest. "Anyway, I just checked. Looks like the school is closed. What do we do now?" I ask.

Reggie fans herself with a pamphlet. "We shall resume our search tomorrow. But for now, a tiny bit of respite might be called for? Maybe even a brief moment to wash our eyes with some local excitements? Yes? Oh . . . just come along. Driver, La Mamounia please. Pronto."

How close is Farouk? He's here . . . somewhere. I can almost feel him. His aura, or soul, or energy. Whatever it is, I'm feeding off it, and I'm so close.

Chapter Fifty

We pull up to a pretty palacey-looking place surrounded by lush palm trees, which seems to be the motif for the entire town. Although once we get into the grounds itself, I can't help but stare. "I think I've said this before, but just in case . . . *whoa.*"

"I know, right? As lush and juicy as . . . Oh, the place. I thought you were talking about my thighs. Yes, this is a pretty remarkable hotel. Used to belong to my family. A long time ago. Or so history says."

"Your family's from here? So many things I still don't know about you."

"Well . . . it was ours, and this was where I . . . I mean, my ancestors grew up, but through some really light fuckery on my end, we sort of lost it?"

"What did you do?"

Reggie chomps on the end of her ponytail. "I might've gambled it away? But no, darling. We shall not lament the past.

I still have oodles of money up my sleeves. Seriously. Watch this."

She struts up to the front desk and slaps her tote on the counter. "My riad, please?"

The man behind the counter clucks his tongue. "Do you have a reservation, miss?"

"I don't need a reservation. It's Mademoiselle Regina Watson. Please don't make me take out my passport. I really don't want to dig through the mess of bottles in my bag right now."

The man lazily glances away, as if Reggie's nothing because she isn't royalty or something, until it seems like the name does register in his brain. At which time he does a somewhat cartoonish perking up, flashing some really impressive whites. "Mademoiselle Watson. Of course. Your permanently assigned riad is ready for your stay." He taps on his keyboard and, seconds later, slides a key card across the counter.

Reggie grabs it, and her tote, and turns to me with a wink. "Privilege, darling boy. Now, let's freshen up a little before we head out."

The man himself leads us through the serpentine corridors until we get to the garden outside. And onto a path. And we keep following. Not quite knowing where we're headed.

Because it's not exactly a room that he unlocks for us but a villa. In a hotel.

Seriously, is this a riad? I creep in like some poor little orphan who's just been adopted by a superrich oil tycoon.

The man's about to leave us to ourselves, but Reggie stops him, stuffing a few dirham bills in his hands. His eyes grow wide at the amount as he makes his way out, the door clicking shut silently behind him.

I stand here in the courtyard, staring at everything around me. A private pool. A dining area. Even a basket of fruit. Who gets a basket of fruit? Oh my god.

I'm starving, so I run over to the table and grab an apple. This . . . I thought I couldn't imagine what the rich live like, but this . . . is . . . it.

"Munch with your mouth closed; gape with your eyes open," Reggie says, appearing with two glasses of something iced but clear. "That's what my dad used to say. Welcome to Marrakech, my little cutlet. Would you like to play a game?"

I set the apple core on the table as she holds both drinks out to me. "What kind?"

"Vodka roulette. Fun game I just invented. One's vodka. One's water."

I try to stick my head out for a quick sniff, but she snatches both hands back. "No cheating. I'll give you a clue, though. I don't want the water."

Ugh. I reach out for the glass on the right, and she pulls it back, hands me the other one. I grab it with a slightly shaky hand and, not smelling anything suspicious, take a sip. "It's really water. Thank you."

"The most pointless thing to have ever been invented, I swear. Why drink that when you can have this?" She takes a sip and exhales slowly. "Yes, that's it. Flow it through my blood-stream. Now, your room is over there. You'll find something to wear in the closet. I keep this place stocked up . . . for guest emergencies. Although, I hope you can find something that actually fits. If not, we'll call that scrumptious front-desk clerk for something for you. And a little naughty-naughty for me, if you get what I— Hey, where are you going?"

"Freshening up." Gotta run gotta run gotta run before she blasts my eardrums with all that talk.

My room is gorgeous. It's fit for a king, not for a lowly peasant like me.

And that's when it hits me.

I *am* a nobody.

But Farouk made me feel like a somebody.

The hours have to count down for one more night before . . . before what? Before he miraculously appears in a school?

There's nothing to do but to keep going.

I shower and find the most perfect black linen shirt and pants in the wardrobe. They fit me nice, too, as I check myself out in the mirror. I might feel like a nobody, but right now, I don't look like one.

Reggie's in a white linen blouse and pants, looking all flowy as she clacks around in her wedges, sipping at a different-colored liquid. She notices my presence and offers a warm smile. "Well, look at you there, mister boy. Who'd have thought you actually had a face under all that worry you've been wearing since I met you?"

I can't help my cheeks heating up. And now, after our amazing food experience in Istanbul, I wonder what we'll encounter here in Marrakech. "Shall we?"

She grabs my arm, and we walk out the door, side by side.

Chapter Fifty-One

Reggie takes me to what's called a souk—a whole series of confusing, tiny walkways lined by vendors with curious smiles and charming words I don't understand. The English-speaking ones compliment me on my style, and I can't help but blush at each remark, even though Reggie's to thank for the sudden upgrade. "Should we at least stop at some of these shops and get . . . like, a spice, or tea set, or what is that leather-looking thing that smells like it's fermented?"

And then I see him. A doppelgänger of Farouk. And my heart wants to rush out of me and slap him across the face, scream *where the heck have you been.* Except I know it's not him. The face is a little too gaunt, the lips not as full, definitely older.

"What's wrong?" Reggie asks, noticing I've fallen behind.

"Uh . . . nothing." That's all I can muster. "Let's keep going."

I haven't really considered what I'll say when I actually *find* him. I didn't consider . . . how angry and scared and sick I may feel.

After another fifteen minutes of twisting our way around, my feet sometimes unsure of left or right, we break through the labyrinth of shops and end up in a wide-open space. A bright throng is gathered under the dark sky, trumpets and flutes and tambourines blasting in the air.

Toward the very center is a trio—a belly dancer, a flautist, and a man with a hat collecting donations.

And there goes Reggie, staring at the flautist. As if she's finally had too much to drink again—a cobra under the hypnotic influence.

The melody is intoxicating; the dancer sways her hips. Makes me a little jealous, that she can seem to dislocate her lower half, forcing it left, right, swiveling all around like that while her upper body stays still. I can't help but pull my phone out to film a tiny bit.

"What're you doing?" Reggie nudges my rib, finally out of her reverie. "Put that away."

Before I can react, the man with the hat shoves his face in my camera and smiles a warning at me before saying something. Expecting something. Uh-oh.

"Here, take it." Reggie tosses a hundred dirham bill into the hat. "Go. Go."

I can't decide if she's saying it to the guy or to me, but I'm off, Reggie right behind me.

"I didn't know you couldn't do that," I say.

"Of course not. It's like . . . stealing a piece of their soul.

You have to give them something in return, and that's usually cash. So from now on, please, for the love of whichever male supermodel you worship, check with worldly little me before doing something like that again. Yes?"

I nod.

We walk away from the ruckus, but what she said nags at me. "Do you believe we have souls?"

She looks all around before pulling a flask out of her pocket and sipping from it. "Why not? You don't think we do?"

"I don't know. I feel like I haven't done enough to redeem mine."

Reggie sputters out a laugh. "Listen to you, old man. What are you? Fifty? You've got a whole lifetime ahead of you to make up for whatever fuckity fuckup you've committed in your oh-so-short life. Don't stress it that much. It gets tiring. Take it from me."

"I *am* taking it from you. And maybe trying to learn as well. You don't seem like you give a shit about anything."

"I don't. And why should I? The world fucks you up regardless of what good you're doing, so I just want to have fun while I'm at it, you know? No, you don't know, do you? I feel like I've wasted seven breaths just with this conversation. Anyway, the point is, you do you, and the rest should just fall in line, right? Like . . . I do what I can to help poor unfortunate miserable souls like you, and what do I want in return? Hmm . . . what *do* I want in return? There's that question again."

I can't decide what's more disconcerting. The fact that I have a lifetime of messing up left to take care of. Or that Reggie might have no idea why she's giving a whole world's worth of niceness in a handbasket . . . to me.

We don't even zigzag five steps before the loudest noise fills the sky. A high-pitched, unrelenting screech that seems to signal the end of the world. And it's not stopping. "What is that?" I ask.

Reggie looks up with doubt and confusion on her face. "I think it's an air-raid siren."

And that's when it happens.

A furor of intense energy fans through the entire mazelike square. Hands raised heavenward, Allah-hu-akbars being uttered, and . . . a lot of packing up by the shops.

We're just caught up in the crowds, people suddenly screaming around us, when . . .

"Sayyed!"

I turn to find Reggie being swept away from me—not on purpose—by the crowd trying to get away. It takes everything that is polite in me to not scream at the jostlers and shovers or to sail over everyone to get to her.

But an endless minute of going against the tide on my end and our fingers reaching for each other's . . .

And we finally make it. I grab on to her and pull her close, dragging her along with me, while tourists and locals continue to run like ants being set aflame.

A mustached man stuffs all his wares, which are prominently on display outside the store, inside as fast as he can. When he sees us approaching, he beckons at us. "Come, come. Not safe."

Reggie doesn't let go of my hand. She seems utterly confused as to which direction to head toward—back or front.
I totally understand, because we have no clue what's going to
happen next.

The man doesn't stop. In fact, his insistence grows louder
and more urgent.

So I grab Reggie by my other hand instead, locking us in a
strange hug, and drag her toward him.

He signals us into the store, and we stumble on in, trying to
find enough room for our bodies to fit within the puzzle of his
tiny space, stocked up with vases, plates, and other glass knickknacks. With the last of his wares in the store, he hurriedly yanks
down the grate and slams the door shut. He leans a shoulder on
it, focusing through the one window giving us a view of the
outside.

The siren continues to pound my eardrums, although a little duller now. "What do we do, Reggie?"

"I don't know, love. But it all looks pretty serious."

I turn to the man. "I'm Sy. Sayyed. Do you know what's
happening?"

The man is half listening to me and half to something else.
"My name is Tareef. This . . . this noise no good."

I don't know how to answer him, because I only have questions. "Are we safe? Is it dangerous?"

He does a one-eighty to face us, then scratches his mustache. "I don't know. Afraid this is attack."

My heart stops. For a few beats. "Attack? Here? In
Marrakech?"

Reggie's so still, even her usually vibrant ponytail seems frozen in place.

"By bad people. Is no good."

And my stopped heart has plonked down right between my feet. "Has it happened before?"

The man shakes his head. "Warning. This is sound warning. I don't know. You stay here until safe."

But how safe are we actually? If someone does declare war on us, we're kinda goners. Do we just stand around and wait? I don't know what it is, but my body's starting to feel real itchy with each ticking second.

The man smiles at us. "You come to Marrakech wrong day. We usually have nice weather, good food, music at night in medina. People dancing. Today . . . sorry."

"Why is someone trying to attack the city?"

"Bad people don't want to see good people happy. We here, good people. We live quiet life. No trouble. Bad people attack our people a lot. They no good."

"Bad people . . . like ISIS?"

An even darker, stormier cloud suddenly floats above him. "They no good. They give good Muslim bad name. They kill many Muslim. So many good men, women die. Bomb. Gun. Many bullets."

Last I heard, there are almost two billion of us. Yet the tiniest percentage decide to stray because they think their twisted version of the story is better. Totally ignoring the fact that there are so many Muslims who go about their lives only wanting to feed their families and put a roof over their heads.

The siren winds down to a low whine, but my nerves still crackle. The sudden silence is not reassuring at all. Because it kinda feels like the calm before the storm.

Reggie shuffles in place, accidentally knocking a tiny salt-shaker off its perch. But she catches it just in time. "Oops," she whispers.

Tareef stares out the window a few more minutes before he finally decides it's safe again, and he reopens the store. "Again, sorry about today. Not every day like this. Once a year maybe? Today not good day. You come back, I give you good discount. Okay?"

I want to tell him there's nothing to apologize for. How is this his fault? He didn't owe us anything. He took us in. But nothing seems adequate to express how I feel. So I just say, "Assalamualaikum."

The square slowly starts to fill up with people again. Wary, a little on edge—I can see it in their eyes. Just like they can probably see it mirrored in mine.

How comfortable is my life, that I don't have to worry about anything like this? Not have to fear for my life?

✦ ✦ ✦ ✦ ✦

The next morning, the rising sun's rays hit my face, and I wake up in a fetal position. It took a while to fall asleep, my nerves had almost fused themselves together after the air-raid siren, but exhaustion finally got to me when we managed to crawl back to the riad.

But Reggie pops into my room, dressed in a denim onesie. "No time to get dressed or shower, my dear boy. We've got to go."

Before I can even croak a single word, I'm ripped out of bed. Everything's a total blur, as my backpack and my body are thrown into a limo.

And we jet through the city. "Where are we going?" I ask.

"He's there." She says it with a wink so conspiratorial, as if she's the one who had a hand in him going missing in the first place.

"At the school?"

Her silence and a wink say it all.

Suddenly, I dare to hope again. What the hell am I going to say when I see him? Maybe I should rehearse something.

Minutes later, we're dropped off on the street, facing a row of shops crowded with tourists and locals. We cut through the crowds at a near-canter, our energy nervous.

And come to a stop in front of the Monte Carlo Language School.

"Here we are. Ready for your reckoning?" she asks.

My stomach tightens. "You think Farouk's here? Like, really here?"

"Yes." Her eyes are bright in this morning light.

My steps are tiny. Takes me a good two minutes to go through the glass door and up to the front desk, where a young man greets us in French.

"What's he saying?" Reggie asks.

"I have no idea."

The man smiles, gives us a shake of the head. "You speak English? Are you our new teachers?"

Reggie spits out a laugh. "No, my dear child. I did not wear this much makeup to teach—"

"What my rude friend here is trying to say is thank you, but no. We're looking for Farouk Hameed?"

The man folds his hands together. "Oh. Farouk. You called earlier. And I said I know Farouk, but you hung up before I could tell you he's not here."

The breath I've been holding whooshes out in frustration. Of *course* he isn't. "Thanks for leaping all the way to misinformation," I say to Reggie.

She looks a little deflated but can only shrug it off, along with a rolling of her eyes.

"Sir, do you know where he is?" I ask. "Please, I've come a long way looking for him."

The young man takes a seat and wears a strange look that says . . . *as if I should know what's going on.* "Farouk Hameed was teaching here. But he left a few days ago."

"Where?"

He pauses, but the desperation on my face probably makes him go on.

"There is a refugee camp close to Essaouira. That's where all the victims from the Al-Darrah bombing—the town that was attacked a few weeks ago—were taken. Farouk went there to help with the survivors. Now, that is all I know. Is there anything else I can help you with?"

Chapter Fifty-Two

THREE MONTHS AGO

Farouk showed up, very excited, at the café one ultra-busy Wednesday evening. He looked like he was tripping over himself trying to tell me something, but I couldn't just leave D in the lurch, so I did everything in superspeed: hustling order after order, sliding them across the counter, until we were in the clear. "What's up, my handsome boyfriend?"

He dragged me outside where no one could eavesdrop. "I think I want to teach."

"Teach? Okay. So you're not going to be a doctor anymore?"

Farouk shook his head.

"Okay, so you're switching majors at USC?"

"No. Not at USC."

My heart almost did a cartwheel. "So . . . you're coming with me to Santa Monica College, then? Pretty sure they have a teaching degree."

He shook his head. "Not Santa Monica College."

"Then . . ."

He grabbed my shoulders. "There's this program where they teach you how to become an English teacher to foreign students, but I don't want to take it here. I think I want to do it in London."

"London? Why London?"

"Never been. Always wanted to. It's a four-week course."

Four weeks. "I guess that's fine. We made do with you going away for two weeks. I can wait."

"Followed by wherever I can get a job teaching after that. And it's probably going to be for at least a year. And then who knows . . . maybe I'll come back and actually pursue becoming a surgeon. Make my parents happy or whatever."

My heart froze over. "Uh . . . what do you mean, *wherever*? Like, if they send you to Macedonia?"

He shrugged. "Could be. But I'd really like to check out Northern Africa or the Middle East. Maybe India or Pakistan?"

"But those are such dangerous places."

He winced. "No more dangerous than LA. You forget we have guns here. Anyway, there are lots of people who need my help. I need to do this. And I want you to come with me. I leave in a week."

The worst thing about doubt is the feeling. That gnawing sensation in your gut, in your chest, the sudden itch on the soles of your feet that makes you shuffle like the earth's about to open up under you. "I don't know . . ."

"What don't you know? I've spent a whole month thinking about it and doing research and I have enough money for the both of us, so we'll . . . Just come with me. Please come with me, Sy. If you love me."

Those words. Those damn words. Sounded so sweet, but with an oily coat of emotional blackmail on their edges. "Farouk, why can't we try to fix things here?"

"Fix things?" He backed off just a single step, which was a widening chasm with every passing second. "Why don't you just say it?"

"Say what?"

"That I'm the one who needs fixing."

"No, that's not what I mean. I love you so, so much, but if you go, if you leave me for this whole crazy idea that you can fix the world by doing this . . . I mean, I can't leave. I have my family here."

"You said you would always be there for me." He pauses and looks down. "Are you breaking up with me, Sy?"

"No, I just . . . can't . . ." The silence that scattered out of my mouth was everything he needed.

"So I guess a promise is only good when it's good for you?"

No hug. No kiss. No wave goodbye. Those were his last words.

For some reason, as he walked away, I couldn't avoid the dreadful feeling that I'd just stabbed the boy I loved so, so much in the back.

And that was the last time I saw Farouk.

Chapter Fifty-Three

My heart dips. "Essaouira? Is that where we need to go?"

"If we're still looking for the same Farouk," Reggie says, "then I bet he'll be there. Let's go, little curry puff."

My stomach churns. *What if . . . something bad happened to him?* The guy said *survivors*. What if he isn't one of them? What if he didn't make it out?

Is that why he's not answering his calls?

I don't even know how to process the possibility.

Reggie leads the way, and we hop into a taxi. She tells him where we're going, and his smile turns to a frown, the mood changes, and we find ourselves kicked to the curb.

Apparently, Essaouira is 120 kilometers away, which is ridiculous by taxi.

Ugh.

After an hour of haggling and begging—mainly on my part—it's clear no one's willing to drive the distance, because what are the chances of finding a passenger to head back to Marrakech? So Reggie does the next most sensible thing.

She gets us a ride to the nearest Mercedes dealership, where she promptly signs on the dotted line for a brand-new car.

Seriously. An hour after we step foot in the place, she's driving us out in a super-sleek silver sports car. With the AC running at full blast, since we're in the desert, the ride is as comfortable as I can imagine it being.

Although everything inside me is a hot furnace of boiling caca.

"Have you traveled everywhere around the world?" I ask. I'm trying so hard not to think about Farouk. About what might happen when I see him. *When I see him.* Oh god. He can't be . . .

Reggie nods. "The world isn't that small, if you think about it. Just look at us. How many days together and we've covered so much distance. When you seriously have nothing better to do but wander about the world, looking for the next exciting and fun thing, you'll see through my eyes."

"And was that how you found me? While you were looking for something exciting and fun?"

"Oh, sweetheart. You were neither fun nor exciting to look at. But jokes aside, I adore a good challenge."

"Challenge? I'm a challenge?"

"Oh. Were we specifically talking about you?" she quips. "I took a look at you that day and decided you needed help. And it seemed like you were out of options."

"But . . . why?"

"Why what? Stop being so vague all the time. I swear, sometimes it feels like you're picking my brain with concepts I don't ever want to consider."

I hold on tight to the door handle, and my patience. "Why help me out?"

Reggie grabs the steering wheel with both hands. "I guess this might not be that important. But I stood outside and saw the pain in your eyes. And there was no way I was going to let you go through life like that."

What? How could she have seen that? I've seen my eyes, and they're not good at telling stories. Not good at showing any emotion, especially when all I felt back then was a near-deadness.

Although she never did explain how she knew Farouk's name when we first met . . . Maybe she did her research on me before she banged herself on the glass door?

My phone vibrates. *Uh-oh.* Do I want to? But I have to. "Umi?" I answer.

"Sayyed. I just had a bad dream." Her voice is soft but raspy. She must've been crying. "I dreamed you were stuck in a cave, and it was dark, and you were afraid to come out into the light."

"Umi, it was just a dream."

"Come back to me, Sayyed. I want you back. Please come back."

"Umi . . ."

"I think . . . I couldn't see for too long. And I need your strength to help guide me."

My strength? But I'm the weakling of the family. "You're mistaken, Umi. Sofia's the better choice for that."

"Just come. I'll make sure everything turns out all right."

Will she?

Can she?

Can *I*?

When I was about eight, I roused from sleep in the middle of the night to Umi's voice. I didn't want her to know I was up, so I just listened to what she was saying.

"Sayyed. Your umi loves you so, so much. When your older brother died in my womb, I cried so many nights. I promised Allah I would do everything right if He would grant me another child. And then you came. You've fulfilled my every wish. To have a son so loving, so forgiving of my many mistakes. Someday you will see that all I've been doing is to protect you from the evils of the world. It hurts me to see you get hurt."

I know she has always tried to protect me. In her own way. But is that really what I need? Or . . . should I be learning . . . to protect myself?

I've never had a brave bone in my body. Umi and Sofia and Dzakir have protected me my entire life, and now . . .

I need to learn . . . to be let go? To not just stand on my own two feet but to make all the mistakes and to figure out how to build . . .

A home of my own?

"Umi, I have to go," I say, and I hang up, even as every part of me feels guilty for it.

Well, that's hilarious. I want my umi to let me go, yet . . . I can't deal with Farouk doing the same. Like I'm a freaking hot potato, being handed from one person to another. "Reggie . . . do you think this is so irresponsible of me? Especially since Farouk might not even be . . ."

She groans out loud. "Dammit, listen to me. You've convinced me that Farouk needs saving. And that's what we're going to do. Save him. You're capable of anything now. You've run away from home and the law, broken into a store, stolen something in front of the police, confronted the man who tried to steal Farouk's heart, and saved us both from a potential air raid. Those are some unbelievable things no seventeen-year-old should be doing, but you did them all."

That is true. "But I don't know if I'm ready to confront . . . whatever is going on there in Essaouira."

"Then just wish your way out of it."

Can I? Is it really that simple? "You said some of your wishers died before they were able to make their third wish."

"That was a joke."

"Was it?" I point to the speedometer. "You're going too fast."

"I can go as fast as I want to, if I want to. I have very good control of my body now, instead of being on autopilot. Seriously, look at this." The car swerves across the deserted road. "Ha, what's that smell? Don't tell me you went in your pants. Oh wait, I think that's just the radiator."

"Can you take things seriously, just for once? I thought it'd be easier talking to you while you're off the special sauce, but obviously, that's not possible." I glance outside the window and take a deep breath so I can calm myself, when I catch sight of an oasis in the distance, fenced in by heavy iron gates. Funny, though, and it must be a trick of the light, because the garden inside looks dark. Pretty random for it to be out here, surrounded by nothing else. Or could it be a mirage? "Why are you so hard up about me making my third wish anyway?"

She blinks once. Twice. Seems like she can't look me in the eye.

"I don't think you'll believe me when I tell you. I'm actually—"

But suddenly, we're doing a backflip. As in . . . the entire car is doing a backflip, while an explosion rings in my ears.

The last thing I hear is Reggie saying, "I did not see that coming."

Chapter Fifty-Four

The smoke clears, but my lungs . . . it feels like I'm breathing bricks instead of air.

My arms . . . are overhead . . . Can't bring them down to my sides because they keep scraping the roof of the car. Something's holding me down.

Or up, I can't tell.

Someone's next to me, dazed, squinting at something, her arms and ponytail glued to the roof.

I think we're upside down, blood pooling in my brain. "Can you hear me?" My voice is a mousy squeak.

The girl next to me tries to shake her head but grimaces. "That was a nasty tumble, wasn't it? Hang on." She reaches down (or up?) and jabs at her belt buckle, until it finally unlatches, sending her tumbling to the roof with a smooshy moan and a crisp crunch of broken glass.

"Can you unlock yourself?" she asks.

I try to reach . . . so slowly. But . . . my world blacks out.

✳ ✳ ✳ ✳ ✳

Someone's grabbed ahold of my arms and legs. A shrill voice bleats like an angry goat. I'm floating. Pretty nice. Why's . . . Reggie (I think that's her name) screaming? She's saying . . . not to touch me . . . or her? And what's this warm, sticky liquid streaming down my face?

Blackout again.

✳ ✳ ✳ ✳ ✳

A rumbling and lots of bumps. Now I'm sideways. Horizontal. Can I go home? Is it time to go home? I miss my umi. Is that her face, staring down at me?

Why do you look so sad, Umi? Promise I'll be home soon.

Sofia? You don't have to be sad too. Say something.

Dzakir? *I've never seen you cry before. Don't cry. You're stronger than that.*

Oh. And Baba. Don't want to talk to you.

Hard to breathe here. *Can someone . . . ?*

Blackout.

✳ ✳ ✳ ✳ ✳

Someone's got my arms this time, dragging me but keeping me afloat. Where is Reggie? I need to . . . ask . . . what we're doing here.

Farouk. Where is Farouk? He's supposed to be here.

"Regggggggg . . ."

A hand grabs mine. "I'm here, silly lamb. Don't stress your-self. You banged your head a little— How dare you touch me! I will talk to my friend if I want to!—What is it, Sayyed?"

My eyelids are sticky and gummy, but a pinprick of light pierces through. "Reggie . . . have you seen Farouk?"

She shakes her head.

"Reggie, have you ever loved someone?"

She looks me straight in the eye. "I've loved many."

"Reggie, have they loved you back?"

Nothing but silence.

"Reggie, have you ever loved someone so much that you're willing to go all over the world for them?"

Something else clouds her eyes, and it looks like a lie form-ing. "Never. Why would I risk my whole life for someone else? Just to fulfill their three wishes and hopefully make them happy? That's just plain ridiculous."

I'll walk through the fires of Hell to save you.

"Is it?" A dull ache pounds my skull. Hard to find the right words. Must focus really, really hard. "Reggie . . . what would you wish for?"

I don't think she's going to answer me again. And then she says, "If I were the loneliest creature with no one I could trust, and I'd traveled the world my whole life to help people who just ended up using me, then maybe all I could want is to find that one friend. Someone I could always count on."

A friend? Oh god. She's being serious.

"Reggie, I don't want to die—"

"You won't. I promised you'd find Farouk, remember? And I never break my wishes." She releases my hand and screams in that shrill voice of hers to people around me. "Where are you taking us?"

"I'm sorry, miss," a voice says. "He needs immediate treatment."

Am I in a truck? Or an ambulance? Or the afterlife?

Chapter Fifty-Five

Hamza said the words, and the imp felt a growing lump in its chest. Hair sprouted out of its head, skin no longer covered in oil.

It asked why. Why he wished for it to become half human?

Because it was deserving of more. That it did not belong there. That it should go out into the world and be amazed. And to help it on its journey, he told it to look for his family in the town of Salamat. To give them his flute and tell them to take it in and treat it like their own daughter, since their only child is now lost.

The djinn hugged her body in her glimmering silver robe and watched the exchange of words, still unsure if Hamza had made the right choice. She asked him what he would do.

He gave her a hug, then, without another word, spun on his heels and headed back, straight into the depths of the Underworld.

The djinn watched Hamza's departure but bore no emotions. She had to move on, because her duties were done. She turned to the girl and held out a hand.

The girl took it and together, they stepped out into the world.

It was only a few days later when the former imp thought she had had enough of the way she was treated, even though Hamza's parents had taken her in without question, but with teary eyes. Boys laughed at her short hair, girls pinched her for her plumpness. She was just glad she couldn't feel any pain.

The djinn appeared in the girl's room one night, sympathetic at the sound of sobs, the tears on her pillow. The girl wanted to go home, back to the Underworld.

The djinn shook her head and explained that the gate was a one-way portal. But the djinn revealed a secret she'd never told anyone.

All the girl needed to do was to grant three earthly wishes for someone who was truly in need of them. And for that someone to use their last wish to help her shed her humanness, so she could step through the portal back home, back into the Underworld.

This last selfless wish by a human would have magic bestowed upon her. The so-called loophole wish.

The girl thought about the proposition and laughed for the first time since leaving the Underworld, because of how easy it sounded.

But the djinn was the last to laugh, because she knew how humans were. She reminded the girl that because she remained half imp, she would retain her immortality.

The girl went to sleep soundly that night, certain she would be returning home by sunset the next day.

But even though Hamza had used his last wish on her, no other human would. They treated her as nothing more than a thing to be discarded once her value was gone.

As the years crept by, and her riches grew, and countless wishes were granted, the girl wondered if there was anyone else like Hamza, as she discovered how futile her efforts were. Because she was to learn the most important lesson of all:

That a wondrous wish was more valuable than her worthless life.

Chapter Fifty-Six

My head feels like it's been squeezed through a whole lot of yeowch. What is this? Gauze? It's like a freaking sandwich of hammering pain.

"Regg—" OH MY GOD. That lightning-sear of a jolt when I part my lips. Totally unexpected.

And my eyes? Did someone staple them shut, because I am having the hardest time even trying to pry one open. It's bright beyond them lids, all right. I can see red. It's definitely daytime.

The accident. Something happened.

"Sayyed? Can you hear me?"

It's Reggie! It's her voice. I have to try again. "Regg . . . ungh . . . gggggie? What . . . I mean, where are you?"

"Right here, silly boy. You got a nasty lump on the old nog right there."

"Are you okay?"

"Dandier than a dandelion dipped in Dimetapp. Seriously. Just look at me."

I try my eyes again. This time, the stickiness parts, and I can actually focus—ever sooooo lethargically slowly—on her. She looks as positively radiant as ever, that ponytail bouncing along as she cocks her head. "Unscathed."

"What's that, love? Doesn't sound like a word I've heard before."

"You're . . . not hurt. Unscathed." .

"Oh, don't you dare accuse me of perfection. Lots of me was scathed. My tote bag is lost somewhere in the desert. My oodles of bottles thrown around, smashed. My heels . . . my favorit-est of heels . . . just wrecked. If I could shed a tear, you know I would."

I want to smile, but it feels like my face is being ripped apart at the sides. "Stop trying to make me laugh. Not fair. This is the most pain I've ever felt."

"Well, it's nothing compared to adulthood, let me tell you that. Which is why I'm sooooo glad I'll never get a day older. Now, take these painkillers."

What the hell is she talking about?

She helps me sit up, pops two round white pills in my mouth, then forces water into my throat to wash them down. "There you go, my little meat puppet."

"Where are we?"

Reggie leans in. "I see a lot of white tents around, so I think we're at the refugee camp in Essaouira. Also, that's what some-one told me."

The camp? "The camp? How did they think to bring us here? And not a hospital?"

"Sayyed, I think they thought we were casualties. Anyway, you should go back to sleep. Get some more rest. Doctor's orders. Well, mine actually. Doctor's not here."

I lie back down, but something's bugging me. "I can't. We need to go."

"Go where?"

"Find Farouk."

"Um . . ."

But something else is odd. "Do you smell that?"

Reggie looks as if she's just swallowed a bag of smuggled diamonds. "What smell? I don't smell anything."

"That's just it. You don't smell of anything."

She looks away. "I guess the accident must've killed your nose, too, because—"

"You haven't had a sip of alcohol."

"I most certainly have. How absurd. I shan't bother with being maligned by such a baseless accusation."

Uh-oh. "If you stopped drinking . . . if you're sober . . . that means something's really serious. What is it?"

She doesn't say a word.

"Wait . . . you were about to say something about Farouk. Tell me. *Please.*"

She *hmm*s and *uhhh*s until finally, with a roll of her eyes, she says, "Farouk's here."

My heart must've leaped into my mouth because I definitely feel like puking. "He's here?"

She twists her ponytail and hugs it close to her neck. "I don't understand Arabic or French, but I've heard people mention his name a few times."

"What? *What?* Why didn't you wake me up earlier?" I scramble out of bed and promptly topple to my knees. "Did you try to find him?"

She looks as if I've just slapped her. "Uh, no. I was too busy by your side for the last four hours waiting for you to wake up."

"I don't care how long I've been out. What about my wish? What about having to fulfill it? I'm not the important one here. He is."

She looks as if I've just slapped her other cheek this time. "You're not important?"

I shake my head. Of course I'm not. I never have been.

The painkillers must be fast-acting, because I can bring myself up to a semi-wobbly standing position. Or maybe it's just the adrenaline. "I need to get out of here."

Reggie rushes over to my side, eyes alert. Grabs ahold of my elbow. "Steady, love. You don't want to fall and crack your head wide open this time. You banged it up real bad. Don't need to make it worse."

"I'm fine." I step out of the tent and into sunlight.

Brine douses the air, and the ocean glitters like stars. All around me are rows and rows of white tents with UNHCR logos on them, where all the displaced victims of the recent attack reside temporarily. I guess we really are at the refugee camp.

I used to think I grew up poor. Chicken was such a luxury.

But our family has always lived in the same house, as tiny as it is, and there's always been food. Baba is a faulty father to his children, but he never failed to keep up with the providing. He always gave us sustenance and a space safe from the outside.

But here, splayed out across several football fields' worth of acreage, is actual, real hardship. Not a single smile. Cries puncture the air—some from women cradling empty arms, others from children. A hint of hopelessness chars the air, swirling with the desert sands. I have never seen anything like this. To say my heart is breaking is the most basic understatement I can make. Because it's ripped into shreds.

And again. I feel so painfully small.

Reggie's eyes are open wide. "You know it's terrible because I have to remind myself to shut up," she says. "Like if you can see my thought bubble, it's literally my face, with duct tape across my lips. And maybe a blindfold, because you know, if you're blindfolded, you don't have to see any of this. I guess earplugs can also help with the noise."

"You're being insensitive."

"You don't have to tell me that. Which is why I really have to shut up. Shutting up now."

So. It. Begins.

What right do I have to pursue anything, in the face of all this realness? Because it kinda sucks when you're thousands of miles away, and you read someone's post about what's happening to people on the other side of the world, like in Syria or Iraq, and you just shrug it off, because you're like, meh, this is just too far away for me to connect with. But it's here and I'm speechless. Because this shit is real, real, real, and life is realer than real.

Everything about me is so insignificant, isn't it?

This is the reason why Farouk had to leave. He wanted to help the world. He understood this.

I'm here for him now.

But I need to find him.

I scan the tents. There's a whole contingent in blue vests who may be aid workers, and I hobble up to a European lady with short hair and a kind face. "Excuse me, I'm looking for . . . Farouk Hameed?"

The lady turns, stares at the photo on my phone. "Maybe he's here. Was he in Al-Darrah? Is he lost?"

"Never mind. I'll keep asking around." I walk off with Reggie close behind as she fidgets with her loose black blouse, taking random chugs from an unlabeled bottle—is that water?

Maybe the locals might know where Farouk is. A boy about my age, hugging a tentpole, stares at me—his face decked with dirt and wonder. I cut across the way and smile, hovering my phone in his face, which I hope isn't too rude a gesture.

He glances at the screen, reaches out a grimy finger, then says, "Farouk."

My heart soars, and I exchange a look with Reggie, who grins with triumph.

The boy takes off, beckoning us to follow.

Past rows of flapping white tents, tens of them, until we get to the one he's looking for. He shouts out "Assalamualaikum" and gets a "Wa'alaikumsalam" in response. A man, maybe ten years older, with a full beard but a worn face, steps out.

Our guide points to us and says something else. I catch "Farouk" in one of the sentences.

The bearded man looks at me with eyebrows raised, and I show him Farouk's photo on my phone. He slaps a hand on his heart and instantly breaks down, yelling to the back of the tent to someone else. A hijab'd lady appears with a toddler by her side, and as soon as she sees his photo, she exclaims "mashallah" and hugs the man tight.

The man starts rapid-speaking to me in a language I faintly recognize, and out of sheer desperation, I run over to an aid worker in a vibrant-green hijab. "Do you speak Arabic?"

The girl carries a large backpack and looks tired but nods anyway.

"Please help me. I need to know what this man is saying."

A minute later, she's by my side, translating.

"This is Aziz; his wife, Maimunah; and their son, Rahmad. He says that Farouk has been helping them the last few days, taking care of their son, helping get them situated. He's been a saint."

Wait, what? Farouk is seriously here? Like, *here* here? Do I start to rub my eyes out, or pinch my sides, or splash ice water on my face?

He is here. My boy is here. And I get to see him soon. Tell him everything about everything for, like, forever and never let him go. Oh my god, how messy do I look? Ugh, I smell like a camel pissed on me. And my head is beyond poundy, so I doubt if I can even behave like a clearheaded person when I see him.

I get to see him. I get to see my Roukie.

"But . . ." She pauses, cocks her head to one side, unsure about finishing the translation.

"But?" I press her. "What happened?"

"He's no longer with us." She looks down, then realizes the meaning of her words. "I'm so sorry." And walks off.

Aziz wipes the tears from his eyes and reaches into his pocket. He pulls out his hand, and in his palm is a shiny band.

The very same ring I gave to Farouk.

Chapter Fifty-Seven

My hands are clasped together, with the last of Farouk nestled inside.

"You all right, love?" Reggie asks.

"I don't know."

I didn't want to look at the bodies—I don't think I can handle it right now. Or ever. And to think his parents are flying in, only for them to be too late, since the dead have to be buried by sundown.

We've walked to the edges of the camp, and there's a whole town ahead of us, about a twenty-minute walk away. But I have no desire to find out what it holds. As far as I know, I've come all this way, to get within a hand's reach of Farouk, only to find out he's gone.

"So it was all for nothing?" I ask, even though I'm not sure I actually want a response.

Reggie licks her lips, as if thirsty for a frosty beverage in this dry desert heat. "Do you think it was all for nothing?"

"Feels like it. I came all this way, and what did I get? A piece of cold metal they took off him?"

"Do you want me to go ID his body? Pretty sure I remember what his handsome face looks like. Gosh, especially now I'm sober. Really need to fix that ASAP."

"I'll follow you in a bit. For now, I just want to sit here and do nothing."

That's what we do. For a good half hour. Just plant our behinds on the sand and stare at everything. And yet nothing.

"I miss my mom and sister," I say.

"My throat feels like the bottom of a cowboy's boot—all dry and leathery. Bloody hell, are we not sharing our personal pains? Carry on, then."

"Can't you take things seriously for once?" I don't know what it is, but her nonchalance is chomping at my nerves.

"But I am. I mean, he's dead, isn't he? Trust me on this—everyone dies. Didn't I tell you this already? Could've sworn I did." She scratches her head, confused.

That's it. "I can't believe you just said that. What's wrong with you? Farouk is gone, and you think it's a joke? Or are you trying to make light of the situation? It's a death—there's nothing light about it."

Her lips curl as she snorts. "Do not talk to me about death. You think I haven't had enough of it? Now, where the hell is a liquor store when you need one?"

I scramble to my feet, kicking up sand as I rise. "That's all you ever care about. Your next drink. You alcoholic who will never face her demons."

"Oh, no you do not. Do not talk to me about demons. You have *no* clue who you're talking to. You want demon? I can give you demon. Seriously. You want it?"

There's a second where we're just facing each other, all squinty-eyed and furious.

Until I give in. "I don't know how to deal with this." Before my whole body just crumples over.

Reggie rushes to me, cradles my head before it can slam against the sand. "I know. I know you don't. Which is why I'm here. I'm not kidding when I told you I know a lot about death."

A hundred yards away, a military truck drives past us. Carrying more dead bodies, I bet. This place doesn't deal with much happy-making, does it?

I lie on the warm sand with my head in her lap. "No, you don't. You're a liar."

"The biggest liar is your heart. You have no idea what it is capable of. It'll whisper all these things to you—like how someone's going to be with you forever. That they'll never cheat on you. Or they'll never give up on you. Or they'll never stop believing in you. Or they'll only want what's best for you. And you keep listening to your weak heart, because you don't know any better. And before you know it, you're by yourself, and . . . everyone just keeps leaving. Yet every now and then, you'll see the one face you will never forget, and you think it's them, but it isn't. You've had the unfortunate situation of losing Farouk. But me? I can't even begin to count."

My breaking heart breaks again—this time for her. "Why won't you trust me?"

"Because, my dear Sayyed, you're going to leave me too." There's an awkward pause. "But I want you to be honest with me. What would you do if Farouk were still alive?"

"I don't know. I'd tell him how much I still love him, and I'm so glad to see he's happy."

"Then I think you should turn around and look up right now."

"What do you—?"

Footsteps in the sand. Behind me.

I whip my head around, and the tall guy just stares at me. And I stare back. Because it can't be.

Reggie props me up, then pushes my body upright.

Takes me a few seconds to figure out how to use my legs again, because . . . it's him. A hundred feet away.

And that's when Reggie, who's appeared next to me, says, "Your wish is granted."

Chapter Fifty-Eight

It's my Roukie.

It's like . . . the world stops.

He's fully bearded now, but always with that smile. The kindest one I've ever seen on anyone.

"Is it his ghost?" I ask.

Reggie lets out a soft chuckle. "Ghosts aren't real, you ninny. Pretty sure that's him."

I want to run to him, to tell him everything, *everything* I've gone through just to find him, but I can't move. My feet feel like they're stuck in quicksand, and I don't understand why. "I need to go to him."

Reggie looks at me. "Why are you still here, love?"

"Because . . . I don't know if I can."

Reggie doesn't leave my side. "Then I'll stay here with you."

He closes the gap between us. Seconds till he's within arm's reach.

"Reggie, what do I say?"

"Quick. Do you have a funny joke? Something to defuse the situation? How about a dig at my never-seen-before sobriety? Because this feels like it's about to get quite serious."

"I know. Do I want to do serious? Or casual? It's hard to do casual looking like this."

But when I turn to her, she's already walking off.

"Reggie, are you leaving me?"

She tosses her ponytail over to the other shoulder as she side-eyes me. "Of course, you silly boy. You wanted to find him, and now you have. Nothing to do with me. I'm going to look for a bar somewhere down there. If there isn't one, I'll start one, where we'll toast each other with rubbing alcohol. I'll meet you when you're done, all right?"

She waves a goodbye.

And then it's just me. Staring at Roukie as he stares back.

Ten feet away.

Five.

Now just inches separate us.

I stare into his eyes while he searches mine for the meaning of my appearance here.

Then he wraps me in his arms, and we just stand together, quiet, tears raining down our faces, as the sun beats down on us.

This. I have missed this so damn much. The safety of his arms.

Only a whisper comes out of him. "I saw you from the truck when we were driving back. Sy . . . your head. What happened? Also . . . what are you *doing* here?"

Why is my throat so dry? Why does it feel like my whole world is about to cave in on me? Because this is the moment I have to make my decision, when I lay everything on the line. "Aziz told me you were dead."

"But I'm not."

"He said . . . you were no longer with us . . ."

Farouk laughs. "Well, I am. I just went with the next shift to pick up some more of the injured."

I feel like a fool as I pull away and twirl his ring in my hand. "Why did you leave this behind?"

He stares at it, not trying to reach out for it. "I'd started to get rid of everything I owned. You know . . . earthly possessions, that kind of stuff. To make the traveling lighter."

I get it. All of it. Sinking in deep down, all the way to my bones.

Then he pulls me in again, and I just let myself melt into him. All of him.

That familiar smell. His smooth fingertips against the back of my neck. His breath against my forehead.

I want to hide here, breathe into the groove of his clavicle, and never leave. "Remember when you came into the café and commented on my cracked phone screen? I wished then I'd had the nerve to ask for your number. And then it turned out you were waiting for me the whole day, to ask for mine instead."

He holds me at arm's length. "You would have never talked to me if I didn't do it first."

"I know that. I know I was always afraid. Of rejection. Of

whatever the whole world might do to me. Of leaving home. See, when you left me, I didn't know what I could do."

His eyes are locked on mine. "I . . ."

I'm not done yet, though. "I wished you hadn't left. I wished we could've stayed together, stayed in love. I wished we could've stuck with our plan of sharing an apartment—a home—together. As scary as all of that sounds, I think we could've made it through anything. Maybe even . . . marriage? Way, way, way down the road."

He stays silent.

"And I wished I wasn't such a chicken, and so I traveled . . . I traveled the whole damn world to find you and bring you home." I laugh a little as his eyes widen, and he winces. He opens his mouth, but I say, "Although lately, I've come to realize how dangerous wishing can be. I wished for you to be alive again, but deep inside, I knew that I'd have to let you go either way."

We both inhale deeply, and I let out the words. "The world is a fucked-up place we have no control over." My grip on his hand is tight but gentle before I continue. "But you want to be out in it. Maybe this is where you need to be. This is your actual path. And I can only wish for you to find peace. So if this . . . if this is where you belong . . ." My eyes look toward the tent with the family he helped. Toward the people walking away from the truck assisting dozens of injured. "As much as it kills me to say this, I'm glad you left me. Because now that I'm done chasing after a ghost, I get to do me now, and my life can finally begin."

I spot Reggie in the distance, chasing after a muscular nurse. "And I know someone who will grant my final wish."

Farouk shuts his eyes, and more tears come. "I'm sorry for how much I've hurt you."

I can only laugh, even though the mirth doesn't last. "You know what? I've gone through worse. If you can believe that."

Then he drags me back into his arms and utters the words, "You truly are the bravest person I know. My Superman."

And with the heaviest of hearts, I pull myself from him, turn around, and walk away.

But unlike Orpheus, I don't look back.

Because I'm finally letting him go.

Chapter Fifty-Nine

I find Reggie leaning against a pole while the handsome nurse desperately tries to escape her. I drag her by the arm before she can do any more damage. "Please excuse my friend. We're leaving."

"Are we leaving?" she asks as she waves goodbye. "Goddammit. What's a girl to do for some fun around here? Also, what a surprise he's not dead. Something-something . . . *Thanks for leaping all the way to misinformation* much, wouldn't you think?"

Way to bring back her mistake at the language school and twisting it to mine. "Fine. I should've asked for a clarification from Aziz."

"Uh, yeah? Could've saved you a ton of trouble, thinking he was dead. Seriously." She throws her hands in the air, like she's just done praying. "Anyway, everything squared away?"

"I'm ready to make my third and final wish."

At this, Reggie skids to a halt, while people stream around us. "I'm sorry?"

"You brought me to Farouk. So it's time for my third wish. And I just want to go home."

What was that? That look that just flickered across her face. Gone in an instant. "All right, then. Just say the words and poof. You'll be there."

But I can't get over that look. For the briefest of seconds, a sliver of hope and . . . regret?

And then it all comes rushing back to me. The things she's said to me this entire journey.

How everyone just uses her.

How she's been alone.

How everyone's died on her.

There is only one thing for me to do. "I . . . wish for you to . . ."

No. I can't do that. What was that thing she said about compulsion? That I can't wish for someone to do something against their will? Someone who's clearly lost and been so alone.

As equally homeless as I am.

I can only want something for myself. And after our entire journey, all I know is how I feel about her. About what I really, truly came looking for.

A home. One I've already begun building.

So here it goes. "I wish to be your family."

It's as if I've just ripped her heart out, the way she staggers back. "What? What did you just say?"

"Reggie, I know why you've been trying to hide your emotions all this while. There were so many things about you I couldn't put my finger on. No one's ever checked up on you. You don't have a place you can actually call home." I pause. "And I'm here for you. I want to be there for you. Always."

She clutches her chest, as if she just grew an entire heart, then glares at me. And without saying another word, walks away from me. Again.

"What? Isn't that what you want?" I say, rushing up to her.

She's walking fast now toward our tent. "You don't know what I want. Also, what are you? A mind reader? If you want me to leave, then why not just say so?"

"I thought that was what you wanted."

We're in the tent now, and she's gathering the bedsheet I laid in, fluffing it this way and that, as if trying to make the bed but never actually having received proper training for it. "Yeah, well. I don't understand why you'd wish for something so pointless. Family? Who wants that? I've already told you there's no fun in people dying on you, leaving you alone."

I don't understand. I thought this would be exactly what she wanted. All the drinking. All the gallivanting. All the searching for friends who never seemed to amount to anything real. Wasn't it all just one big cry for help?

Or was it all just her being so set in her ways?

Reggie refuses to talk to me, which makes it so, so much worse as she negotiates our way back to the city. Back to the tarmac, back to the plane.

My head is still a horrific level of ouch. It's a wonder Phoebe even lets me on board. But fatigue drugs me into slumber all the way home, and I interact little with anyone. Not even Reggie, who, for the most part, is a remarkably different person, even remaining sober the entire time. She's rejected the flight attendant's many offers of alcohol—for the first hour at least. And even when she does finally have a drink, it sits there for a good hour, barely touched.

We land at Santa Monica Airport in the middle of the night.

"Reggie!" I say as she starts to walk away.

It just feels . . . so weird, to walk away from her. After all we've been through. Was this really . . . nothing to her? Was I a nobody all over again?

She turns back to me, and her face, with a smile that may as well have been a frown, is a mask that betrays nothing. "This won't be the last time you'll be seeing me—"

There, right there! Just the tiniest of problems. I can't tell if she ends that sentence with a definite period. Or is it a question mark?

But then my Uber arrives, and she disappears. Leaving me standing there, wondering how one tiny, undefined piece of punctuation can pack so much damn meaning.

I don't know if I'll ever figure her out.

✦ ✦ ✦ ✦ ✦

I make it to the hospital and have to bribe the receptionist to let me see my family since it's way past visiting hours. It's amazing how a hundred dollars can change someone's mind very quickly.

The wing's silent except for machine beeps and groans from

tired throats. I ask a nurse where I need to go, and she points the way. People always talk about a hospital's smell, that of death, but I think it's the air. There's something clean about it—the filtration maybe?—and that's the opposite of death, isn't it? Everything in a hospital is designed to prolong life, not to take away from it.

Sofia and Umi are perched on a bench outside the room. My sister's head is on my mother's lap. I don't think I've seen them this tired before—faces, shoulders, whole bodies just sagging. When Umi opens her eyes and sees me, it's the fatigue that finally breaks me. She shakes Sofia's shoulder, which awakens her, and together they watch my approach, my sister seating herself upright.

I drop at Umi's feet, staring up into her eyes. All I can say is, "I'm sorry."

She runs her fingers gently through my hair and stares at my wounds, and then her eyes search mine, almost as if she's convincing herself that I'm here, I'm really, really here. She rests a trembly chin on my head and says, "My poor son. What happened to you?"

I look at my sister, trying her best not to cry, and I know I am loved. These two people, the most important people in my life—I should be adoring them. And that was pretty much what I decided all the way home.

That they should be my home.

Sofia punches me on the shoulder. "You are such a dick, you know. What happened to your face?"

Umi *tsk*s. "Don't talk like that."

I laugh, and it feels good. "I know I've been a dick."

Umi *tsk*s again. "Language, you two."

I hug Umi so tight by her legs. "I promise never to make you worry ever again."

Umi sighs. "Sayyed, you're almost a grown man. But I will worry about you until the day I die, and that will never change. I just don't know what to do with your baba and you." That's said with a kiss to my forehead.

I don't dare tell Umi that I may move out as soon as I'm eighteen, to live life by myself because I'm no longer afraid to be alone. There's just one more source of fear I need to conquer.

I glance at the room beyond them. "How's he doing?"

Sofia punches me on the shoulder again. "He's fine. Surgery went well, and he's sleeping now. He's been having terrible dreams."

✳ ✳ ✳ ✳ ✳

I drag myself to my feet and stride through the empty doorway and into room 4327. There he is, in a hospital gown. I tiptoe to his side, not wanting to wake him, but he opens his eyes. He's weak; I can tell, but even so, he raises a hand to wave at me.

I've never seen Baba worried before, looking so human, when the impossible happens—the smallest tear leaks out of his eye. The situation has reversed. He's the one full of fear now. He looks so normal. So like me. Which floors me, taking all my anger over the last seventeen years with it.

He chokes out a strangled cough, and I grab a cup of water

with my free hand and offer him a sip. He swallows, his eyes on me the entire time. When he's finally able to speak, he does so quietly. "My parents died when I was a baby. You know that, right?"

I nod.

"My brothers and sisters raised me, and even though they did a good job, I still had to find strength to survive on my own. It wasn't easy, but I thought the only way to be a man was to be this."

"This?"

He points to himself. "Angry. Scary. I thought to be a man, I had to be mythical. Someone who demands respect from everyone. But then something like a heart attack happens, and it makes you see . . . that everything you love can be taken from you in . . . what they say . . . a blink of an eye. No matter how scary you are."

I give him a moment to catch his breath. "Baba, I'm sorry for what happened to you, but I came back because I needed to tell you this. I will not be terrorized any longer. I am no longer afraid of you. I do not care why you did what you did, but all I know is that if you dare try again to lay a hand on Umi or Sofia or me, then I will charge at you with everything that I've got." And I repeat the most important words I've ever said in my life.

"I am no longer afraid of you."

His fingers tremble as he tries to speak.

But I cut him off. "And there is another thing I came to say. I'm giving you the chance to make an important choice. Either be my father, the father you're supposed to be, and learn to love me—your gay son—for who I am and have a relationship with me, or remain the bigoted monster you've always been."

He has nothing left for me.

I walk out of the room, my feet so light.

Because I refuse to run away from my home any longer.

Chapter Sixty

Once I'm able to tear myself from Umi's grasp—which takes a whole three days—I decide to pay Dzakir a visit. He literally jumps up, sliding over the counter the moment he sees me, his flailing arms threatening to joust at me. "Oh. My. Eff. God. What happened to your head?" He sweeps me into his arms in the most intense of hugs.

"I've missed you too, D. Careful of the nose," I say, returning the embrace with a peck on his cheek.

He pulls me away, scans my body, notices something in my eyes. "Are those crow's feet? How'd you get them being gone less than a week?"

"How could you." I plant a drama slap across his face as he swings his head in the same direction. "Anyway, so many things to tell you."

"I know. You better start before the rush crowd comes in."

I spend the good part of an hour divulging all of the last

week to D, to horror and laughter and disbelief. To too many gasps to even count.

By the end of his shift, I've told him everything. We laugh at the hysterics of my replacement help having to serve the residents of West Hollywood. So far, it's been nothing but a disaster. "So when do you think you'll be ready to get back to work?" Dzakir asks.

"I need some time to myself for a while. Maybe a week or two. And when I'm back, I need a new nametag that says 'Sayyed.'"

He drapes a hand over mine and gives a reassuring squeeze. "You do you as long as you like. I'm just glad to have my mister-sister back. And the request will be taken care of."

As he says those words, my gaze pulls out and across the Boulevard. At the appearance of an all-too-famous ponytail swishing by.

My eyes meet hers as she walks right into the stop sign with a bang. But she sidesteps the pole and continues on, undazed and unfazed, as if nothing in the world has changed.

But yet, everything has.

"You okay?" Dzakir asks.

I turn back to him and give him a smile. "I will be. Just give me a sec, will you?"

The door dings behind me as I dash across the street, toward that ponytail I've gotten so used to seeing this past week. I grab her by the shoulder and spin her around, then say, "Hey."

Reggie—in a red tube top and short skirt—blushes.

She actually blushes and says, "Hey right back at you."

"Where've you been?"

She twirls her ponytail. "Oh . . . I'd say to hell and back. But that's a little too on the nose. It's not like we're in a TV series filled with beautiful twentysomethings pretending to be teens."

"I'm glad you're here."

"Of course you are, my little moppet. Who wouldn't be?" she says. "Anyway, I've thought long and hard . . ."

"About?"

"Your third and final wish."

Here it goes. "Reggie, I haven't changed my mind one bit. You have no idea what you've done for me. And it hurts me to know that you've gone your whole life without someone you can trust. Someone to confide in. Someone to . . . watch your alcohol intake."

"Wait, what? Are you, Sayyed Nizam, telling me you've been the reason for my sobriety as of late?"

Uh, guilty.

"Well, I must admit this is all new to me. I told you my parents died a long time ago."

I grab her hand. "I know. And I'm so sorry. I don't ever mean to replace them, but I've discovered lately that there's a strange twist to this thing called love."

"Oh? Pray tell, service me with your wisdom."

"See, a friend told me days ago that we get to choose our own family. That we're not just stuck with the people we were born to or with. That I get to choose you, the wonderful Reggie, as my own family."

She gives me the crookedest smile. "Sounds like poopie-poops. But whatever. Your wish is granted."

Reggie doesn't let go of my hand.

"Maybe you can even help me figure out what I should do with the rest of my life," I say.

Our steps are awkward at first, but we finally get into the groove of it.

"You could be a wine taster," she says. "Or vodka somme-lier. If there's such a thing."

"Uh, no. That's all you."

"Therapist? You have a way of convincing random strang-ers. Not me, of course. I'm absolutely un-convince-able."

"Oh god no. I can't listen to life problems all day long."

"Travel reviewer? You do have experience."

"Don't want to do it alone."

"You are being extremely difficult right now. But tell you what. You're seventeen. I find it strange that the world expects you to decide right this second. Just . . . take your time."

I can only balk. "How do you make so much sense? It's unbe-coming. Anyway, there are some people I want you to meet."

Together, we make our way to the café. So she can meet Dzakir. No surprise at how easily they get along.

Later that evening, I introduce Dzakir and Reggie to the rest of my family where we sit down for dinner. To Umi and Baba, both shocked at her super-short skirt and at his colorful nails. And to Sofia, who interrogates them on being as fabulous as they are.

And as I watch them all—even my father, whose lips are zipped together into a fine line, learning to understand his son and friends—a sense of calm wraps itself around me.

I had to be kicked out, get lost halfway around the world, to finally make it back home.

And this is my home.

The home that I wasn't given but that I have dared to make.

While everyone's busy wrapped up in getting to know one another around the table, I find Reggie staring at me—her expression utterly and completely indecipherable—and I stare back.

There she is.

And here I am.

I can't help but think about how far we've come in such a short time. How she helped me get over my fear of the world.

Reggie helped me escape. In order to find me. In order to find this.

So I pull out my phone and quietly but calmly text her:

Me: Thank you for being my loophole *winky face*

ACKNOWLEDGMENTS

How odd is it that the first three letters of "Acknowledgments" are "A-C-K," amirite?

Because . . . Ack! That's the sound coming out of my throat! I can't believe Sayyed's story is an actual book. Can you believe it? I can't. But here it is!

So here I am, trying to thank everyone I can remember. Which means I'm bound to forget someone, so if I do, I blame my memory, and you can too. In any case, a million apologies in advance!

First of all, I want to thank my mom, Mariam. The bravest woman on the planet, and the one who had to let me go, so I could choose my own path. Thank you for always putting up with me. I know I haven't been the easiest child, but I'm trying to make up for it.

My sister—Noor Bee—for being the most amazing sibling

out there and supporting me through the years of siblinghood. Soooo muccchhhh nagging! But I don't love you any less ☺

My partner, Benson. Thanks for all the wonderful laughs. Can't believe I get to go on this journey with you, and you won't ever grumble about it. Because you know how it all goes anyway!

Alex and Raffe! The best doggies ever. I have only one thing to say: *Woof woof woof growl arrrrrr woof woof woof woof woooooooooooooof!* I know, right?

Anna Gracia—partner in crime. Our hushed secrets will go to the grave with me. I promise. You know I need the fuel you give me to keep going.

Erik J. Brown, Susan Lee, Brian D. Kennedy—I'd be so lost without you three. Naggy Shrews forever!

Dante Medema, J.Elle—thank you for your kind words, and for being the most supportive friends ever. Our many chats have helped me navigate this industry and also everyday life!

To Mark Oshiro—I can't believe you made drunk Naz cry with your wonderfully kind words at YALLFest 2021. I'll never forget that moment. So, thank you, friend.

Brigid Kemmerer! Thank you for welcoming me so warmly to the Bloomsbury family. You reached out to a nervous author and intro'd yourself and have always been super kind. Can't believe we're publishing sibs! YAY!

To Charlie Barshaw, Tiffany R. Brown, Kathryn Merlo, and Eric Poole— It finally happened, after all that time in our critique group, since 2015? Those were so many hours, and I will cherish them always. Me and my writing would not be here without the four of you.

The 99 Dead—you know who you all are. Can't believe we've been together since that first DVpit! Yay to our safe space!

Speaking of . . . Thanks, Beth Phelan, for everything you do for DVpit. What an amazing opportunity for marginalized authors.

To the Author Mentor Match family, especially Alexa Donne, for trusting me and my mentoring ability.

And to the SCBWI family, for introducing me into their world, where I have met the most wonderful friends.

To fried chicken—I wouldn't be anywhere in the world without you as a primary motivator. Y'all may think I'm kidding, but I started early. And there's a whole history to this food!

I'm saving some significant people for last. Because this marathon is all about making it to the end. And here we are!

Kate Sederstrom and Claire Stetzer, for believing in the early drafts of this book. Thank you for putting your faith in me.

Shazleen Khan, for the most amazing illustration ever for the cover. Look at the faces, and all the detail in the background. I'm still stunned to this day!

And John Candell, for a wonderful design. Everything came together so well, and I can't wait to see it on bookshelves.

Phoebe Dyer, Beth Eller, Alexa Higbee, Jasmine Miranda, Kei Nakatsuka. Still so impressed by everything you've come up with to make this book a success. So much love for you all and your team.

Sarah Shumway— Wow, could I have asked for a more

wondrous editor? You helped make this book into the perfect alchemical magic that it is. Three stories bound into one. I couldn't wish for a better end.

Finally, to the most important person in my writing career. I wouldn't be here without my agent, Natalie Lakosil. Thank you for believing in me and my writing. And for not giving up even though I was close to it at times. You've helped me so much, and I can't wait to keep doing this with you.

I want to close by thanking all the queer teens out there who've picked up this book. It was written for you, so you can hopefully unearth that tucked-away, brave part of you, which you may need one day to keep going when life gets too unbearable.

Find that means to an escape.

Find your loophole.

Ever hopeful,
Naz Kutub